DYEING TO BE LOVED

WITH BONUS PREQUEL, FATAL REACTION

AIMEE NICOLE WALKER

Dyeing to be Loved
(Curl Up and DYE Mysteries, #1)

aimeenicolewalker@blogspot.com

ISBN: 978-0-9974225-3-5

Cover photograph and interior photos © Wander Aguiar - www.wanderaguiar.com

Cover art © Jay Aheer of Simply Defined Art - www.jayscoversbydesign.com

Editing provided by Pam Ebeler of Undivided Editing - www.undividedediting.com

Proofreading provided by Judy Zweifel of Judy's Proofreading - www.judysproofreading.com

Interior Design and Formatting provided by Stacey Ryan Blake of Champagne Formats - www.champagneformats.com

Other Books by Aimee Nicole Walker

Only You

The Curl up and Dye Mysteries

Fatal Reaction (prequel)
Dyeing to Be Loved
Something to Dye For
Dyed and Gone to Heaven
I Do or Dye Trying

The Fated Hearts Series

Chasing Mr. Wright, Book 1
Rhythm of Us, Book 2
Surrender Your Heart, Book 3
Perfect Fit, Book 4
Return to Me, Book 5
Always You, Book 6

Fatal Reaction
A Curl Up and Dye Mysteries Prequel

aimeenicolewalker@blogspot.com

Editing provided by Pam Ebeler of Undivided Editing,
– www.undividedediting.com

Proofreading provided by Judy Zweifel of Judy's Proofreading,
– www.judysproofreading.com

This book contains sexually explicit material and is only intended for adult readers.

FATAL REACTION

CURL UP AND DYE MYSTERIES PREQUEL

AIMEE NICOLE WALKER

PROLOGUE

I SHOULD'VE LISTENED TO MY MOTHER. I SHOULD'VE TRIED HARDER to ignore the gypsy blood that ran through my veins, but I couldn't turn my back on people who needed help. Well, that and I needed money because my day job of pouring java at The Brew didn't pay much. So, I started seeing clients in my home and had myself a nice little business going until I got an unexpected reaction – a fatal one. Unfortunately, the fatality would be my own.

I saw my death in a vision and accepted it as my destiny. I hadn't trusted my instincts when a particularly tall, dark, and handsome man approached me for help and it would seem that I'd be paying the ultimate price. He came to me looking for help with his love life. Things had grown stagnant in his marriage, and he wanted to spice things up a bit to remind his wife of how strong their love had once been. Apparently, the love potion I gave him to use backfired, and his wife realized she was in love with his best friend. I honestly hadn't seen that coming. In my defense, they didn't come to me for a couple's reading, or I would've known that they weren't meant to be together.

One would think I learned a lesson about meddling in peoples' lives after seeing my fate, but I decided to help one last man on the final day that I would walk the earth. He too was tall, dark, and handsome, but his aura showed him to be a good man despite the sadness I saw in his eyes. Unbeknownst to the dashing detective, Gabe, I slipped a little something extra into his coffee. I called it Love Potion #7 for the number of ingredients I used. Its purpose was to open his eyes to love. I recognized a man who sorely needed love when I saw it. The potion wouldn't make him fall in love with a particular person or compromise his judgment; it would simply open his mind to possibilities.

As I stood at my kitchen sink washing my dinner dishes, I let my mind imagine a world where Gabe brought his love into the coffee shop, and they lingered over java and pastries as they stared into one another's eyes. There would be soft smiles and longing looks exchanged as the morning ticked by lazily.

Noise from outside the kitchen window startled me out of my reverie. I looked across the expanse of my back lawn to the alley that separated my property from the neighbor. Josh "Jazz" Roman was taking the trash out to his bins after closing the salon he ran from his house. He turned and waved at me, and I waved a soapy hand in return. He was one person I'd sorely miss.

A shiver worked its way down my spine as I realized that the wave and smile I shared with Josh was exactly what I'd seen in my vision. My time was almost up, and my brain scattered to think of a way to let the police know who killed me. *Why hadn't I thought of that already instead of daydreaming about a cop I hardly knew?*

I pulled my hands out of the soapy water and quickly rinsed and dried them. I turned to find something to write with and saw that *he* was already standing in my kitchen. The rage I saw in his eyes sent fear coursing through my body, and all but one thought slipped my mind.

"I'm so sorry, Mama," I whispered out loud before I released a blood-curdling scream. I would not leave the world quietly!

ONE

"Man, it's the sweet lady from the coffee shop," said my partner, Adrian Goode. "Who would want to hurt her?" As detectives, we had seen a lot of shit in our lives, but that didn't mean we were immune to it. The young woman lying in a pool of blood from where someone had slit her throat wouldn't sit well with the most hardened veterans.

"Bianca," I said to him. "Her name is Bianca." And someone had done a real number on her too. The facial bruising indicated her attacker had struck her several times and the kitchen furniture knocked haphazardly all around suggested she had put up a struggle.

"Bianca Dragomir, age twenty-four," the first responding officer said. "Call came in from the neighbor behind her. Josh Roman said that he'd seen Ms. Dragomir standing at the sink washing dishes when he took out the garbage around six thirty. They waved at one another. He said he was almost back inside his home when he heard her scream. He said even from across the alley he could hear a lot of scuffling and loud banging. He immediately called nine-one-one, but by the time I arrived, she had already bled out from her wound."

"Did he get a look at the assailant?" I asked Officer Perkins.

"Mr. Roman was deeply distraught, and I didn't get much out of him. Maybe you guys should take a crack at him. His friends are sitting with him, and maybe he's had time to calm down."

"Yeah, sure," Adrian said, closing his notebook. He looked at the medical examiner who was bagging Bianca's hands to preserve any DNA evidence she might have beneath her nails. "I hope you're going to help us nail the son of a bitch who did this to you, kiddo."

"She put up a hell of a fight, Detective Goode," Dr. Melissa Chan replied from where she squatted beside the body. "We have to send all the DNA evidence to state crime lab in Columbus for analysis, so it might be a while before we receive the results. If this guy is in the system, then we'll have him." That was something at least. Even though the dead didn't talk, they often told us quite a lot about the person who killed them.

Adrian and I left Bianca's house and began a silent walk across her back yard to her neighbor's house. I had moved to Blissville, a sleepy southern Ohio town, to get away from big city crime. Okay, I moved to Blissville with my then boyfriend when he wanted to move back home and take over his grandfather's veterinary practice when he retired. Still, I had been looking forward to a slower pace as Kyle, and I built a life together. A year later, Kyle and I were no longer a couple, but I kept my position on the police force and rent-ed a small house of my own. I hadn't lived here all that long, but I got the impression that a murder wasn't something that happened very often.

There was a light on in the rear of the massive, two and a half story home owned by Josh Roman. A large portion of the home was converted into a full-service salon called The Curl Up and Dye that was popular with the local ladies. I had seen the owner many times since I moved to town but never spoke to him.

He was a few inches shorter than my six-two frame and very slender compared to my bulkier build I earned working off my sexual frustration in the weight room. His hair was so blond that it was nearly white and he often wore a colored streak in his bangs. He had a sway to his hips when he walked and an "I don't care what you think about me" air about him. He was clearly comfortable in his own skin, and that was something I admired, even if I wasn't attracted to him.

Adrian knocked loudly on the back door of the home, and after a few moments, a gorgeous African-American lady in her early 20s answered. "I'm Detective Goode, and this is my partner, Detective Wyatt," he told her. We both held up our badges, which she scrutinized before she stepped aside so we could enter.

"We'd like to ask Josh Roman a few questions if you don't mind, Ms…"

"Meredith Richmond," she replied. "Jazz is a mess right now. He truly loved Bianca, and he's devastated by her death. Could he possibly do this tomorrow?"

"I'm afraid it's very important that we speak to him while things are still fresh in his mind," I told her. "We'll try to make it quick."

"Okay," she said reluctantly. "Follow me."

She led us through the kitchen and into an elegant, yet cozy looking, sitting room decorated in earth tones with bright bursts of blues and greens. Huddled together on the couch were two men. Josh's stooped shoulders shook as he cried silently. The other guy sat with his arm around Josh and his forehead pressed to Josh's temple.

It spoke of a very familiar, if not intimate, relationship.

"I should've done something more," Josh said, unaware that we'd entered the room. He was looking down at his lap and running his hands over the long, furry body of a ferret. "She was my friend and I..."

"No, baby," Meredith said, taking up the open space on the other side of him. "You would've gotten yourself killed too."

Behind the trio sat a gorgeous Siamese cat who pinned me with suspicious blue eyes. Her chocolate-brown ears twitched, and her tail swished from side to side in annoyance at the scene that played out in front of her. I was about to clear my throat to announce our presence when a shrill whistle split the air. I whipped around to see the source of the noise and found a vibrantly blue macaw watching me through his cage.

"Hey there, sexy thing." The bird let out another whistle and then bopped its head in excitement. "Come give Daddy a kiss."

"Looks like you made a new friend," Adrian said from beside me. "It's been a long dry spell for you. Maybe you give this guy a chance."

"Savage, behave," said a soft voice from behind me.

I turned around and found myself caught in a pair of huge hazel eyes that were wet with tears of anguish. It wasn't the time to catalog every fine, almost delicate feature on Josh Roman's face, but I couldn't help myself. It was the first time I'd seen him up close and personal, and his beauty shocked me. I hadn't thought of men in terms of beauty before, but it was the only way to describe him.

His wounded eyes held onto mine for several long moments, and I wondered what he thought about when he looked at me; then wondered why I cared. I had a job to do, and it wasn't to get a date for the following weekend, even if he had been my type. Our eyes stayed locked on each other until Adrian spoke. Josh was the one to break eye contact to focus on him.

"I'm sorry about the loss of your friend Bianca," Adrian said compassionately. "Your friend Meredith is right though, Mr. Roman. You could've been hurt or killed if you'd gone over to her house. You called nine-one-one, and that was exactly what you should've done."

"It doesn't feel like the right thing. I can't believe Bianca is dead. Who in the world would want to hurt her? She was the kindest person I'd ever met." He shifted his eyes back to his lap where he had resumed petting his ferret. "It makes no sense."

"It seldom does," I said, speaking for the first time. Josh jerked his gaze back up to mine. "Did you see the assailant entering or leaving her house? Have you seen anyone hanging around that appeared out of place?"

He shook his head slowly. "I didn't see anything at all. She was washing dishes, and I waved to her as I took the trash out. I didn't see anyone outside her house at that time, so maybe he was already inside, or he rounded the corner and entered her house right after I turned around to come back inside."

"Which means he might've been familiar with your nightly routine or he was watching and waiting for you to go inside," I said, thinking out loud. I heard a collective sharp intake of breaths and looked at the three people sitting on the couch.

"Is he in danger?" Meredith asked, looking ashen.

"Oh my God, Jazz," the other guy said. "You need police protection." His blue eyes were bugging out of his head. He ran his hands through his light brown hair in agitation. "You will protect him, won't you?"

"Calm down," Adrian said, his deep voice sounding as if God spoke. "There's nothing to indicate that the killer thinks Mr. Roman saw or heard anything at all. Detective Wyatt was mentally piecing together a scenario, not fact." Adrian pinned me with a dark look that let me know he wasn't happy I had riled up the witness and his friends. "I know it's been a difficult night for you, so we won't stay any longer. We'll give you our cards, and you can call us if you think of anything at all."

"Or he gets death threats," the brown-haired guy added.

"Knock it off, Chaz," Meredith said calmly. "If the detectives thought Jazz was in danger then they'd do something about it, right?" She pinned us with a "don't mess with me" look that had us both nodding in agreement. "See there," she said softly to Josh. "You're going to be okay. I'm going to stay over tonight because you need a friend, but *no one* is in danger." She looked back at us. "Give him your cards, gentlemen." We rushed to do Meredith Richmond's bidding and then said we'd show ourselves out.

Once we were out of earshot, Adrian leaned toward me a bit and said, "He's cute, huh?"

"Stop, Adrian." The last thing I needed was his attempt at matchmaking.

"Come on, man. You and Kyle split up over a year ago. It's time you got back on the horse or allowed yourself to be mounted – whatever you're into." He waggled his brows at me and made me smile.

I truly lucked out when I was partnered with Adrian. Police departments haven't always been LGBTQ friendly places, and a lot of cops stayed in the closet. The world was changing, and there was more acceptance to be found, even if there was still a lot of room for improvement.

"He's not really my type," I said with a casual shrug.

"Why ever not?" Adrian sounded genuinely confused by my answer.

"He's just a bit too…"

"Feminine?" A soft voice with a bite of anger finished my sentence. Adrian and I stopped and turned to find that Josh had followed us. Some detectives we were that we didn't even know. A defiant look replaced the wounded one I'd seen in his eyes moments prior. The way he held his head high told me that he had survived many an asshole in his life and I was sorry he would include me in that category. "You're one of those 'masc only' guys, aren't you?" His use of fingers to quote the words in the air would have been cute had I not been mortified. "Don't worry, Detective Wyatt. I'm not into tall, dark, and dickish men, so you're safe from my affections." I just stood staring at him, unable to say a word.

"Was there something that you thought of?" Adrian asked, steering us back toward a more appropriate conversation and saving me from more embarrassment.

The sadness returned and flooded his expressive eyes. I'd be lying if I said it didn't move something inside of me, something that made me want to reach out and pull him into my arms where I could tuck him under my chin and keep him safe. The protectiveness I felt toward him was a development I hadn't expected.

"Did she suffer?" Josh finally asked.

"She died quickly," Adrian replied softly. I noticed he didn't say anything about it being painless, but he didn't lie to Josh.

"Thank you." He nodded quickly and returned to the comforting fold of his friends.

Much later that night when I was alone in bed, I couldn't help but wonder how Josh was doing. Was he able to fall asleep? It upset me that he overheard what I'd said to Adrian. It irritated me even more that I had left him with a bad impression of me. What bothered me the most was that I was wide awake in the middle of the night thinking about sad, hazel eyes and wishing I could take his pain away.

TWO

Before Bianca's murder, I might've seen Josh Roman around Blissville once a month, which was saying something because the community only had a little over six thousand residents. Since I embarrassed myself in front of him, I'd seen him at least once a week. Each time, I'd hoped to redeem myself and each time I failed miserably.

I ran into him once outside the Sac-n-Save. I was going in, and he was coming out with three or four canvas shopping bags in each hand. I thought I was a gentleman when I offered to help carry some of his burden to his teal green convertible Mini Cooper.

Instead of accepting my help, the feisty shit batted his eyelashes at me like a simpering southern belle and said with an exaggerated southern accent, "Why, Detective Douche, I do declare that is the sweetest offer I've had in days. I'm sorry you think my wrists are so limp that I can't carry a few groceries to my car. I appreciate you offering your big manly assistance, but I got this. Bye bye, Detective."

I couldn't help but notice he added an extra sway to his hips when he walked away and if I wasn't so pissed at the way he insulted me, I might've admired his taut, bubble butt. Instead, my face burned with anger over my rejected offer. Regardless of what he said, those bags looked like they were overflowing with groceries as if he planned to buy just a few things and ended up buying half of the store.

The next time I ran into him, it was at the coffee shop. I stood behind him in line and tried hard not to notice the way his fresh scent tickled my nose. His hair was still damp like he'd just gotten out of the shower. When it was his turn, he ordered a plain black coffee with two sugars. Once he paid for his drink, he moved off to the side to wait. Josh turned and found me watching him and a scowl formed on his face as he looked at me.

"What's the matter? My coffee too butch for someone like me?"

I opened my mouth to speak, but the guy behind the counter walked up with his steaming hot coffee. Josh turned away from me, grabbed his coffee cup, and left the shop without another word. I fought the urge to follow him, to find out who in life hurt him so bad that he carried such a huge chip on his shoulder. Instead, I stepped up to the cashier and placed my order for a French vanilla latte. I couldn't help but wonder what Josh would think of my preference for flavored coffee.

These incidents went from a weekly occurrence to bi-weekly, and I became more and more frustrated each time. Why? Simple, I could never find the words to refute his generalized statements;

something about him twisted my tongue in a knot and prohibited me from arguing or at least apologizing for what I had almost said about him in his home. As if that wasn't enough, I couldn't stop thinking about him. I found myself constantly creating interesting ways to shut his smart mouth—most often it involved his lips wrapped around my dick.

The weeks that followed Bianca's death, Adrian and I went through boxes and boxes of evidence taken from her house. We learned from interviewing her coworkers and friends that Bianca ran a business from her home where she read tarot cards and palms. She gave advice about love and even sold potions to help the lovelorn. None of the documents we found in her home indicated the names of her clients or what she discussed with them. We found initials instead of clients' names, codes we couldn't decipher for the services she performed for them, and the amount she charged them per visit.

She was doing well for herself financially, and it appeared that she had a lot of repeat clients. I felt certain that her line of work was the reason behind her murder. She had zero known enemies, there was no indication that she'd been robbed, and we found nothing suspicious looking in her finances. My gut told me that someone didn't like what she had to say or one of her potions didn't go well, and she died because of it.

"I don't know, Gabe," Adrian said when I told him my theory. "I'm not sure I believe in all that spiritual stuff." His dark scowl matched the late afternoon sky. We'd been at it all day and were no closer to an answer as to what happened to Bianca. She deserved justice, and it looked like it might not happen if we didn't catch a break soon.

Bianca's aunt arrived to escort her body home to New Orleans once Dr. Chan completed the autopsy. Questioning a bereaved family is a tight line to walk; you needed to find out if they knew anything that could produce a suspect while showing as much compassion as possible. Unfortunately, the family had nothing to give us. Bianca wasn't seeing anyone that they knew of and she never spoke of a client who was angry with her.

"If they're all clairvoyant or have spiritual powers then why can't they tell us who killed Bianca?" Adrian asked, his voice filled with the same frustration that I felt at not being any closer to catching her killer. "Somebody has to know something, and they're too afraid or too embarrassed to say anything. They don't want people knowing they're consulting a psychic, gypsy, fortune teller, or whatever she went by." There was no derision or scorn in his voice, just a desire to solve her murder. A little over a month had passed since her death, and the case was getting colder than ice with no leads in sight.

I wasn't sure how to answer Adrian's question about Bianca or her family's abilities. I wasn't sure what all was involved in reading tarot cards, palms, tea leaves, or whatever tools she might have used. I wasn't even sure I believed it worked, but a lot of people did, judging by the earnings in Bianca's ledgers.

We sent the only physical evidence we collected off her body to the labs for analysis, including hair and fibers that we believe belonged to her assailant. However, we didn't find her attacker's fingerprints or blood at the crime scene. He was either incredibly lucky or had killed before and knew what he was doing. My opinion was that all killers made mistakes, even seasoned ones. We just needed to find it.

We had decided to call it a day because Adrian had an anniversary dinner planned with his wife, Sally Ann. I just needed to get laid. I had a level of sexual frustration that no amount of jerking off could ease. Josh Roman had me turned inside out and I almost hated him for it. Gone was my peaceful existence and in its place was a constant state of arousal and irritation. Fuck, I wanted to kiss the hissing and spitting right out of him but damned if I'd make a move on someone who I obviously repulsed. I had no choice but to drive to a bigger city and find someone to work out my frustrations with; someone who didn't look at me with disgust in his eyes.

Just as we were about to leave, a wide-eyed young woman entered the police department. Apprehension and fear rolled off her in waves. Adrian was too busy texting his wife to notice her at first. I heard her tell the desk sergeant that she might have information regarding the Bianca Dragomir case and that caught Adrian's attention.

"Listen, why don't you go on home to Sally Ann and let me take care of this. I promise to fill you in tomorrow morning. There's no need to be late for your reservations and upset your wife." Canceled plans and super late nights were one of the reasons that Kyle and I didn't work out. I jumped at the chance to move to a smaller town so that I wouldn't have many late nights to save our three-year relationship. I didn't realize it then, but it was already too late. We'd grown too far apart to repair our relationship.

"Are you sure?" Adrian asked. "We're partners, man." I could tell he struggled between doing his job and making his wife happy.

"I'm positive, Adrian. Go home and take your gorgeous wife out to dinner." I loved Sally Ann like a sister. She had been nothing but kind to me the minute I moved to town. Adrian didn't bat an eye when I told him I was gay. Living a lie wasn't something I was willing to do, and I needed to know I had a good partner. I ended up with a partner who felt more like a brother to me.

"Call me bright and early," he said, pointing his finger at me. He walked over to the front desk and talked to the nervous lady. He placed a calming hand on her shoulder and pointed in my direction. The smile he gave her was kind and assuring.

I watched as the lady smiled tentatively back at him before she headed toward my desk. It was a small police department, so she didn't have far to travel. We didn't have a fancy setup like in some cop shows, but it functioned well enough to suit me.

"I'm Detective Wyatt," I said, extending my hand to her. I hoped the smile I gave her was as assuring as Adrian's. I was relieved when she visibly relaxed. "How can I help you?"

"My name is Tara Evans. I don't live locally, I don't read the papers, and I don't watch the news because it's depressing..." Her voice broke, and I gave her a minute to gather herself, knowing if I were patient she'd finish telling me what she'd come to say. "I didn't know about Bianca's death until I showed up at her house this morning for my monthly appointment." She choked a bit on her words and wiped tears from her cornflower blue eyes. I handed her my box of tissues so she could wipe her face.

"The sweet guy who runs the salon saw me on her porch and came over to break the news." *Sweet guy? Had she met Josh?* A fresh wave of tears flooded down her face, and once again I sat and waited them out. "Bianca was such a kind person, Detective. She helped me out so much, and I can't understand who would want to hurt her."

"Do you know something that could help us solve her murder?" I asked, trying to steer her to the reason she came to the police department.

"I saw her a few days before her murder, Detective. I noticed something odd; *someone* odd, I should say. Bianca never scheduled clients close together to assure absolute discretion. There was never anyone coming or going near our appointment times, no waiting room or reception area, and she kept her doors locked during our sessions to ensure privacy and to make sure we weren't interrupted."

"But that wasn't what happened on your last visit?" I asked.

"There was a man leaving her house, a very angry man. He practically ran me over as I was walking up the steps to her front door. He didn't apologize or anything." Tara looked shocked that assholes existed in her world. "Anyway, Bianca was standing on her porch watching him as he walked away. She had this odd expression on her face," Tara squinted as she concentrated, "it was a mix of shock and horror, Detective. Whatever he said to her shook her something fierce. She was off during our session, and she politely rejected any attempt on my part to talk about what bothered her. I left with an uneasy feeling, and it turned out that I should've been."

My heart sped up with the information that Tara gave me. "Did you see his face or what he was driving?"

"I did get a good look at his face, but he must've parked around the corner from her house. That cute neighbor Josh might've seen what he was driving though. Josh had been jogging from that direction, and the two of them met at the corner and nearly collided. The guy practically shoved Josh out of his way. Josh turned and yelled something after him, so if he got into a car, he might've seen it."

"Thank you so much for coming in, Tara. I don't know if who you saw killed Bianca, but I'll do everything I can to track him down and question him. I have one favor to ask you." She nodded exuberantly, all traces of fear from earlier were gone. I realized that her dread from earlier wasn't so much about talking to the police; it was fear of being judged. "Do you mind working with our sketch artist to see if you can come up with a likeness I can use?" As small as we were, we had one hell of an artist on the force.

"Anything to help," she replied, as I signaled for Officer Jayna Murkowski to come over. "You'll talk to Josh, won't you?" Tara asked me.

"I'll head over to his salon as soon as we're finished."

I hoped my smile covered up the internal grimace I had going on. All roads led to Josh it seemed, which also meant I had to gear up for another round of verbal sparring. Okay, he sparred, and I took it on the chin because I felt guilty. He was going to need to retract his claws because neither of our feelings was what counted right then. I had a murderer to catch, and he might be my key witness.

THREE

I STOOD JUST OUTSIDE THE DOOR OF HIS SALON TRYING TO WORK up my courage. I always felt out of place at salons and boutiques. Groups of women made me nervous; being gay didn't change that for me. I was never anyone's GBF, I didn't have any sisters, and my mom knew more about sports and cars than she did about shopping and hairstyles. Duty called so I sucked up my awkwardness, squared my shoulders, and walked into that salon like I had a right to be there.

All noises came to a screeching halt—hairdryers were turned

off, talking ceased, and all eyes were on me. I felt like a giant fish out of the water, and I wondered if my mouth was gaping open like one too. There were four occupied chairs in the salon, but I only recognized two of the stylists—Josh and Meredith.

"Howdy, Detective," Josh's friend, Chaz, said from behind the reception desk. He looked me up and down appraisingly; I had a feeling I was a shared topic between the three friends. Unfortunately for me, I didn't think they sang my praises when I wasn't around. "Jazz, it's for you," he said loudly as if he had to yell to be heard. Maybe I was the only one who noticed the still silence.

I looked at Josh, and he met my gaze with an exaggerated eye roll. The guy hated my guts. I fought the urge to turn around and walk out, not because I was a coward, but because I was afraid I'd lose my cool and say something equally as shitty to him in return.

From within the salon, I heard Josh's crazy bird sing out, "I like big cocks and I cannot lie." The bird broke the silence, and soon the ladies' laughter filled the salon.

"My word, Jazz, wherever did you get that crazy bird?" One of them asked after she wiped her tears from her eyes.

"Brook's Pet's," he replied. "Someone passed away, and their family wasn't sure what to do with the foul-mouthed bird, so they took him to Brook. I walked in to get Jazzy and Diva some treats, and there he was bopping his head and spewing filthy language at me. I just had to have him." I guessed that Diva with her sparkly crystal-encrusted collar was the cat and Jazzy was his ferret. Josh returned his attention begrudgingly back to me and said, "Why don't you head on into the sitting area and keep Savage company until I get Mrs. Hendrickson under the dryer."

I recognized dismissal when I heard it. However, I needed Josh's help and didn't have a choice but to indulge him. I took my chances with the bird, but luckily all he did was whistle at me and call me a hot stud. I still felt a little violated by the time Josh walked into the room. I could tell by the arrogant lift to his brow that he deliberately kept me waiting longer than necessary. Again, not like I could call him on it. Yet.

"What can I do for you, Detective Dick Breath?"

It was the proverbial straw that broke the camel's back. "Drop the bullshit, Jizz." Maybe making fun of his nickname was tacky and immature, but I'd had enough of his mouth. I marched forward until our bodies almost touched. I used my height to my advantage and forced him to tilt his head back to look at me. I saw wariness in his eyes, and it reduced my boiling rage down to a simmer. I took a step back for both of our sakes. He was scared and being near him made me horny. Damn him! I so badly wanted to suggest what he could do with his mouth instead of sniping at me all the damn time.

"I had a witness come forward today who thinks she might've seen the person who killed Bianca. She also said that you got a look at him and possibly saw the vehicle he'd driven to her house." I repeated what Tara had told me. All the animosity he'd felt toward me disappeared in a flash. The only thing on his mind right then was helping me find Bianca's killer.

"I did get a good look at his face and his car, but it was parked across the street facing me and didn't have a front license plate on it. All I can tell you is that it was a new black Audi sedan, but I'm not sure which model." He sounded disappointed that he couldn't do more.

"No, Josh, that's great. I can add the description of the car with the sketch our artist comes up with and give it to the media." My mind was already back on work, focusing on solving this case for Bianca and her family. Her aunt had been heartbroken about burying both of Bianca's parents and then her too; she could use the closure.

"We have a sketch artist in our police department?" he asked.

"Yes," I said, laughing softly at his surprise. "Would you mind sitting down with the sketch artist too? It would be great if the descriptions you give are similar to Tara's."

My laugh seemed to startle him; he narrowed his eyes and studied me as if seeing me for the first time. "I'd be happy to do it. Mrs. Hendrickson is my last client for the day, so I can head to the station after her appointment. Will that work?"

"Perfectly," I replied. I didn't have anything else to say, and it probably would've been a good moment to apologize for the first night I met him, but for some reason, I didn't. "Well, I'll get out of here and let you get back to work. I'll be in touch if I need anything else. You have my number if you remember anything, right?"

"Right," he answered softly, studying his feet as if they were the most interesting things he'd ever seen.

"You threw it away, didn't you?"

"Burned it," was his reply. He looked back up at me and shrugged nonchalantly.

I dug out a card from my wallet and held it out to him. "Just in case." I left his salon without another word after he reluctantly took it from my hand. Too bad the tension I felt in my chest didn't diminish once I left. In fact, it increased every time I was near him until I thought I might explode.

There was only one avenue open to me to work it out of my system—a hard fuck.

FOUR

The closest gay club, Vibe, was nearly an hour away, but the only place I wanted to be that night. Some might've thought the drive was too long for a night out, but I wasn't looking to get drunk. I had beer at home, but I didn't have a willing male body in my bed. It wasn't like Kyle and I hadn't hooked up out of loneliness since we ended things, but I couldn't keep doing that to myself. We both deserved better.

I loved the multi-level functionality of the club because it had space for people who wanted to dance and it had space for guys who just wanted to shoot pool or throw darts. I was not a dancer; I usually spent my time on the second level picking up guys… like me? Was I as shallow and close-minded as Josh had implied? Would it hurt me to spend time at the bar and try to expand my outlook on men?

That was how I ended up at the bar with my eyes locked on the dance floor. I couldn't take my eyes off him. Everything about him—from the way the colored lights hit his platinum hair to the way his lean body swayed and moved so fluidly—held me captivated. Well, that was until a tall guy moved in behind him and put his hands all over Josh Roman's lithe body.

I hated that dickhead and the urge to pull him away from Josh so that I could take his place stunned me. Hell, I didn't even like Josh Roman so why did he ensnare me so much? Why did my dick throb and ache to know him up close and personal? I turned away from the action on the dance floor and caught the eye of a guy at the other end of the bar. A month prior, I would've been all over the silent invitation he sent me, but I was too caught up in hazel eyes and hair so blond it outshone the sun.

Fuck me!

The object of my desire came to the bar to get a drink and blinked in shock when he stopped beside me. The alcohol in his blood must've slowed down his cognitive skills because it took him a few minutes to say, "Well, hello, Detective D…"

I stopped his drunken words with a firm kiss on his mouth. I couldn't be certain if it was shock or want that made him open his mouth and extend an invitation to taste him, but I didn't stop to ask. I tasted the fruitiness of his cocktail on his lips and tongue, which clashed with the one beer I had allowed myself to drink when I came downstairs to scope out the dance floor. Our drink choices were complete opposites, like the two of us, but maybe it was what I needed in my rather dull life.

I kissed him until someone bumped into Josh hard enough to

jolt him. He pulled back and stared up at me with shock, and I probably wore a matching look. It was no ordinary kiss, you see. It felt like the little imp burned himself beneath my skin and I wasn't sure what the fuck to do about it. Then he opened his mouth and took the decision away.

"Did that feel like kissing a girl to you?" He leaned in and pressed his lips against my ear. "I might be on the lean side, but that's because I do yoga and I'm extremely limber. I can reverse cowboy like you can't even imagine. Well, you'll have to use your imagination because you're not man enough to act on the desire I see in your eyes. You think you'll be less of a man or less gay if you sleep with a guy with soft skin and a lean body. To men like you, fucking guys with big muscles on manly frames makes you feel more masculine yourself."

"You don't know shit about me, Jizz." I sounded like a sixth grader, but his accusations stung. Hard.

"I've known your type my whole life, Detective." He shook his head like he pitied me.

"My name is Gabe."

"Okay, *Gabe*." Josh rolled his eyes as if I was stupid; maybe he was one of those that thought all jocks were dumb; I was neither a jock nor dumb. "A lot of guys want to fuck me, to use me as their personal blow-up doll with ready orifices to please them until the next strapping stud comes along to grab their attention. I'm never the guy they take home to meet mom and dad. I'm not good enough."

I heard the hurt behind his words and I wanted to punch anyone who'd hurt him—including myself. Maybe he had jumped to conclusions that night and finished my sentence, but he had been right. It was what I was going to say. Looking at him now, I didn't see anything feminine about him. Yes, he was lean, and he had more delicate features than I, but that didn't make him girlie. He was beautiful, and his anger made his large hazel eyes more luminous than they already were. If I weren't careful, looking into those eyes would get me into a lot of trouble.

"Come on, baby, let's dance." I hadn't seen the asshole from the dance floor approach because I had been captivated by the blond fury that stood before me.

"Get lost," I snarled at the intruder. I would rather sit there and listen to Josh flay me alive than go home alone. In the end, it wasn't really up to me.

"Don't you go anywhere, honey," Josh practically purred at the guy. "Our evening is just getting started." Josh's eyes were on mine the entire time he spoke. He was putting me in my place and daring me to watch him getting close to the other man. The sly smile he gave me made me ill. I didn't want to think of him naked with the other guy, but it was the picture he painted so vibrantly. I left Vibe as soon as they returned to the dance floor. Maybe it was cowardly, but it was the only option for me.

I tossed and turned into the wee hours of the morning, my body hard with desire and my brain tortured by all the things I should've said or done differently. I realized that I'd probably never get the chance to make it right. I more than burned my bridge with Josh.

Imagine my surprise when I found him sitting on my front porch step after I returned from helping my elderly neighbor next door. "Josh?" I asked like I wasn't sure. "Is everything okay?" I would've asked how he knew where I lived, but it was a very small town, and probably everyone knew where to find me.

He held up a plastic container as if it explained everything. He had a flushed face, and I couldn't help but wonder if his entire body was that pretty shade of pink. Of course, my dick wanted in on the action.

"I made you cookies as an apology for the way I acted last night," he said softly. "I said some harsh things that I had no business saying." He rose from his feet, and his eyes met mine as he held out the container for me to take. I saw exhaustion and weariness in his eyes; I wanted to make them go away.

"Come inside and have cookies with me," I said in invitation. I was shocked when Josh nodded his head in acceptance rather than kick me in the balls.

He followed me to the kitchen and sat quietly at my table while I made us some coffee. I handed him a cup of black coffee with two sugars. "Do you have any cream? I hate black coffee." I looked at him in confusion because that was how he ordered it that time I was behind him at The Brew. "I was just doing that to prove a point," he said sheepishly.

I said nothing as I opened the door and pulled out two types of flavored creamer I had on hand. Josh raised a brow in surprise, and I pinned him with a "don't fuck with me" look. I made our coffee and sat across from him at the table, and we dug into the cookies.

"So good," I said around a chewy, gooey bite of chocolate chip cookie. "You can insult me every day if it gets me these cookies." I looked at him then and saw a smear of melted chocolate at the corner of his mouth. I couldn't resist leaning across the small table and licking it away.

Just like that, we both went up in flames, reaching for one another like we were half-starved for each other's touch. I stood and pulled Josh to his feet, slung him over my shoulder in a fireman's hold, and carried him up the stairs to my bedroom. His laughter and the sound of him slapping my ass rang throughout the hallway to my room and made me smile.

I not so gently deposited him on my bed, and we immediately tore the clothes off each other in between hot, greedy kisses. My dick begged for me to take, take, take, but I took my time learning the different textures of his gorgeous, leanly muscled body. "Beautiful," I whispered against his skin.

Once I had him spread beneath me, properly stretched open, and my dick suited up, I slowly slid inside his tight heat. My God, he threatened to burn me alive as I pushed inside him until I couldn't get any closer to him. If I could, I would've crawled inside his body because I wasn't nearly as close to him as I wanted to be.

I didn't know if he'd gone home with the guy from last night, and I didn't have the right to ask, but I wanted to obliterate the memory of every lover who'd gone before me like some chest thumping Neanderthal. I pumped into him slowly, allowing his body to adjust to my size. I could see it in his eyes and feel it in the way that he dug his nails into my ass cheeks that he wanted it harder and faster.

Harder and faster meant that it would be over too soon and I might not get another trip to nirvana. Josh fit me so perfectly like he was made just for me. Jesus, I was wrapped up tightly in emotions I hadn't felt in a long time, if ever.

I rolled over on my back and pulled him on top of me. I wanted to watch him ride me, to take me into his body and love the way I made him feel. I wanted to see his "limber" in action. It was all I had been able to think about once those words left his mouth.

"Ride me, Josh." My voice sounded tortured as I waited for him to move. I needed to feel friction along the length of my cock again, to know it was him, my personal tormenter, who was bringing me so much pleasure.

Josh began a slow ride that drove me crazy. I gripped his hips hard enough to leave bruises, but he didn't seem to mind. Instead, my insane need seemed to spur him on. He held me tight between his thighs as he rose and fell on my cock. His head was thrown back in ecstasy, he ran his hands through his hair, and the mewling sounds that came from his throat drove me fucking wild.

I bucked up into him, needing more friction, more heat, more everything. Josh lowered his head and smiled wickedly at me before he gave me the ride I craved. His mesmerizing hips snapped back and forth fluidly as he rode me like I was a prize stallion. I'd never seen anything as sexy as him in my life. I reached for his cock to help him, but he slapped my hand away.

"Won't need help." Moments later he shot all over my stomach and chest before he collapsed on top of me in exhaustion.

His ass still had a chokehold on my dick, and I drove up into him as I held his body securely against mine. I roared as I filled the condom, burying my dick deep inside him over and over until the last drop left my body. "Jesus," was all I could manage to say afterward.

"Leave him out of this." Josh's voice was muffled by my chest because he hadn't moved an inch since he landed there.

I rolled him gently onto his side so I could remove the condom and throw it away. Exhaustion like I'd never felt before descended on me. The last thing I remembered doing before I fell asleep was pulling Josh tight against me, tucking him beneath my chin, and pulling the covers over us.

When I woke up hours later all alone, I started to doubt that Josh had even been there, but then I smelled him on my pillow and saw his dried release all over my chest. It bothered me more than I wanted to admit that he just got up and left without saying goodbye. I wanted to hunt him down and kiss him until he came back to bed, but I got up and showered off the remnants of our afternoon, hoping it wouldn't be the last time.

FIVE

THE FOLLOWING MONDAY, A SKETCH WAS ISSUED ALONG WITH THE description of the car owned by our person of interest. DNA results still had not come back from the lab over a month after Bianca's death, so the info sent to the local news stations and papers was all we had to go on for the time being. We suspected the guy wasn't a local because no one recognized him.

Adrian and I kept busy investigating burglaries and drug-related crimes, but my mind never strayed too far from a certain blond guy who had my insides all twisted up. Somehow he'd been avoiding me, and I was too uncertain about things to approach him. I carried his stupid plastic container around in my car hoping to run into him, so I'd have an excuse to talk to him.

I got my chance a week after he disappeared from my life without a goodbye or fuck off. He was loading groceries into the trunk of his Mini when I pulled up beside him. He looked my way, and I didn't need him to take off his sunglasses for me to know he was irritated about my appearance.

Undeterred, I got out of my car anyway and walked to him. "I thought you might want this back for the next time you insult me." My attempt at humor failed epically.

Josh shut the trunk, turned to me, and took the container from my hand. "There won't be a next time, Detective." *So we were back to formalities.* "What happened between us was a mistake and I can't… don't want it to happen again. I'm sorry."

I wasn't sure how to respond. No one had referred to me as a mistake before, and it was entirely unpleasant, much like the time I fell off the seesaw in kindergarten and broke my arm in two places. In fact, Josh's verbal stab to my heart stung a little more.

"Yeah, you're right. We don't fit," I said, lying through my teeth. We fit perfectly together, and I could tell by the downturn of Josh's luscious mouth that he knew it too. Whatever was keeping him from trying anything with me was done out of self-preservation. I wasn't the guy to knock that chip off his shoulder, so I did what he expected. "See you around, Princess." I hated myself and the words I slung at him the moment they left my mouth.

"Fuck you." Josh's snarled response echoed in my ears for hours afterward.

I figured I'd never hear from him ever again, so I was shocked when my phone rang at eleven o'clock that night and his voice was on the other end. Gone was his cool detachment or snarl from earlier in the day and in its place was panic and fear. I was pulling on my sweats and T-shirt before he finished his greeting.

"Gabe, someone just broke into my house through the back door. I heard glass crashing followed by footsteps. It's probably Bianca's killer. He knows I'm the one who gave the description of his vehicle to the police." His voice was almost hysterical. "Send help."

"Do you have a landline? If so, call nine-one-one but keep me on your cell phone. I'm on my way." Later, I'd wonder why he chose to call me first instead of emergency services, but all I could think about right then was getting to him. I grabbed my gun and badge, slid my feet inside my sneakers, and ran out of my house like it was on fire. I was only two blocks away, and I could get there faster on foot by cutting through yards rather than jump in my car and drive over.

"I hear him on the steps. Gabe, I'm not ready to die." I heard tears in his voice.

"Can you barricade yourself in your room? Push a dresser over in front of the door?" I was almost to his house. I had his back door in sight as I ran down the alley between his and Bianca's house. The back door was gaping open from someone kicking it open. "I'm almost there, Josh." As soon as I said the words, I could hear wood splintering like his bedroom door had been kicked in.

"He's got a knife, Gabe."

"You should've kept your mouth shut, you little fucker." The voice coming through Josh's cell phone was eerily calm but very deadly.

I heard Josh drop his cell phone and yell before I heard a scuffle; it sounded like Josh was trying to avoid the madman hell bent on killing him. I dropped my phone as I ran through the back door and up his stairs as fast as my legs could carry me, praying I wasn't too late. I saw what that bastard had done to Bianca, and it would kill me to find Josh dead too.

When I got to the top of the landing, I saw that a dark figure had Josh pinned to his bed, his knees in Josh's chest. That position made it hard for Josh to get the air he needed to fight off his attacker.

The assailant had both hands wrapped around the handle of a wicked knife and was pushing it toward Josh's throat while Josh had his hands wrapped around the assailant's wrists to keep the knife from stabbing him.

"Police! Freeze!" The dark figure on the bed ignored me, and I didn't have a good angle to take a shot. I couldn't risk hitting Josh instead.

As I ran toward the bed, the mirror hanging above his dresser and a decorative vase burst and shattered, creating one hell of a noise. It was so surprising that the killer sat up straight and looked in my direction. I had a clear shot and took it. The bullet from my Glock sent the killer tumbling backward on the bed.

"Call nine-one-one," I told Josh, knowing he didn't have the chance before hell broke loose.

I rounded the bed and moved the knife away from the killer. I checked for a pulse and found that he was dead. I stepped away from the body and placed my gun on the dresser so that the boys in blue didn't accidentally shoot me.

I turned and found Josh standing as far away from his bed and the dead body as he could get. He had his phone up to his ear and told the dispatcher what happened then he hung up. I opened my arms to him, and he crashed into me. His body shook all over; I ran my hands up and down his bare back to comfort him and give him some peace.

"Thank you." My T-shirt muffled his voice.

"I'm right here, Josh. I'm not going anywhere." I held him tighter and just breathed him in; ecstatic to know he was alive and well. I heard the sirens coming and knew they'd separate us for questioning soon, so I enjoyed the quiet moment with him while I could. "You can thank me with some more cookies." My response got a tiny chuckle out of him, which was my goal and made me happy.

EPILOGUE

THE MOMENT MY ASSHOLE KILLER DROPPED DEAD, I COULD FEEL A difference in my spirit. I was happy I could provide the distraction that Gabe needed to save sweet Josh. I hated that my mistake brought trouble to his front door.

I looked at the two beautiful men holding one another and knew I'd done the right thing by slipping that potion into Gabe's coffee, although I had a feeling they'd have found one another anyway. Their auras told me that their road to happiness would be a bumpy and sometimes ugly road. I almost wished I was sticking around to watch it all unfold, but a bright, shining light was starting to form, and I knew that my path was clear.

"You're on your own now, fellas," I said to the two men who were oblivious to my presence.

The light got brighter as I began walking toward it. I could already hear my mama raising a ruckus, and even heaven bound, I knew I was in for it.

"I hear ya, Mama. I hear ya."

DYEING TO BE LOVED

AIMEE NICOLE WALKER

DEDICATION

To Nicholas Bella,
You're an amazing friend, writer, and human being. I treasure our friendship, our chats, and our TV nights. I'm grateful for you every day and convinced more than ever that God sends the people we need into our lives at just the right time.

ONE

Josh "Jazz" Roman

My day started out like a typical Friday at my salon, Curl Up and Dye. I drank my coffee and looked around the business with pride that I had built from scratch. I purchased my childhood home from my parents when they retired and moved to Boca Raton, Florida. They offered to sell the house to me, their only child, for what they paid for it in 1975. The grand dame, as I referred to my home, was appraised at nearly $400,000, but my parents sold it to me for just over $60,000. With that much equity, I was able to borrow enough to renovate the first floor into the most beautiful salon.

I stressed and fretted over every square inch of the design plan making sure it was perfect. I had been miserable in the space I had rented for five years from Harold Kingsley. The man had no vision and would not allow me to make the most minor of enhancements to the building I leased from him. Needless to say, I jumped all over my parents' offer when they made it. Thanks to them, I could expand my business to make it one of the most popular salons in southern Ohio.

Gone was the tired, dated look of yesteryears that I had grown up with, and in its place, was a warm space with real mahogany floors and walls that I painted a neutral ivory that allowed the artwork and glamorous accessories throughout the salon to shine and take center stage. Each of my stylist's stations looked like old Hollywood glam rather than an ordinary booth you'd expect to see at one of those chain salons. I wasn't running some $5 hair emporium. No! If my name was listed as the proprietor, then people were going to get wowed. They were getting the Cadillac experience when stepping into my salon, not the Ford Pinto.

Some people drove for an hour to my tiny town in Blissville, Ohio to have their hair styled and get pampered by my staff and me. I passionately loved my job and looked forward to it every day, even though not all clients were created equally. We had our hands full with quite a few of them, but I had yet to meet a woman that I couldn't win over.

So, my day might've started out like all others, but my harmony and bliss didn't last much later than noon. My best friend and receptionist, Chaz Hamilton, had been out all week with strep throat. My stylists and I tried to take over his duties the first day he was out but quickly realized that we would be better off if I hired a temp to fill in for him. I called Terry, who ran the only temp agency in our county, and she sent us Krista Howard, who was as sweet as apple pie and fit right in with the rest of us. Unfortunately, she committed the one cardinal sin of our salon.

I put a message at the top of our scheduling calendar on the computer that said: **Never Book Georgia Beaumont and Nadine Beaumont on the same day. Ever!!!!** It was written in bold letters, was underlined, and had many exclamation marks to show its importance. It appeared at the top of the calendar every single month because Chaz could sometimes be a spaz and forget things. Nadine and Georgia in the same room was something I wanted to avoid at all costs, so I wrote it out plainly for everyone to see. I couldn't take the chance that one of them would show up early for her appointment while the other's ran over, so I made the rule that they couldn't have an appointment on the same day. It was a good business decision—one that Krista either failed to see or completely ignored and my lovely salon and I paid the price.

I had just removed the foils from Georgia's hair and shampooed her, making sure to massage her scalp a little longer than I did with most clients. She wasn't an easy person to get along with, in fact, some would say I was one of the few who did. Where everyone else saw a bitter, older woman who lost her husband to a younger woman, I saw a person who only wanted to be loved. Yeah, that acerbic tongue she used on people didn't back me up, but I saw through her act.

Georgia was one of my first clients when I opened my doors at the squalor I rented from Harvey. She loved the name of the shop, and as the mayor's wife wanted to stop in and congratulate me on opening a small business. I thought that Georgia was an attractive older woman, but I wanted to yank the license of whomever did her hair color. She caught me staring and perhaps I was biting my lip to avoid saying anything blunt. I had been known to pop off at the mouth with the first thing that came to my mind. It was a bad trait I worked hard to overcome. The last thing I needed was to make Georgia angry so that she warned my potential clients away.

"You keep staring at my hair," she said bluntly. "You're making me nervous."

"I'm sorry," I replied, shuffling my feet nervously from left to right.

"Go ahead and tell me. I can take it," Georgia replied. I could tell she was bracing herself for bad news.

I didn't know it then, but beneath her confident - sometimes arrogant - veneer was a very insecure woman. Had I known, I might've used kinder words than, "Your hair color ages you. It's too blonde, and it makes it look like you're trying to appear younger than you are. It detracts from your beauty rather than enhances it."

Georgia narrowed her eyes at me for several long moments, and I wondered if I'd just killed my career before it even began. Finally, she tipped her head slightly to the side and said, "I like you." Then she sat down in my empty chair and said, "Fix it." So I did, and she became a loyal customer who told all of her friends—or frenemies in her case—about my business. I credited her with my early success and she gobbled up the praise like someone who was desperate to hear positivity in their lives.

For whatever reason, I was one of the rare people who got to see her softer side. Georgia treated the rest of the town like they were beneath her somehow. I would see people cower in her presence or cross the street to avoid her when they saw her walking toward them. It made me sad that the rest of the town didn't know her as I did. Even though I knew of her reputation, it shocked me to see her in action when we came out of the shampoo room, and she laid eyes on her nemesis. Nadine Beaumont.

Rocky's second wife was a much younger version of the original model. Nadine used to be Georgia's personal assistant until she was caught assisting Rocky with things not on Georgia's agenda. The affair itself was pretty big news, but Nadine's unplanned pregnancy was even bigger. Georgia didn't take the humiliation very well, but who the fuck would in her shoes? Three years had passed, and it was obvious that the hurt and embarrassment was just as raw as the day she caught them in the act in her own bed.

"You fucking cunt," Georgia yelled loudly to be heard over the noise of hair dryers, softly piped music, and conversations between stylists and their clients. "Disgusting, husband-stealing whore!"

Nadine was standing with her back to us looking at nail polish for a mani/pedi. My nail tech, Dee Hayslip, and I stared at each other with bulging eyes. Both of us were wondering how the hell it happened when I caught the shocked expression on Krista's face. I had looked at the salon schedule that morning like I always did, and Nadine's name wasn't on it.

Nadine whirled around, her expression going from shocked to downright evil as she took in her adversary wearing a salon cape and her hair wrapped in a towel. She held up a bottle of bright red nail polish in her left hand in a way that the afternoon autumn sun caught her ginormous diamond and sent prisms of light all over the walls.

"Well, if it isn't Rocky's dried out ex-hag. I stopped by to get a manicure and pedicure before I celebrate my anniversary with my husband tonight. I picked a shade to match the new lingerie I bought for the occasion." She smiled evilly and then addressed me. "Josh, honey, I think you're going to need more than a little hair dye to help make her presentable again." Nadine was not a good person, and I didn't like her at all. I would never refuse service to a client just because I didn't like them; it was bad for business. However, I was seriously starting to rethink my business philosophy.

Georgia stood rigid in front of me and I could feel the anger rolling off her in waves. There stood the woman who was thirty years younger and could give Rocky what she couldn't—children. I knew how much it hurt Georgia when Nadine gave birth to their first child. The town gossips lauded the baby over her head, hell-bent on having a good time at the expense of others. The town treated the mayor and new first lady like royalty and their son like a prince. It amazed me that Georgia chose to live remain Blissville after the divorce, but then I realized she had too much pride to be run out of the place she called home. It made me proud to know her and call her a friend.

Well, that was until she let out some banshee-like battle cry and launched herself at Nadine. She grabbed two handfuls of Nadine's Blonde Bombshell hair and began yanking it. Nadine drew back her hand and slapped Georgia so hard her towel fell off her head.

"You fat, sterile cow," Nadine screeched before she wrapped her hands around Georgia's throat and began to squeeze.

It happened so fast that I was slow to react, but I flew into action once Georgia head-butted Nadine and broke her nose. I grabbed for Georgia while my best friend, and fellow stylist, Meredith, grabbed for Nadine.

"Georgia, settle down now." I tried to calm her down while Nadine wailed and screamed, covering her bloody nose with both hands. At least her hands were no longer around Georgia's neck.

"Yeah, settle down, Georgia," Nadine said, wiping away at the blood on her face with the back of her hand. "Too much exertion at *your age* can kill you."

I seriously thought about dropping my hands from Georgia's shoulders and helping her whip Nadine's ass. Business be damned, that hateful shrew wasn't welcome back, and I'd tell her as soon as I knew the fight was over.

"Don't listen to her, Georgia," Meredith chimed in. "Be the classier woman that we all know you to be." Well, at least I knew Mere would have my back when it came time to give Nadine the boot.

It was as if our words didn't register with her because Georgia shook me off and tackled Nadine to the floor. Meredith leaped out of the way in the nick of time or would've been taken down with her. Georgia straddled the younger woman's hips and began to choke her in earnest. Nadine's eyes looked like they were going to pop right out of her head and I had to do something.

Meredith and I tried to pry Georgia's hands off Nadine's neck. We were able to loosen the grip she had on the younger woman and just about had her pulled off when Nadine took advantage of the situation and rolled Georgia over. Instead of pinning Georgia down, she kept rolling until they crashed into my display case that held my hair products and styling tools for sale.

I watched in horror as the glass unit wobbled and threatened to tip over. The force of the hit broke a few of the shelves on the bottom. Glass and bottles of styling products crashed on top of the two women, but that didn't stop them. Instead, they rolled in the other direction, screaming profanities and yanking each other's hair the entire time. It looked like we were on the set of Dynasty instead of standing in my salon.

They barreled into my legs, knocking me over. I hit my head on the receptionist's desk hard enough to see stars. It usually took a lot to make me angry; trashing my salon and nearly knocking me out was enough to do the trick.

I shook off the stars and quickly got to my feet. "That's enough, Nadine and Georgia!" They completely ignored my yelling, so I made a grab for whoever was on top as they rolled on the floor. Instead of grabbing ahold of one of them, I got a fist to the eye for my effort.

It took my three stylists and me to break the women up. They stood panting like rabid dogs as they glared at one another. Georgia then turned her gaze to me and looked at me with wounded eyes. "You betrayed me by allowing *her* into your salon," she said, her voice filled with hurt. She pointed her finger in Nadine's direction and raised her voice when she added, "I made you, Josh. You were nothing when I first walked into your cheesy salon five years ago. Your success, this beautiful salon," she gestured around at my pride and joy with both hands, "is all because of me." Georgia's face twisted with rage. "I will just as easily destroy you. Do you hear me?"

Not waiting for a response, she whirled around and left the salon. The autumn breeze kicked up as she walked down the front steps, making the cape she still wore billow up in front of her body. She looked down at the cape then whipped it off and tossed it to the ground before she stomped on it with both feet.

"She left without her coat or purse," Meredith said softly beside me. "I'll take them out to her, honey."

I turned to face Nadine while Meredith retrieved Georgia's things. I knew that I should've been the one to take them to her, but I also knew she needed time to calm down before we spoke again. Georgia had been very instrumental in my early success, but she did not make me. She might've sent a lot of clients to my door, but I was the one who pleased them and kept them coming back for five years. Still, I didn't want there to be any animosity between us. I decided to wait until the morning and then I'd give her a call or stop by her house.

Someone had brought Nadine a towel to hold to her bleeding nose. I could hear her mumbling about pressing charges beneath the cotton. She looked at me when she felt my attention on her. Nadine must've seen how angry I felt because she at least had the smarts to look a little nervous.

"You are not welcome here again, Nadine." She removed her towel in preparation to argue with me, but I held up my hand. "This is not up for debate. Curl Up and Dye is my salon, and I decide the clients I will and will not see. I am aware that Georgia threw the first verbal barb, but the things you said to her were cruel and uncalled for. You are persona non grata around here from now on."

She stood taller in her indignation over my criticism. "Wait until my husband hears about this. He'll destroy you for treating me this way."

"I really don't care what your sleazebag for a husband thinks about me," I replied. "I'd like for you to leave now or I'll be forced to call the police. I could press charges for the property damage." I gestured to the broken glass all over the floor. "Or even assault," I added, pointing to my eye that was starting to throb.

"Fuck you," Nadine said, flipping me the bird on her way out the door. Such a classy act from our town's first lady.

I shook my head and turned back to face my employees. "Back to work, everyone."

It wasn't long before the normal buzz of the salon returned. Since Georgia left early, I had a few hours before my next client. I got out a broom and cleaned up the mess before I retreated to the sitting room between the salon and massage areas with a cup of coffee.

"Fucking cunt!"

I looked up at my blue macaw, Savage, and grimaced at what he just said. He already had the filthiest mouth on the planet when I took pity on him and bought him from the pet store. His previous owner had died, and his family didn't know what to do with him, so they took him to the pet store. Brook, the owner, took him in before she discovered his vocabulary. I walked into the pet store one afternoon to buy treats for my Siamese cat, Diva, and my ferret, Jazzy, and was immediately propositioned by the bird for a blow job. It was love at first sight.

Normally, his raunchy talk made me laugh and brought a smile to my face, but not right then. It reminded me of how hurt Georgia was when she left the salon. I wanted to find her and make things right between us, but I had several more clients on my schedule, and I figured she needed more time before she would want to talk to me.

I tried calling her when my day was over, and I was alone in my living space on the second floor, but my call went to voicemail. Instead of leaving a message, I hung up. I decided it would be best if I talked to her in person.

TWO

Gabriel Wyatt

IT WAS A RARE OCCURRENCE FOR ME TO GET CALLED INTO WORK ON a Saturday once I moved to Blissville two years ago. My then-boyfriend, Kyle, wanted to move back home and take over his grandfather's veterinary practice when he retired. At that time, Kyle and I had been together for two years and lived together for one. Our relationship had become strained from both of us working such long hours, and we both thought the move to a smaller town was what we needed to repair our relationship. We tried for another year but realized the chasm between us had grown too large to bridge. We parted on good terms, and I decided to stay in the quaint town, rather than start all over someplace else.

It had been a sleepy existence until Bianca Dragomir was killed in her home by a client who didn't like the results of a love potion she gave him. Not only did her death shock the community of just over six thousand citizens, but it also brought a new person into my life who confused me on every level. I pushed thoughts of Josh Roman aside as I jogged up the steps of the mini-mansion that belonged to the town's former first lady, as they referred to a mayor's wife in Blissville.

"I figured Bianca's homicide would be the quota for our community for the next twenty years," my partner, Adrian Goode, said once I reached the wide porch. "Sadly not."

"Let's look at what we have," I said to him. We slipped on blue booties to make sure we didn't contaminate the crime scene then entered the house.

There was a team of officers dusting for fingerprints and looking for any signs of evidence or blood that might belong to someone other than our victim. We often caught killers because of a negligently tossed cigarette or the victim making their attacker bleed during the struggle. Those were the cases where you got lucky; other crime scenes were clean and offered very little in the way of clues. We found our medical examiner, Dr. Melissa Chan, in the upstairs master bathroom.

We stayed outside the bathroom door until she said, "Come on in, Detectives." She looked away from the body and offered us a strained smile. Dr. Chan was a petite woman with shrewd, dark brown eyes and a rapier wit. I enjoyed talking to her, but not over top of a dead body. "Gentlemen, this is Georgia Beaumont." She gestured to the woman who was lying in bloody bathwater with a pair of scissors protruding from her neck. "It looks like she was attacked while taking a hot bath, reading a book and drinking a glass of wine."

"You're certain it was a homicide and not self-inflicted?" Adrian asked.

Dr. Chan pulled one of Mrs. Beaumont's hands out of the water and showed us the cuts on her palms and the outside of her hand. "Defensive wounds. Mrs. Beaumont held her hand up to ward off the attack," she explained, then gestured to the book floating in the water. Dr. Chan pointed to the scissors and said, "The angle is all wrong for a self-inflicted wound, and it's not likely she would've stabbed herself more than once." She pointed to the other puncture wounds on the victim's neck with her gloved finger. "The carpet was dry by the time the police arrived this morning to arrest her, but it was obvious that the blood-tinged water had been splashed all over the carpet around the tub. That indicates foul play to me, fellas."

"Arrest Mrs. Beaumont?" I asked. I knew of her, of course, but didn't know her on a personal level. I had heard she was quite a force to be reckoned with, but the idea of her getting arrested seemed absurd to me.

"Apparently, she and the new Mrs. Rocky Beaumont got into an altercation yesterday. The officers downstairs could tell you more," she said then returned her attention back to the body. "I'll have tox screens and a preliminary report for you guys as soon as possible." Dr. Chan dismissed us so she could finish her work and send the body to the morgue.

Adrian and I went downstairs and asked around until we found the responding officers, Hank Jones and Marley Kasey. "What brought you to Mrs. Beaumont's door so early this morning?" I asked Hank.

"She and Nadine Beaumont got into a huge fight at the salon yesterday." I almost visibly flinched when Hank mentioned the salon because I knew exactly which one he meant. An image of Josh's platinum blond hair and hazel eyes popped up in my brain, and I had to force him out of my head to focus. There had never been another guy who tied me up in as many knots as Josh did. "Rocky and Nadine stopped by the police station last night, and Nadine insisted on pressing assault charges against Georgia. It was obvious that Nadine had a broken nose and she said it was from Georgia's head butting her. It was equally as obvious that Rocky had tried to talk her out of it, but she wasn't listening to him She wanted Georgia arrested, and that was final."

"We showed up this morning to arrest Georgia, but she didn't answer the front door," Marley told us. "We noticed that the door was open when we came around back and knew something wasn't right. Temperatures dropped to nearly freezing last night so she wouldn't have left it open to let in fresh air." It was abnormally colder than usual for that time of year, and I agreed with their decision to enter the premises. "We found her dead in her bathtub and called it in."

"Did our killer leave behind any clues?' Adrian asked.

"No blood beyond the bathroom," Hank replied. "Our killer was pretty clean on entrance and exit. No finger or hand prints."

"Nadine Beaumont mentioned something in her report last night," Marley added. "She said that Georgia physically and verbally attacked the salon owner, Jazz Roman." I hated when people called him Jazz instead of by his name. "According to her, Georgia also threatened to destroy his business right before she stormed out."

I could tell she was hesitating to say more. "What aren't you saying?"

"Well," she paused for a second then continued, "the scissors used to kill Georgia look like a pair of shears a hairstylist would use."

I felt as if she punched me in the stomach. I knew to the depths of my soul that Josh Roman was many things, but a killer was not one of them. Granted, the amount of talking we did was minimal during my investigation into Bianca's death that led a madman straight to Josh's door and nearly cost him his life. Josh and I got off to a horrible start when I stuck my foot in my mouth and made an ass of myself. I spent weeks trying to atone for it, but he wanted no part of my apologies.

There was one glorious afternoon when we quit hissing and spitting at one another long enough to do what we wanted. As long as I live, I'll never forget the look on Josh's face or the way his lean body moved over mine when he rode me like a stallion. It was only once, but there wasn't much I wouldn't do to get us back there again. If I were honest, I would admit there were many things I wanted from Josh but doubted I'd ever get them. Two months had passed since I shot and killed Bianca's killer in his bedroom and we hadn't spoken. Sure, we'd seen each other in town and nodded at one another in acknowledgment, but that wasn't good enough.

"Come on. Josh?" Adrian asked, pulling me out of my thoughts. I was happy to hear Adrian was as doubtful as I was.

"I don't know, Detective," Hank said to Adrian. "That business is all that he has, and maybe he retaliated after she threatened him."

The business wasn't all he had. Josh had friends who loved him, pets he cherished, and a long client list who adored him. Hell, even I knew that and I sadly didn't know much about him. Well, I knew the face he made when he came from the pleasure he got from my dick. I knew that he tucked up nicely against me when we cuddled afterward. I also knew that someone or perhaps several people had hurt him badly enough for him to erect a shield around his heart. I couldn't prevent my mind from wandering back to an encounter we had at a gay club called Vibe.

I kissed Josh until someone bumped into him hard enough to jolt us. He pulled back and stared up at me with shock, and I probably wore a matching look. It was no ordinary kiss you see. It felt like the little imp burned himself beneath my skin and I wasn't so sure what the fuck to do about it. Then he opened his mouth and took the decision away.

"Did that feel like kissing a girl to you?" He leaned in and pressed

his lips against my ear. "I might be on the lean side, but that's because I do yoga and I'm extremely limber. I can reverse cowboy like you can't even imagine. Well, you'll have to use your imagination because you're not man enough to act on the desire I see in your eyes. You think you'll be less of a man or less gay if you sleep with a man with soft skin and a lean body. To guys like you, fucking men with big muscles on manly frames makes you feel more manly yourself."

"You don't know shit about me, Jizz." I sounded like a sixth grader, but his accusations stung. Hard.

"I know all about guys like you, Detective." He shook his head as if he pitied me.

"My name is Gabe."

"Okay, Gabe." He rolled his eyes as if I was stupid; maybe he was one of those that thought all jocks were dumb; I was neither a jock nor dumb. "A lot of guys want to fuck me, to use me as their personal blow up doll with ready orifices to please them until the next strapping stud comes along to grab their attention. I'm never the guy they take home to meet mom and dad. I'm not good enough."

The next day he had shown up at my house with cookies as an apology, and we ended up in my bed. When I woke up, he was gone, and he wanted to pretend it didn't happen when I approached him to talk about it. He referred to it as a "mistake."

"Anyone is capable of murder," Marley said as if we needed a lecture. She just shrugged when I aimed a dark scowl in her direction. Their attention to detail was appreciated, but I didn't need them playing junior detective.

"I think we've done all we can do here for the time being," Adrian said. He looked at me and said, "I guess we better head over to Curl Up and Dye and talk to Josh."

"Yeah," I agreed. I had too many emotions warring inside of me; I just needed to shove them aside so I could focus on doing my job. Georgia Beaumont, regardless of how she lived her life, deserved my undivided attention. I had myself totally convinced I could do it until we walked outside and the man himself was standing on the sidewalk in front of her house.

I couldn't tell how long he'd been standing in the cold, but his pink cheeks and nose told me it had been awhile. I saw the small bruise beneath his eye and knew it must've been from the assault that Nadine mentioned to the police. His large, expressive eyes were wide with fear, and it was all I could do not to reach out to him. I knew my gesture of comfort would be rejected, not to mention completely unprofessional since I had to treat him like a suspect. The concern in his hazel eyes turned to irritation when he saw me. I blew out a quiet, frustrated breath and prepared myself for his hostility.

"What happened?" he asked between chattering teeth.

"Let's talk in my car," I said to him. I hit the button to remote start my Dodge Charger and gestured for him to precede us. He looked hesitant, but he bit back whatever reply he had for me because of Adrian's presence.

Adrian got in the back seat, leaving Josh to climb in the back seat with him or take the passenger seat beside me. I knew he'd rather sit with Adrian, but must have figured it would look weird so he reluctantly climbed in beside me. I hit the ignition button to fully start the car before I cranked up the heat and turned on the heated seats for Josh.

"Georgia Beaumont was killed sometime last night or early this morning." I kept my eyes on him to gauge his reaction. The devastation in his eyes was exactly what I expected. "The M.E. hasn't released the time of death yet."

Josh closed his eyes and shook his head, trying hard to find his composure, but my words cut him deeply. He bit his lip, but not before I saw it tremble. "Poor Georgia," he said softly. "She just wanted to be loved."

"We heard about the fight between the past and current Mrs. Beaumont. Can you tell us about it?" Adrian asked.

We listened as Josh described the event in great detail, including how he had rules in place that they were not to have appointments on the same day. I could tell the altercation upset him and he wasn't happy about banning Nadine from his salon.

"Is that when Georgia Beaumont struck you?" I asked.

Josh raised his hand and touched the tender spot beneath his eye. "I'm not sure which one of them hit me. It could've just as easily been Nadine." He went on to explain he was struck while trying to stop them from rolling all over his floor and wasn't sure who hit him.

"Where were you last night, Josh?" Adrian asked. I was glad he did because I wasn't sure I could.

"Home alone," he replied, then swallowed hard. "Am I a suspect because of Georgia yelling at me? I didn't take it personally. I knew she was just upset and I didn't blame her. She and I would've kissed and made up." Josh sounded certain. "I know not many people liked Georgia, but I did. I could be myself and didn't have to tiptoe around her." His lips trembled again, and tears escaped his eyes before he could blink them away. "I would never hurt her or anyone."

He turned his wounded gaze on me. I wanted to reach for his hand and tell him I believed him. I did believe him, but I kept my mouth shut and my hands to myself. Fuck! This guy had me all twisted up inside and damned if I knew what to do about it. The truth was, even if I could make all my feelings for him go away, I wasn't sure I would.

"She just wanted to be loved," he repeated.

"I don't have any more questions right now. Do you, Gabe?" Adrian asked.

"No, not right now." I couldn't tear my eyes away from his.

"You're free to go, Mr. Roman," Adrian said, "unless there's anything you want to add."

He stared back at me for a few long moments, and I wanted to know what he was thinking. He closed his eyes briefly and shook his head. “No, nothing,” he said when he reopened them.

I could tell Josh was trying hard to keep it together in front of us and I truly felt bad for him. He'd been through a lot during the last few months. First, his neighbor, and friend, Bianca, was killed. Her assailant attempted to kill him when a sketch with his image was given to the press and broadcasted. Now, another person Josh obviously cared about was killed.

Josh got out of my car without another word. I watched him walk toward his teal Mini Cooper. He walked tall and proud like he normally did, but he wasn't fooling me. Beneath that confident veneer hid a lot of vulnerability that I wanted to make disappear.

“Careful, buddy,” Adrian said from the back seat. “You look like you're awfully attracted to him despite your claim that he's not your type.”

I had said that once and I meant it at the time. A lot had changed since then, and I wasn't sure why. All I knew was that Josh Roman got to me on so many levels and I didn't know what to do about it. “I'm not sure that I even like the guy,” I told Adrian honestly.

“Well, ‘like’ doesn't always have anything to do with it,” he replied with a chuckle. “Just wait until the case is over before you scratch that particular itch.”

Adrian was right to caution me, but it was too late for that. I had already done the scratching, and all it did was make me itch more. Instead of confessing the truth, I said, “I hear ya, buddy. I promise to behave.”

Early that evening, I stood on the sidewalk in front of Josh's salon and home, willing myself to keep my promise to myself and my partner. Yet, I knew I'd break it if Josh gave me any indication that he wanted me as badly as I wanted him.

I was a grown-fucking-man, not some horny, hormonal teenager that popped wood every time the wind blew. It was time I started acting like it. I looked over the front of his home while trying to get my body and breathing under control. I had to say that Josh's home was the most unique I'd ever seen.

The two-and-a-half story home had a Victorian feel to it with a turret on the right side of the house. The home was a soft gray color that seemed to contrast with Josh's bold personality. My favorite parts of the home were the huge porch on the front that rounded at both corners and the black metal roof. The porch invited you to sit and drink lemonade while you watched the world go by on a summer day. The roof made me think of lying in bed on a rainy day and listening to the music the rain made on the tin.

I stood outside for so long that I started to feel like a creeper. I needed to decide whether I rang Josh's doorbell or just walked away. Leaving would've been the smart thing to do, but my traitorous heart wanted to be certain he was okay after he learned about Georgia's death. I couldn't forget the sadness I saw in his expressive eyes.

"Are you just going to stand out there all night or are you going to grow a pair and ring my doorbell?"

I looked up to the second-story where I knew his bedroom was and found him leaning out his window. I saw the challenge written all over his face even in the fading sunlight. I started up the sidewalk to his house even though I knew I should've left. I headed around to the back of his home because I knew business was in the front and personal was in the back—sort of like an 80s mullet.

He was waiting for me at the back door when I climbed the steps. I told my heart to settle the fuck down when his lips turned up in a smile slash grimace. I reminded the dumb organ that he didn't like us much and trying to get close to him was like hugging a porcupine. The frustration and hurt weren't worth all the hot and cold vibes he sent me, yet, I couldn't turn away.

"Evening, Detective Dickface," Josh said, stepping aside to let me in.

So, not worth the abuse, but that didn't stop me from wanting to kiss him until he begged me to fuck him.

THREE

Josh

GEORGIA WAS DEAD. THOSE WORDS PLAYED THROUGH MY HEAD all day long while I tried my best to function for my client on her special day. Jessie Miracle booked my salon for her bridal party months ago, and I couldn't let her down. Jessie's joy and happiness were contagious, and it was just what I needed to push my sad thoughts aside while we got the bride and her party ready.

Once they left, my heart felt very heavy, and I was grateful to have the next two days off so I could hide inside my home and try to come to terms with Georgia's death and the fact the police had asked me for an alibi. Seeing Gabe again rattled me more than it should. I might've only been in his car for ten minutes or less, but the smell of him and the sound of his voice were permanently etched in my brain. Every time I thought I had worked him out of my system, he reappeared and sent me reeling all over again.

I locked up the salon once everyone left and headed upstairs to my private residence. There had once been four large bedrooms and one bathroom upstairs. I knocked down the wall between the master bedroom and a spare bedroom so I could have a master suite with a large bathroom and a walk-in closet. I also tore down the walls between the third and fourth bedroom and turned it into an open concept living room and kitchen. The contractor had tried to talk me into leaving a guest bedroom in place for resale purposes, but I rejected him outright. I planned to live in this house until I took my last breath. Besides, the third story attic was huge and I could easily convert it into a guest suite someday.

I took a very long, hot shower and let the water ease the aches I had in my shoulders and neck from a long day of blowouts, updos, and applying makeup. I hadn't eaten anything except for a small pastry for breakfast, and my blood sugar was letting me know it. I wasn't a bit hungry, but I knew I had to eat or I'd end up with a massive headache.

Speaking of headaches, I happened to see one very sexy and frustrating detective standing on the sidewalk in front of my house. Gabriel Wyatt. I could tell by his body language that he was very hesitant about knocking on my door. Could I blame him? I wanted to; I truly did, but I knew I was the reason he hesitated. I ran hot and cold with him, and I knew it had to fuck with his mind. It wasn't something that I did intentionally, but I doubted he would believe that.

I stood in my window and just looked down at him while my mind replayed every run-in I'd had with him over the last few months. I had seen him around our small town plenty of times, but we never spoke until Bianca's death. I had heard my friend's screams and called 911. That night, Detective Dark and Dangerous showed up at my house to ask questions. I felt something sizzle and spark inside me the first time I looked into his eyes.

My attraction to him died a quick and painful death when I followed him and his partner out of my sitting room downstairs to ask a question about Bianca's death. They didn't know I trailed them, so they felt free to talk amongst themselves. What I heard that night left no doubt in my mind that the dark-haired, dark-eyed detective was no different than the rest of the guys I mistakenly fell for in the past.

"He's cute, huh?" his partner had asked tall, dark, and dreamy.

"Stop, Adrian." His response was surprisingly firm.

"Come on, man. You and Kyle split up over a year ago. It's time you got back on the horse or allowed yourself to be mounted—whatever you're into." I couldn't see the expression on Adrian's face, but I imagined he was waggling his eyebrows or something silly.

"He's not really my type," Detective Dreamy said with a casual shrug. Right then I knew where this was going, and I should've just turned around and gone back to my friends, but I couldn't. I had to know what he was going to say.

"Why ever not?" Adrian sounded genuinely confused by his answer.

"He's just a bit too..."

"Feminine?" I finished for him. I could hear the edge of anger in my soft voice. The detective duo whipped around to face me, shock registering on their faces. The look of shock on Gabe's face turned to shame in an instant when he realized I knew what he was about to say. I held my head high and stood straight and proud in front of them like I'd taught myself to do over the years.

"You're one of those 'masc only' guys, aren't you?" I even used air quotes for emphasis. At least he had the decency to look mortified at

getting caught. "Don't worry, Detective Wyatt. I'm not into tall, dark, and dickish men, so you're safe from my affections."

As first meetings went, it was terrible. He had approached me with an apology in his eyes several times during the weeks that followed, but I didn't want to hear it. He wasn't sorry he thought it or that he was about to say it. He was only sorry that I overheard him. It was a battle I'd faced all my life, and quite frankly, I was tired of it. So, I insulted him at every turn before he could get a word in edgewise.

Gabe took it like a champ each time until his patience ran out; then he kissed me. I didn't react very well to the kiss—okay, I did during the scorching kiss, but not afterward. In the process of setting him straight, I exposed some of my insecurities to him, flirted with another guy, and insinuated that I'd be going home with him to make Gabe jealous. In essence, I'd made an ass of myself.

I barely slept after I returned home from the club alone. After tossing and turning for hours, I got up and baked apology cookies and took them to Gabe later that morning. I wasn't sure what kind of reception I was going to receive but was surprised when he welcomed me into his home without any wisecracks. Instead, he made us coffee, and we sat down to eat cookies at his kitchen table. I wouldn't have been as forgiving or as nice as he was that morning had the situation been reversed.

Gabe moaned and groaned indecently around his bites of my chocolate chip cookies. My dick didn't care about how big of a mistake it would be to get involved with him. He looked at me, his eyes honing in on my lips, and told me I had a little chocolate on my mouth. Gabe leaned forward, and I thought he was going to wipe it off with his finger, but instead, he licked it off.

That small gesture was like throwing gasoline on a bonfire. Gabe threw me over his shoulder then carried me upstairs to his room where I rode him like he was a bronco. After I had bragged about being limber in one of my tirades, I had to show him what I could do. I thanked the yoga gods when I saw his dark eyes burn with unadulterated lust when he looked up at me. He gripped my hips so hard he left bruised fingermarks that lasted for days, and it turned me on every time I saw them.

I snuck out of his house and did my walk of shame home and then avoided him for days afterward. When he finally pinned me down, I told him what we experienced was a mistake and would not happen again. I wanted to mean it, but I also knew there was something about him that made me want to take a chance. Later that same night, I got the scare of my life when Bianca's killer broke into my house and tried to kill me. I had called Gabe in a panic when I heard the glass in my back door shatter and knew what was about to happen. I could've called 911, but if those were my last minutes on earth, I wanted to hear his voice one more time.

He saved me that night. He shot and killed that guy in my bedroom and then held me tight when fear and shock rocked my body like an earthquake. The police came and separated us so they could take our statements, and I immediately missed the heat of his body and his arms around me. After everyone had left, we looked at each other for several long moments.

I wanted to ask him to stay; I think he wanted to take me back to his place to tuck me away nice and safe. In the end, neither of us said anything of the sort. He watched as I pulled spare blankets out of a hall closet and made up a temporary bed on the couch. That bastard died on my bed, and I'd never sleep on it again.

"*I'm going to need to buy a new bed tomorrow,*" was what I ended up saying to Gabe. I didn't thank him for running to the rescue and saving me. I acted like I always did, I pushed all thought of the incident aside and focused on what I could control. I couldn't change what happened in my home, but I could buy a new bed and bedding.

Gabe reluctantly left that night, and we went back to pretending we were strangers for the weeks that followed. I'd seen him about town, but we never spoke again until the morning outside Georgia's house. Looking down at him through my window, I could see how twisted up he was about stopping by to see me. I should've kept my mouth shut and let him make up his mind, but instead, I yelled out the window and issued a challenge that I knew would work in my favor. Regardless of what my brain said, I wanted to see him again and breathe in the scent of him—sandalwood, citrus, and man.

I met Gabe at the back door and insulted him like a school kid would, but it didn't faze him. He just smirked at me and walked into the kitchenette the staff, and I used for the salon. I shut the door and turned to face him. The way he chewed his lower lip and his furrowed brow led me to believe that he was feeling uncertain about being in my home.

"How are you doing?" he asked, his deep voice filled with concern. I liked it almost as much as when his voice was gravelly with need when he came.

"Who's asking? The cop or the guy who..." I let my words trail off because I wasn't sure how to classify him.

Gabe could've come back with a witty, snappy reply, but he didn't. He was obviously a better person than me because I would've jumped all over that opening. "I'm not here on official police business," he replied. "You've been dealt many blows lately, and I wanted to make sure you were holding up."

"You want to come up for a cup of coffee?" I think we were both shocked by my question—probably me more than him. "And I mean coffee, nothing more." I had seen the little flare of hope in the dark depths of his eyes and I had meant it when I said we weren't having sex again. He was just too damn dangerous for my heart.

"Sure." Gabe offered me a sly grin and followed me up to the second story.

I wondered if he was thinking how different that visit was from the previous one. I still woke up with nightmares of that man pinning me to my bed with his knees on my chest. I couldn't breathe, and I was quickly losing my strength as the sharp end of his knife got closer and closer to my throat. Sometimes I dreamed other people were trying to kill me. In fact, one dream included the dashing detective with a knife to my throat. Dreaming of him pinning me to my bed wasn't new, but in all my previous dreams I was panting, moaning, and begging for more, not fighting for my life. I felt that dream was symbolic of my internal struggle to resist him.

Gabe took a seat on the sofa while I popped a K-Cup in the Keurig to make him a cup of coffee. I remembered how he liked his coffee from my only visit to his house. It was good host manners and nothing more that encouraged me to add the hazelnut creamer and sugar to the brew for him.

"Thank you," he politely said when I handed his cup to him. "So, how are you holding up?" he asked when I returned to the living room with my cup of coffee. I sat in the club chair rather than beside him on the couch. The smile on his face was almost a smirk. Did he think I didn't trust myself to sit beside him? *Well, he wasn't wrong*. I feared he was my kryptonite.

"I'm still shocked," I replied honestly. "This seems like a really bad dream."

"Tell me about the Georgia you knew," Gabe said. He didn't sound like he was asking as part of his investigation. He sounded like he genuinely wanted to know as if he cared.

"She was a tough nut." I closed my eyes and pictured the Georgia I knew; the one she rarely showed to the world. She smiled, she laughed, and she told bawdy jokes. She didn't care that I was gay. She only cared that I was always honest with her. It wasn't something that happened when she was the mayor's wife. People told her what she wanted to hear and she lost respect for them. Then there was the ordeal with Nadine and Rocky's affair. That was the ultimate betrayal, and she felt her entire adult life had been a lie. "I knew a different side of her than most. She trusted me." Emotion choked my voice when I added, "And I let her down."

"How so?"

"I could've refused Nadine as a client, but I thought it was bad for business to choose sides. Personally, I always chose Georgia."

"Were you upset about what she said to you?" Gabe set his coffee down and leaned forward when I didn't answer right away. "I'm not here as a cop. I'm trying to be a..." He paused for a few moments as he searched for the right term. "Friend," he finally said.

"Friend," I repeated, testing the word on my tongue. The thing was, I couldn't be sure I even liked Gabe, so a friendship wasn't something I wanted from him. I chose to ignore it and answer his damn question for fear I'd give myself a goddamned migraine if I thought too hard. "I wasn't worried," I told him, but I had already said that earlier in the day. "She would've forgiven me. I was going to make it up to her."

Gabe looked at me for a few seconds before he picked up his coffee and took another sip. "Look, I've wanted to say something to you for quite some time now and..."

"Don't." My words were firm and resolute, to the point that he jerked back a bit in his seat. "I know you want to apologize for what you almost said the night Bianca died. I've seen the apology in your eyes many times, but I honestly don't want to hear it." His mouth dropped open in surprise, so I took advantage. "I wish I could tell you it's water under the bridge, but it's not. By now you've learned it's a very sore subject for me. Guys like you..." I broke off because I was stereotyping just like he'd done to me because I'm leaner than most men, there's a sway to my hips when I walk, and I'm vibrant. To a lot of men, that made me feminine, and it pissed me off. "You know what, it doesn't matter."

"It does matter, Josh," Gabe said. "I hurt your feelings, and I *am* sorry for it. I'm not going to bullshit you by pretending I wasn't going to say it or that I didn't mean it at the time because I did. That's not what I was going to apologize about." *Kudos for honesty.*

"Then what are you sorry for?" I asked, tilting my head to the side in puzzlement.

He rose to his feet and set his coffee cup down. "For being narrow-minded."

"Oh," was my awe-inspiring response. Gabe Wyatt had done something that not many had over my lifetime; he rendered me speechless.

"I'm going to show myself out now. You've had a traumatic day, so you stay up here and rest. I'll lock the door behind me." He nodded his head when I sat there staring mutely at him. "Okay then, I'll see you around." He made it to the top of the stairs before I finally found my voice.

"Detective," I called out. He stopped and looked over his shoulder at me. "Do you honestly think I'm dangerous?" Did he think that I could hurt another person? I needed to know.

"Not to anyone but me," Gabe said in response. His mouth quirked up in a half-smile before he descended the steps.

My heart pounded in my chest, and my brain throbbed over the possibility of his words. Did he mean that I was dangerous to his *heart*? Couldn't be! It had to be my low blood sugar playing tricks on me. And if I *did* understand him correctly? Then what?

FOUR

Gabe

THE SKY OPENED AND RELEASED A TORRENT OF COLD RAIN AS SOON as I was inside my car. I had almost walked the two blocks to Josh's house, but I was glad I drove when my wipers couldn't keep my windshield clear on max speed. Rather than risk an accident, I pulled over and decided to wait until the rain let up a bit.

I would've normally groaned about the cold rain, but I was still buzzing from being in Josh's presence and not being on the receiving end of his cutting tongue. For once, things weren't tense and awkward between us. Weird feelings stirred within me when he handed me my coffee and I saw it was exactly how I liked it. It meant he had been paying attention to me and I liked that a lot more than the simple act warranted. It made me feel bolder and gave me the courage to speak up.

Did I just flirt with Josh? I did, and I shocked him so much that his mouth gaped open and no words came out. That was a first. Usually, he was the one who left me tongue tied. Of course, my mind immediately went to the gutter, remembering the way our tongues tangled during our hot kisses and trying to figure out how to get more of them.

The truth was Josh had me completely enthralled with him. It went beyond his looks because I had seen him many times before, but the way I responded to him was different. I wasn't in love with the guy. Hell, I wasn't even sure I liked him. There was something about him that captured my attention the first time he opened his mouth and blasted me with his sarcasm. Josh was prickly, untouchable, and carried a chip on his shoulder the size of Texas. And damned if I didn't want to knock that chip off. I decided it was straight-up lust. If so, it would fade over time, and I could get back to solid footing instead of feeling like my equilibrium was fucked up.

The way he challenged me was new to me and it turned me on beyond sanity. *What kind of guy wants someone who doesn't want them back?* I mean, I've seen that behavior before and I always shook my head in confusion, but, yet, there I was in the same boat. I craved Josh Roman like an illicit drug. Why? Because he was a challenge? Because he was completely different from any guy, I had ever dated? I didn't have the answers to my questions.

All I knew was that he sparked something inside me that I didn't want to squelch. That one afternoon I spent with him showed me that something huge had been missing in my life for a long time—passion. I had loved Kyle deeply, I truly had. Our sex life for the first year and a half of our relationship had been stellar, in my opinion.

Things had slowly fizzled out between us, and I had blamed our careers and the time apart, but even when we were together, we lacked spark. Sex had been more perfunctory, as if we were going through the motions, by the time our relationship ended.

I felt guilty thinking about Kyle in those terms, but it was true. Even after our cordial breakup—and it had been very amicable—we still hooked up a few times because it was easier and safer to have sex together rather than look for it with strangers. At the time, I thought it was no big deal. We weren't hurting anyone, and we both got what we needed, but I was wrong. We were hurting ourselves by not going out and finding someone more suitable for us.

Sure, Kyle and I had a lot in common, but we didn't push each other to become better. We didn't spark an insane need to be inside one another. Playing it safe with our emotions wasn't going to enrich our lives on any level, and I suddenly wanted that for myself at thirty-five years old.

I wasn't implying that Josh was "the one" I would grow old with, but I knew he was "the one" I wanted to take a chance on—if only he could find a way to like me after I botched things. I had tried on numerous occasions to apologize to him. I was glad that he never let it happen and that I had to force my words on him that night. Truthfully, my earlier apologies would've been based on my guilt rather than enlightenment. I meant what I told him that evening.

I had been narrow-minded in my thinking and I failed to recognize that beauty exists in more places than just ripped muscles, chest hair, and deep voices. I don't know when I changed, or how, but I suspected it was just something about Josh himself that had me sitting up straight and taking notice. I admired his long, lean frame and the fluid way his body moved while walking, dancing, and fucking. Josh had appropriately proportioned muscles to fit his frame and the smoothest skin that I had ever felt. I discovered I liked the differences between our bodies—from our heights, our skin tones, and our weight. I never once thought of his attributes as feminine when I had him in my arms or my bed. I had been a judgmental ass, and I was determined to prove that my old way of thinking was well and truly in my past.

The rain let up and became just a downpour instead of a monsoon. Since the visibility had improved, I drove the rest of the way home. I ran from my car to my house faster than I did when I was trying out for the first string tight end for my varsity football team in high school. I worked hard during the offseason in the gym and on the track to gain physical strength and speed. It was something I wanted really bad, and I worked for it.

I knew I needed that same dedication if I was going to win Josh over. *Win him over?* I shook my head, more from my surprising thoughts than from my drenched hair, as I unlocked my door and let myself into my house. A cold chill permeated my body, so I kicked the furnace up a notch and decided to make another cup of coffee.

Once I warmed up, my thoughts went right back to Josh, and I began to catalog the differences I noticed in him since the night of his attack. The first thing that stuck out to me was that he had grown a beard that was a shade or two darker than his platinum hair. I liked the way it looked on him; I liked it a lot. I wanted to run my fingers over the beard to see if it was soft or bristly, then I wanted to feel it against other parts of my body.

The wariness in his eyes when he looked at me had faded somewhat. It was still there, but not as strong. It used to be that his wariness lingered in his eyes longer than the annoyance or dislike he felt for me. He still had his reservations about me, but they weren't as strong.

On some level, he knew he could trust me because I was the one he called the night of the attack, not 911. I suspected that he had put my number in his phone rather than pull out my business card from his wallet. That was precious time he didn't have that night.

A shiver worked through me as I recalled just how close he

had come to dying. Shooting and killing a man wasn't something I enjoyed, even if he was a cold-blooded killer. I still relived that night for a solid month in my sleep and had to work with the police psychologist to make sure I was still capable of doing my job. I had a support system, but did Josh?

I had called to check on him the days that followed, but he either didn't respond, or his answer was the same, "I'm fine." He made it clear that he didn't want to talk to me about the situation, which only made me worry about him more. I didn't push Josh because I knew I would lose any ground I had made with him, which I suspected was very little.

He let me hold him tight against my chest and comfort him until the police officers arrived on the scene, but he rejected the hug I tried to give him when I left his house that night. I had wanted to ask him to come home with me, but I could tell by the look in his eyes that the answer would've been no, even if I promised to sleep on the couch.

Damn, the guy drove me nuts. There had to be someone out there that I was attracted to *and* didn't drive me crazy. Okay, what I felt for Josh was more than the garden variety attraction, but my concept was right. I just needed to talk myself into looking for that other person, but hell, I wasn't ready to give up on Josh yet.

Dinner was a frozen square of lasagna that took forever to bake in the oven, a bowl of salad, and cold beer while I watched college football on my big screen TV. It wasn't an exciting evening by any stretch, but it was peaceful, if not lonely. I thought about Josh's pets and wondered if maybe I should get a fur buddy of my own. I felt content in my life at the moment, but I wouldn't go so far as say that I was happy.

I looked around my living room and tried to see it as a stranger would. I saw oversized, non-descript brown furniture surrounding a large glass coffee table that I ate my dinners on nightly. My TV was the most predominant piece of furniture in the room, taking up a huge portion of the living room wall. I had CDs and DVDs sitting on my bookshelves, but no decorations or pictures of my family. I didn't have art on my walls or throw pillows on my couch to accent the curtains. My bedroom was just as nondescript. I had a large, comfortable bed, a chest of drawers situated across from my bed with a TV on top, and two bedside tables. Hell, even my bedding was a boring navy blue with white pinstripes. *It sure looked good against Josh's fair skin though.*

Josh's house was opposite in every way. I could tell he spent a lot of time making each room look nice, yet comfortable at the same time. His house wasn't like my grandmother's where everything was for looks only. We were afraid to sit on her furniture or breathe near her fancy hand towels in the downstairs guest bathroom. It wasn't pleasant spending time there as a kid or even as an adult. Josh's living space was warm and inviting, not fussy.

I went to bed once the game was over. I told myself I had done enough self-reflection for one evening but couldn't seem to shut my brain down when I climbed between the sheets. It was the same thing that happened to me every time I ran into Josh. The emotions had changed a bit over the past few months, but I was still baffled when it came to him. He was an exotic animal I wanted to pet but feared it might bite me.

I was chuckling at my inner musings when I heard a pitiful whining sound coming from outside. It sounded like an unhappy dog was right below my bedroom window. The mournful whining became a hopeless howl and tugged at my heart. The temperature was supposed to reach the freezing point, and then the rain would turn to ice. It was not fit for man or beast out there, which was why I got dressed, put on my coat, and went outside to get the dog.

I found the animal just below my window as I suspected. The dog looked at me so woefully when I rounded the corner, as if he or she was afraid of me, but realized I was the only hope on a night like that. I felt a strong tug on my heart and squatted down to its level so that I'd look less threatening.

"Come here, pooch," I said in the softest, non-threatening voice I could muster. "I'm not going to hurt you, buddy." I extended my hand out, and the dog hung its head for a few seconds before slowly walking toward me. I didn't reach out to pick the dog up because I wasn't sure how scared it was and I didn't want to get bitten. The shaking could've been from being scared or the cold, but I suspected it was both. "I have a warm towel and some lunchmeat with your name all over it." I rose to my feet and started walking backward. I coaxed him with my hands until we were both in the house and out of the cold rain.

The dog shook all over, sending rain and mud all over my foyer. It eyed me cautiously, and I wondered what kind of hell the weary animal had been through before I found him. "Hmm, let's get you a snack and then we'll get you cleaned off in a warm bath." My new friend cocked his head to the side like it knew what the word meant.

I gave the dog a few pieces of ham and then coaxed it into the bathroom. I discovered during bath time that I was working with a boy dog. He looked grateful that he was getting clean when I lathered and rinsed him twice. Once I finished, I checked him over for wounds and was pleased to find none.

He was a pretty boy and looked to be a shepherd and lab mix. I hadn't seen him in the neighborhood before and wondered how far he had traveled. I toweled him off good and took him back downstairs to get a bit more to eat and a bowl of water. I didn't have a dog bowl so I used a mixing bowl that my mom bought me on the off chance that I would bake. It was like she didn't even know me sometimes.

"I'll hang up some posters and see if I can find your family since you're not wearing a collar," I told him while I got out an old comforter from my closet and laid it on my bedroom floor for him to use as a bed. He tipped his head to the side as if he understood what I said and the sad look on his face made me think his family no longer wanted him. It was hard for me to imagine since he was such a beautiful dog, but people tossed aside beautiful things all the time. Josh appeared in my mind just then, and I realized that he too could fit into that category.

I pointed to the dog's bed and said, "Lie down, buddy. It's time for bed. Tomorrow is a new day, and we'll figure out what to do." The dog surprisingly lay down like I commanded—well, after doing the three spin move that dogs are known to do.

I climbed into bed and tried to shut my brain down so I could get some rest. I told my brain not to conjure up images of Josh, or I'd never get to sleep. It didn't listen, so I lay awake for quite some time. My new friend must've thought I drifted off to sleep because he boldly jumped on my bed and made himself at home. He let out a relieved sigh and then soft snores drifted up from the foot of my bed.

Instead of thinking about Josh, I began to think up names for my new dog. I had a strong feeling his owner wasn't coming forward, and there was no way I was dropping him off at a shelter. No fucking way. Bandit. "What do you think about Bandit?" I asked the sleeping dog. He raised his head up and looked over at me. The dog would've shrugged if it were a possibility. "Okay, I'll keep thinking." After a few more minutes I asked, "Roscoe?" That time he didn't even acknowledge me. He just snored louder. "No go," I said, then yawned as sleep finally moved in. "I'll figure something out tomorrow."

I woke up the next morning, and the dog was no longer by my feet, but was instead, lying beside me with his head on the spare pillow. "Listen, buddy," I said, "I'm hoping to reserve that pillow for a human." The dog wagged his tail when I said "buddy," and I realized that would be his name.

"Buddy?" I questioned just to be sure. That time the tail wagging was accompanied by a doggy kiss on the side of my face. The dog had a name, and I had a companion. It was a great way to start off a Sunday.

FIVE

Josh

People would often see my bold color choices for my clothes or the colored streak I'd sometimes wear in my hair and figured I was a spontaneous, exciting person. In reality, I liked consistency and routines because I could always count on them. That hadn't always been my experience in my late teens and early 20s. The things I thought would happen didn't, and it left me spinning with feelings of disappointment and disillusionment. People would let me down, but I could rely on routines.

For example, on Sundays, I would always go to Brook's Pets to get whatever supplies I needed for my fur babies after a leisurely cup of coffee and a pastry from The Brew. That morning, I sat at my usual table and noticed a flyer hanging up on the window about a lost dog that someone found. It had a picture of the pooch and a phone number where the owners could call and claim their dog.

My heart kicked up several notches when I recognized the pattern of tile on the kitchen floor and the phone number. Although I only dialed it once, I thought about calling and texting that number on several occasions. Only memories of past hurt kept me from dialing Detective Hung Dick's number, even to thank him for saving my life. I would've baked him cookies, but we just would've ended up fucking again, and I couldn't let that happen.

I stared at the flyer and smiled at the thought of Gabe taking the time to print and hang them up around town. I wondered if he truly wanted the owners to come forward or if he was just doing the right thing. The dog sure looked happy to be in Gabe's kitchen.

I got the answer to my question when I walked into Brook's and found Gabe studying the display of collars, harnesses, and leashes very carefully. I should've just picked up the things I needed and got the hell out of there because he was so focused on making good choices for his new friend that he didn't know I was in the store. Instead, I stood there noticing how the sun brought out golden caramel streaks in his dark hair. I knew how soft that hair felt between my fingers and…

No! Not going there now or ever. It was a one-time thing, and I didn't want it to happen again. Okay, I wanted it very badly, but I wouldn't *allow* it to happen. Still, I stood silently and observed until he picked up a leather studded collar and harness combo and smirked. I could not pass up an opportunity like that.

I approached him stealthily, and once I was standing directly behind him, I said, "I didn't take you for a leather daddy." I laughed at the shocked look on his face when he looked over his shoulder.

Was it because I startled him or was it because I sought him out? I got the ball rolling so why stop? I leaned forward and lowered my voice so only he could hear. "Do you have a dungeon in your basement?"

Gabe hung up the studded items and turned to face me. He leaned in until his lips were nearly touching my ear. I fought off a shiver that wanted to ripple its way through my body due to his nearness, but I think he knew the effect he had on me. "Do you want me to?"

Did I? No! I wasn't really into that kind of thing. I mean if he wanted to spank me a little or… *No, no, no!* "It's not my thing," I replied after I pretended to ponder his question. I must not have sounded too convincing because his lips tilted up into a crooked, wicked smile as if he was picturing me tied down and… I commanded my brain to cease and desist immediately. "What are you doing here?" I asked as if I didn't just see the flyer at the coffee shop. Not like I was going to confess I had his kitchen tile and phone number memorized.

"There was a dog whimpering outside my bedroom window last night in the pouring rain. I couldn't just leave him out there so I brought him in, bathed him, and gave him something to eat to tide him over until I could get him some legitimate dog food. I have no idea what I'm doing here. You'd think after dating a vet that I'd…"

He let his sentence fade away as if he thought bringing up Kyle would upset me. I already knew he moved here to be with Kyle and that their relationship ended a year later; it was a very small town after all. Knowing and liking wasn't the same thing though. I didn't like picturing him with Kyle, and I refused to think about why.

"You should call him and make an appointment to have your new friend checked out," I recommended. "In the meantime, Brook can make some good food suggestions for you. I've never had a dog, so I wouldn't be much help to you." Not that he asked.

"I already called Kyle, and Buddy has an appointment tomorrow night." He turned back to look at the display once more, and I was glad to have his keen eyes off me so that I didn't accidentally give away any of the emotions he made me feel.

"Buddy, huh?" I reached around him to pick up a simple navy blue collar that reminded me of Gabe's comforter. I felt Gabe stiffen when my body brushed up against his. I tried not to get busted as I breathed the scent of him into my nose. He smelled just as masculine and sexy as I remembered from our one afternoon together. "Here," I said, holding out the collar to Gabe. It looked sturdy and reliable—adjectives I was starting to associate with Buddy's owner. Still, I wasn't going to trust him with my heart and body.

Gabe took the collar from my hand then picked out a leash and harness in the same color before he turned around and looked into my eyes. "Thanks."

"You're welcome." It was the friendliest exchange we'd ever had up to that point. *I don't know, having his dick in my ass was pretty friendly.* I could tell that he wanted to say more, maybe even push for more, but I wasn't ready for that; I might not ever be ready. So, I took a step back and briefly broke eye contact. "Well, I better get my stuff and get on the road. I have several stops to make before my company comes for dinner." *Why was I telling him so much?*

"Company?" he asked, his brow furrowed as if he didn't like the idea.

I didn't owe him an explanation, so I was surprised when I responded. "Mere and Chaz come over for Sunday dinner every week. Family Sunday dinners have always been a tradition, but my parents moved south after my dad retired. Mere and Chaz are my family, and I cook dinner for them every week."

"What are you serving?" Gabe asked. I didn't know how I expected him to respond, but that wasn't it.

"Meatloaf, mashed potatoes, green beans, and baked banana pudding with meringue on top." His eyes glazed over; I half expected to see a little drool form at the corners of his mouth. For a brief second, I almost entertained the idea of inviting Gabe over for dinner, but I squelched that quickly. Sunday family dinners were sacred, and he wasn't my family. Mere and Chaz had brought boyfriends to Sunday dinners before, and that was fine with me because it didn't have the same significance to them as it did me. If I invited a guy to Sunday dinner, then it meant he was very important to me, as in maybe "the one." That had never happened, and I doubted it would anytime soon, if ever.

"That's a lovely tradition," he said softly, almost distantly. It made me wonder where his mind had gone just then. Did he think about his family or the way things used to be for him and Kyle? Why did that last thought stab me right in the heart? He wasn't mine; he would never be mine. Yeah, he wanted to fuck me, but that was nothing new. He would be like the others; he'd take what he wanted and then move on when someone better came along.

I shook off the melancholy and offered him a half smile and said, "I need to take off. I hope everything works out with Buddy." I took a few steps backward and nearly knocked over a lady who was looking at dog sweaters. "Sorry," I told her before I looked back at Gabe. "See you around, Detective." I could feel an embarrassed flush creep up my neck and face.

"Thanks for your help," he said, holding up the items in his hand.

I'd already said too much and made an ass of myself, so I simply nodded and left. I was halfway to the grocery store when I realized I didn't pick up the things I'd stopped at Brook's to get, which meant I'd have to stop back by on my way home. *So much for consistent, reliable routines.* I knew damn well who was to blame—that dark-haired, dark-eyed demon in the guise of a sexy man.

"I can't believe the police thought you could hurt Georgia," Meredith said as she set the table. "Detective Wyatt might be sexy, but he can't be that observant if he's thinking of you as a murderer."

"He's hardly had an opportunity to observe me, Mere," I said over the noise of my mixer as I mashed the potatoes.

"He watches you every chance he gets," Chaz contributed. He placed the rolls on the counter and shut the oven door before he swatted me on the ass with the oven mitt he removed from his hand. "That man wants you sooooo bad." Chaz said the last bit in a sing-song voice that made me smile.

"Whatever," I replied, blowing it off. Neither of them knew about my afternoon in Gabe's bed, which was strange because they knew *everything* about me. I didn't know why I refused to share with them what had happened between Gabe and me; I just knew that it felt wrong.

"That one is trouble," Meredith said. She stood at the table with her hands on her hips. The vibrant pink sweater she wore complimented her dark skin. She looked as fierce as she did the day I met her.

Chaz and I have known each other since kindergarten, but Meredith didn't come into our lives until high school. Chaz and I were the only "out" gay kids in our school, but we both knew that there were plenty of closeted kids who were either gay, bi, or curious about what our hands felt like wrapped around their cocks. Chaz and I felt like outcasts in the school, as a lot of gay kids probably do. Meredith was the only African-American student in the school, so we formed our own little band of rebel misfits.

I loved her from the moment I laid eyes on her. Like with Chaz and me, Meredith had her heart broken when the boy she fell in love with refused to acknowledge their relationship for fear of what his parents would think. He was an idiot and not nearly good enough for my queen. Meredith realized that for herself later on, but at seventeen it was a very bitter pill to swallow. I think rejection colored her dating decisions as it had mine. Hence, the reason I kept Gabe at a safe distance—or tried to anyway.

"Yep, trouble," I repeated. Meredith narrowed her intelligent eyes at me, and I worried she could read my mind.

"There's more here than what you're telling us," she shook her finger at me, "but I'll let you keep your little secret. For now," she clarified before she finished setting the table.

We gathered around the table and held hands while Mere said grace. Afterward, we passed the serving dishes around and loaded up our plates with good food. As I preferred, there was no topic that was off limits for discussion over dinner. I wasn't at all surprised when Chaz brought up Georgia's death again.

"I heard she was stabbed with a pair of shears, so that's why they're probably looking at you," he said.

"It didn't help that she screamed she was going to destroy your business the day someone killed her," Meredith added. "I guess I can see why they'd at least question you."

"They're just doing their job," I replied. "At first, I was pretty insulted, but I got over it. They didn't haul me into the station for a formal interview. They just asked a few questions in Gabe's… I mean, Detective Wyatt's car."

"Gabe, huh," Meredith asked. "On a first-name basis now, are we?"

"He did save his life, Mere," Chaz stated. "That warrants a first-name basis in my book." Chaz tipped his head to the side and tears filled his eyes. He had always been an emotional person, but feeling sick the past week brought his emotions closer to the surface. "I'm so glad you didn't die."

"Thanks," I said cheerfully, hoping to change the topic. "So am I."

"Time for a toast," Meredith said, raising her glass. Chaz and I did the same. "To not getting killed," she said with a smirk.

"To not getting killed," Chaz and I repeated before we laughed.

"I was kind of hoping you were going to say something about

getting laid," Chaz told her. "It's been a long dry spell for all of us."

"You got that right," Mere agreed.

I didn't dare say a word, choosing to keep forking savory food into my mouth. Apparently, my silence spoke volumes because I could feel their intense focus on me right then. I risked a glance at their faces then wished I hadn't. I could feel my face starting to turn red like it had when I nearly bowled the lady over at the pet store.

"Is there something you want to share with us?" Chaz asked primly.

"No," I said around a mouthful of mashed potatoes.

"Oh, I think there is," Mere commented. "That is the face of a man who's been keeping a secret from his so-called best friends."

"I agree, Mere," Chaz said, a bright smile spreading across his face. "I think he wants to confess that he's doing it with the detective."

"Doing it?" Meredith repeated his phrase questioningly. "No, that sexy hunk of man meat doesn't 'do it,'" she told Chaz and then turned her shrewd gaze on me. "Honey, tell us the truth. You got your freak on with that detective, didn't you?"

I was busted; I knew it, and they did too. The arrogant smiles they wore on their faces told me so. I neither confirmed nor denied their accusation. I wasn't sure I could if I wanted to since it felt like the last forkful of mashed potatoes was stuck in my throat. I reached for my wine and gulped down half of the glass.

Meredith leaned over and placed her elbows on the table. "It was good, right?" I knew she was talking about the sex I had with Detective Hot Lips and not the damn wine I just chugged.

"Soooooo good," I admitted, but then added, "which is why it can't ever happen again." And I meant it.

Meredith and Chaz looked at each other then burst into raucous laughter. They laughed so hard they had tears running down their faces. I debated spitting in their pudding when I served it, but even I couldn't be so cruel.

"Twenty bucks says he holds out for two weeks," Chaz said.

"I got fifty that he doesn't make it past another week," Meredith said.

"Fuck you both," I replied but couldn't keep a smile off my face. I thought about betting against Chaz and Mere, but then my mind conjured up a memory of the way Gabe looked in the pet store as he fretted about making the right purchases for his new furry friend. I wasn't so sure I could resist him if I found myself alone with him again. Instead of placing a bet, I looked at them and said, "Traitors."

SIX

Gabe

As cold as it was, it didn't take Buddy long to go outside and do his business before he wanted back in the house. When I first rented the house on Jasper Street, I liked the fenced-in back yard but didn't think I'd have a need for it beyond keeping people away. Well, I was pretty damn grateful for it on my second morning as a dog owner when there was frost on the ground. I let Buddy out to do his business and watched him from the comfort of my kitchen while drinking coffee. He was safe, I was warm, and we were both happy.

I knew it was wimpy behavior, but I still hadn't adjusted to the colder weather in the midwest after living there for two years. I was a Florida boy, born and raised. Kyle had gone to graduate school for veterinary medicine at the University of Florida and then had stayed there to work. It wasn't until his grandfather announced his retirement that Kyle decided to move back to Ohio. Looking back, it was probably his way of trying to break things off with me. Back then, I thought he was happy I was moving with him, but it didn't take me long to realize I had been wrong.

As much as I disliked the cold weather, Josh appeared to embrace it. It was pretty pathetic that I engineered my dog doody supervision to be the same time that he would run by my home. It wasn't hard to do because the guy was like clockwork. He ran by my house every other day and always at the same time, regardless of the weather conditions outside. To say he had me tied in knots was putting it mildly. What was more pathetic was me pressing my nose to the window to get a better view as he ran along the chain-link fence. Cold glass and hot breath equaled a steamed-up window, so I had to wipe off the glass with the sleeve of my navy dress shirt. *At least I wasn't drawing fucking hearts in the condensation. Yet.*

I had noticed him jogging by before and even admired the way his legs looked in the shorts he wore during warm months or the running tights he wore in cold ones. What was equally as predictable as his schedule was that whatever ensemble he wore would be bright and captivating. That morning was no different. His jacket was neon orange, and his running tights were dark gray with ribbons of that same neon orange running up his legs, which made them look even longer.

Woof! Woof! Buddy's bark grabbed my attention, and I realized that Josh had already passed by and I was still staring out the window like a lovesick fool. I shook my head in frustration and let my new bestie in the door. I looked at my watch and saw it was almost time for me to leave. Whoever invented remote start, heated steering wheels and leather seats for cars were some of my favorite people. A garage didn't come with my rental house, but those three modern conveniences at my fingertips made the loss bearable.

Most garages in the neighborhood were only large enough for one car if that. Had there been a garage on the property, it would house my 1970 Dodge Charger I affectionately named Charlotte. Instead, Charlotte was stored in a rental unit not too far out of town.

After clicking my car on, I put up the dog gate so that Buddy would stay in the kitchen with his new fluffy dog bed, toys, and his food and water bowls. Brook recommended that I confine Buddy to one room rather than a crate to see how he did. It was obvious he was no longer a puppy; I hoped he had outgrown his instincts to destroy. Could I be so lucky? I'd see how he did for a week before I risked letting him have full run of the house.

I squatted down to give him a good ear scratching and tried to ignore the tug at my heart when I saw the sadness in his eyes that I was leaving. In such a short time, he'd become my dog, and I honestly hoped his former owners didn't call and claim him. If so, I'd have to give him back no matter how much I didn't like it. I tried to assure Buddy I'd be back and then I forced myself to leave, or I'd never do it. Hell, I wasn't even to my car yet, and I was already looking forward to returning home and spending time with him.

I figured that must be what a happy relationship felt like. Adrian always looked forward to heading home to Sally Ann each day. I think I would've felt the same about heading home to Kyle in the beginning, but our careers had us home at different times from the very start. Other couples seemed to make that work, but we didn't. I stopped feeling sad about the end of our relationship quite some time ago, but I still carried doubts that I had what it took to be in a happy, healthy relationship.

I got another glimpse of Josh as he turned a corner a few blocks down heading in the opposite direction from the way I needed to turn. Very indecent thoughts of Josh replaced the ones of my failed past with Kyle. That afternoon we spent together ended quicker than I had hoped and I sure as hell didn't like waking up to find that Josh had left without a goodbye. I liked even less hearing that he thought it was a mistake when I thought it was the best thing to happen to me in ages.

He seemed to be thawing out towards me a bit. The look in his eyes at the pet store was nothing like the distant one I had become used to receiving from him. I wanted to think it was progressing and that there was a tiny sliver of hope that just maybe I'd get a chance with him—not just for sex either. That aloofness he wrapped around him like a cloak intrigued me, and I wanted to know what made him tick. I got a glimpse of the vulnerabilities he hid beneath his confident veneer when the alcohol loosened his tongue at Vibe.

My goals for the week were to wrap up the Georgia Beaumont case and then I could see just how thawed toward me Josh had become. Well, those plans crashed and burned as soon as the M.E. report landed on my desk not ten minutes after I arrived. It wasn't the pathology or lab reports that shocked me to the core; it was a photo of the scissors that had been removed from Georgia's neck. At first glance, they appeared to be a regular pair of shears that a hair stylist would use. It was what we discussed at the crime scene, so having that confirmed wasn't the problem. No, it was the engraved name on the scissors that made me feel like I could vomit.

I couldn't help but reach out and touch the photo, my finger tracing over the letters that spelled ***Jazz.*** It didn't matter that I knew in my gut—and my heart—that he wasn't a killer. I had to take this seriously and do my job, which meant we had to bring him in for formal questioning on video.

"Fuck," I said beneath my breath. "Just fucking great."

"What's wrong, partner?" Adrian walked by me and sat at his desk that faced mine. He wore a grin that stretched from ear to ear.

"What's going on with the Joker smile this morning? Did you

have an awesome weekend or what?" Adrian practically glowed like the sun.

"You could say that," he said before leaning forward. "Look, it's early on, and we're not telling many people yet, but you're not just people." He took a shaky breath and said, "Sally Ann is pregnant."

I was out of my chair and around my desk giving him a congratulatory hug in a blink of an eye. "That's fantastic, Adrian. I am so damn happy for you two. You'll both be amazing parents." I knew it was true. I'd been to barbecues at their house and seen them interact with their nieces and nephews enough to know how lucky their baby would be. "I won't say a word until you guys are ready to tell everyone. I am so honored that you wanted to tell me."

I felt like I'd hit the lotto when I was partnered with Adrian. He never once gave a damn about who I was attracted to, all he cared about was that I was a good cop. In the two years that I worked with him, he went from a friend to my family. No one deserved happiness more than Adrian and Sally Ann.

"So, the look on your face and the cursing under your breath indicates that all is not right in your world. What's up, partner?"

I said nothing; instead, I flipped the photo around and handed it to him. Adrian let out a soft whistle before looking up at me. "We have to bring him in and officially question him," I said.

Adrian held out his hand for the file, and I gave it to him. "There's nothing hinky in the toxicology reports or her stomach contents." I saw sympathy in his eyes when he looked at me. "I'll send out a unit to bring him in."

I just nodded my head, grateful I didn't have to give the order. I would do it if I must because I had sworn to uphold the law, to protect and to serve. I couldn't make exceptions just because I wanted to fuck the prime suspect. I cringed at my inner thoughts because I knew what I wanted from Josh was more than a fuck. I didn't proclaim to be in love, but I sure as hell wanted more from him than to spread him out below me in bed.

Dreadful anticipation built inside me until I felt like I would implode while waiting for the officers to bring Josh in. I felt his presence in the precinct and slowly turned my chair to face him. I wanted to close my eyes, so I didn't see the hurt and betrayal when his gaze connected with mine. Everything about the situation screamed how wrong it was and not just because I wanted him. I saw how he interacted with his clients, his friends, his pets, and people at the fucking grocery store when he didn't realize I was watching. Okay, I sounded like a damned perv, but it just went to show how much I had seen with my own eyes. Josh Roman was no killer. I hated the situation more than he hated me right then. He was led to interview room one, and I was grateful to be away from his accusing stare, even if it was for just a minute.

"Look, why don't you let me take care of this interview. You can watch on the monitor," Adrian offered.

I shook my head. "No, Adrian. I can and will do my job. I will push my personal feelings aside and do what I've been hired to do."

"Okay, but…"

"I got this," I said, stepping around him and heading toward the interview room.

I could feel Josh's hostility as I strode in the room with Adrian on my heels. I let Adrian take the lead by reading Josh his rights after I turned on the video camera. Josh refused to look at me, choosing to keep focused on Adrian.

"We already established that you don't have an alibi for the night of the homicide when we last talked, Mr. Roman." Adrian pulled out the photo of the scissors from the file, turned it around, and slid it in front of Josh so he could see it. "Care to tell us how your scissors ended up buried in Georgia Beaumont's carotid artery?" Josh flinched sharply before all of the color drained from his skin. I wanted to kick Adrian beneath the table, which was wrong because I would've approved of his method had it been anyone else.

"I-I-I-did not do that to her. I could *never* do that to someone."

Josh's voice and eyes pleaded for Adrian to understand. He still didn't look at me, and I needed to change that.

"Everyone is capable of murder," I told him. The cold look he gave me said what he thought of my statement. I couldn't let that sway me, so I pressed on. "You didn't answer the question, Mr. Roman. How did your scissors end up at Mrs. Beaumont's home?"

He turned back to look at Adrian and said, "I gave them to her a few years ago when I opened my new salon. She gave me a brand new blue set of shears as a congratulatory gift. In return, I gave her the first pair I had ever bought—the ones I had used to cut her hair for years." His voice had cracked with emotion during the last few words, and he closed his eyes in what I thought was an effort to gather his composure.

"We need to get your fingerprints. You can volunteer, or I'll get a warrant," Adrian replied. "What will it be?"

"I'll do it, but I already know my fingerprints will be all over them unless she wiped them off since then." Josh turned and looked at me. His eyes went from cold to downright mean, and his next words cut me to the bone. "I do have an alibi for the night of Georgia's death. I had an overnight guest who can testify to my whereabouts from seven o'clock until the time I left and ran into you outside her home."

"Why didn't you tell us about your alibi then?" Adrian asked.

"I didn't want *him* to know," Josh replied, nodding his head in my direction so that there was no doubt who he meant.

Inside I was seething, but not at him. He'd done nothing wrong, owed me nothing. I was furious with myself for fantasizing about a guy who truly meant what he said when he claimed not to want me. He had moved on and was trying to be discreet. I needed to put him behind me and do my fucking job.

"We're going to need the name of your alibi and a way to reach him to confirm." I slid a notepad and a pen to him. He narrowed his eyes at me, but then looked down at the notepad as he wrote down what I requested.

Once he finished, Adrian took the notebook from Josh before I could then he escorted Josh to have his fingerprints and palms scanned into our database for comparison. I tried not to bristle too much over Adrian's heavy hand in dealing with the information Josh provided. I knew he was only looking out for my best interest, but it wasn't like I was going to ask the guy for a blow-by-blow of how their evening went. Or, at least I didn't think I would. I immediately regretted the *blow-by-blow* thought as soon as it crossed my mind because it was too easy to imagine a faceless man enjoying Josh's mouth on him.

I must've stewed in my chair for a good twenty minutes before Josh and Adrian returned. Josh looked smug, and Adrian looked indifferent. Josh took a seat, and Adrian motioned for me to join him in the hallway outside the interview room.

"His alibi checks out, and we can't hold him even if the fingerprints match. Like he said, they were his scissors, and his prints should be on them. He even offered to show us the card that Georgia gave him with the new set of scissors."

"He still has it?" I asked.

"He said he keeps things like that because when people take the time to do something nice, it deserves to be treasured." Adrian shrugged and added, "Besides, I think the guy did care about Georgia Beaumont. This guy isn't our killer."

"I've known that all along." I blew out a frustrated breath and said, "I'm going to take him home."

Adrian looked at me skeptically and said, "Gabe, I don't think..."

"This is something I need to do, Adrian. I promise I won't fuck up the case." I thought about what it meant that he'd recently had an overnight guest. "There's no future for us and no harm in me taking him home."

"Okay," Adrian agreed after a few more moments of hesitation.

Too bad Josh wasn't as agreeable. "I'd much rather walk." He was so huffy that it almost made me smile.

Adrian shut off the camera and said, "I'll just let you two work this out." The asshole didn't bother to keep the smile out of his voice. I glared at him as he exited the interview room.

"I don't have to accept a ride home from you," Josh said as he rose to his feet.

"What exactly are you afraid of?" I asked him. "I only want to talk to you."

"I'm *not* afraid of you." He stood taller and lifted his chin arrogantly.

"Good, then you don't mind accepting my offer." The look I shot him in return was just as arrogant.

Josh reluctantly followed me to my car. We spent most of the short ride to his home in silence. "I just want to reaffirm that I do not think you killed Georgia Beaumont. I'm sticking my neck out by telling you this."

"Don't do me any fucking favors." Josh's words were as icy as the frost covered lawns he stared at through the window as I drove.

His attitude was starting to piss me off, but I stamped down the temper that was brewing inside me. I pulled up in front of his house and parked. "Look, I think you understand why we had to interview you. I think your irritation is directed at me and not the fact that we brought you in."

"No shit, Sherlock." He finally turned his angry eyes at me. "You could've at least been the one to come and take me in."

"I thought it would make it worse," I replied.

"Because you're Detective Dumbass," he said nastily. He ran his hand over his forehead as he worked to calm himself down. "Look, I don't know why the hell I'm telling you this because it means nothing to you. *I'm* nothing to you," he amended. "My overnight guest, Merrick, wasn't there for the reason you think."

"How do you know what I'm thinking?" I wanted to ignore the way Josh's words eased the tension in my body.

Josh looked at me like I truly was the idiot that he accused me of being. "I didn't have to see the look on your face to know how pissed off you were at the thought I had been sexing it up with someone other than you. The anger rolled off you in waves."

"So why are you telling me?" I couldn't help but ask. I tried to school my features into a mildly curious expression instead of the hopeful one I felt.

"Damned if I know."

I wanted to reach over and pull him into a kiss to show him why he told me, but I did nothing. Instead, I quietly sat as he got out of my car without another word. Yes, I watched the exaggerated sway of his hips that irritation seemed to bring out in him. Yes, I sat there in my car longer than I needed to while I debated following him, but I didn't. I put the car in drive and headed back to the station while my thoughts remained on Josh. Was that his way of taking the next step in whatever was brewing between us?

SEVEN

Josh

I PACED THE FLOOR OF MY SALON INSTEAD OF TAKING INVENTORY like I normally did. God, that man drove me bat shit crazy. I ran my hands through my hair, not even caring that I destroyed the look I carefully styled after my shower. After I had dressed, I had two cops at my back door informing me that they had to take me in for questioning in the death of Georgia Beaumont.

I was confused as to how they came to the point that I was a suspect, regardless of the blustering Georgia did before she left my shop. I was angry that Gabe wasn't the one to pick me up, although I wasn't sure why I felt that way. We weren't friends nor would we likely be, but I had thought we had become friendlier to one another or at least civil. I was scared that I would somehow go down for a crime I didn't commit, even though I knew damn well, there had to be evidence pointing the finger at someone else since I didn't harm a hair on her head. As much as I had cared about Georgia, I wasn't blind to how she treated others. *She just wanted to be loved.* The thought ghosted through my mind again for the umpteenth time since I learned of her passing.

Then they pulled out the photo showing an older pair of my engraved scissors. I wasn't lying when I said that I gave them to Georgia as a memento. I should've told the truth about my alibi when they first asked about it, but I didn't want Detective Crusty Butt to know my personal business. I knew the conclusion he would've drawn, and I wanted to avoid that conversation at all costs. It turned out I had to confess to having an overnight guest after all.

Merrick wasn't just my usual type of friend. He happened to be my former fuck buddy, and we still hung out platonically every once in a while. The man who swore he'd never fall in love had gone and done just that. At the time it happened, I was disappointed that our sexy times would come to an end, but I was not angry with him. Merrick and I entered our agreement with our eyes wide open. Both of us had a history of hurt and was only looking for occasional sex. My heart had been safe with him because I didn't love him and he wouldn't hurt me.

Anyway, he called me up out of the blue and asked if he could come over. He'd had a nasty argument with his boyfriend when he discovered that Kevin had been cheating on him with a coworker. I had to admit I was shocked because Merrick and Kevin seemed to be the perfect couple, even though I knew there was no such thing. Still, I couldn't resist a heartbroken friend who needed someone to talk to, regardless of my being surprised that I was the one he chose. Once he arrived, it made sense; things were safe and simple between Merrick and me.

I couldn't say the same thing about my *feelings* for Gabe Wyatt. Every particle in my body wanted to know every particle in his. I wanted to learn things about him like what made him tick, what kind of music he liked, or how the hell he was getting along with his new dog. Yes, a tad bit—okay a lot—of jealousy flared up inside me when he told me he was going to meet up with his ex to have him look at Buddy. I didn't remember what day he said he was taking him because I was too busy castigating myself for the way I felt.

Therefore, when Chaz called me in a panic that something was wrong with Harry, his hairless cat, I didn't hesitate to drive to his house to pick them up and take them to see Dr. Vaughn. Chaz was too worried about Harry to be driving, so I felt it was the right thing to do. I regretted my decision when I pulled into the parking lot and saw Gabe's badass Charger parked in front of the building. All the feelings of jealousy and—I hated to admit it—insecurity came flooding back to me. My brain immediately began coming up with ways I could drop Chaz and Harry off without drawing suspicion from him, but I knew it wouldn't work. Besides, I wouldn't let that man chase me off and make a fool of me.

I sat stiffly in a chair next to Harry's cat carrier while Chaz signed him in. Gabe was nowhere in sight so he and Buddy must've already been in one of the exam rooms. Try as I might, I couldn't help picturing the detective and the doc rekindling their love connection. I don't know why I cared, but I… I just did. My imagination didn't seem like much of a stretch when the hunky doctor walked Gabe and Buddy out to the lobby, which he never did. I'd been there on enough visits with my pets to know he usually shook your hand before moving on to his next patient.

I couldn't help but stare at them as they stood looking at each other. Gabe and Kyle had similar builds and heights, although it looked like Dr. Vaughn spent more time in the gym than Gabe did.

They had similar dark hair but wore it styled differently. Gabe wore his hair a little longer while Dr. Vaughn wore his stylishly short. I talked him into trying something different last year on one of his visits to my salon, and he had kept it up nicely. I figured that Gabe got his hair cut at Burt's Barber—more like butcher—Shop. I wanted to get my hands on Gabe's hair, but that wouldn't be a very good idea. Normally, I'd be gloating inside over Kyle's transformation, but he was standing too close to Gabe, and they were obviously having a serious conversation. Then the good doctor reached out and gripped Gabe's bicep. I just knew he was turning his gorgeous blue eyes on Gabe and pleading for... Nope! I'm not going there.

At that moment, I hated them and the ridiculously beautiful way they looked together. I bit my lip hard to keep from saying something snarky. Gabe looked shocked by the way his ex boyrfriend reached out to him. The hand holding Buddy's leash went slack and Buddy made a run straight for me.

Fuck! I had hoped Gabe wouldn't discover me, but that must've been just too damn much to hope for. Buddy stopped when he reached me and put a paw on my knee as if to introduce himself. I couldn't help but smile at his soulful brown eyes and big doggy grin. No wonder Gabe was crazy about him.

"Hi there, Buddy," I said, giving his ears a good scratching. The dog closed his eyes, and a blissful expression crossed his face. Too bad it wasn't enough to calm my anxiety when I saw his human break off his conversation with Doctor Fuck Me and head my way.

"I didn't expect to see you here tonight. You're not following me, are you?" Gabe's attempt at humor might've worked on someone else, but I wasn't in the mood. I was feeling pretty bitchy at witnessing him getting groped by his ex-boyfriend.

"Hardly." I rolled my eyes to let him know how I felt about his question. "Chaz's cat is sick, and he was too upset to drive."

Gabe squatted down, looking into the cat carrier as he grabbed Buddy's leash. "That's a cat?"

"Yes, a hairless one," Chaz said when he returned from completing the paperwork.

"Chaz, come on and follow me back to exam room two," Doctor Smooth Talker said. "Let's see what's going on with Harry."

I swore I could see an excited shiver work its way through Chaz as he picked up the carrier and followed the vet. I could barely refrain from rolling my eyes again. Okay, so Kyle Vaughan was a sexy beast, but a person should at least aim for a bit of self-control. I mean, he wasn't as good looking to me since he became the enemy. *Wait? What, and since when?*

Once we were the only two people in the waiting room, Gabe just had to open his mouth and make me angrier. "You don't have to be jealous," he said softly. He started to walk backward, which was a good thing because I could feel my temper begin to boil. Especially when he said, "It's not what it looked like so there's no need for you to be upset or angry."

I sat stunned for a whopping ten seconds, which was enough for him to exit the building. I don't know why I didn't leave it alone, but I just couldn't. I was up and following him out the door. I heard his remote start fire up on his Charger and stood there as he put Buddy inside the warm car before he stood and faced me.

"I'm not jealous of you and Kyle," I told him. "I can't imagine why you'd think that."

"You wouldn't look me in the eye, and you had your teeth clenched so damn hard I was afraid you'd snap off a tooth." He let out a frustrated breath and added, "It was probably exactly how I looked today when I learned you had an overnight guest Friday night."

"Listen, Detective Ego," I said marching toward him. "I'm not a bit jealous of you. Someday I might meet the man who makes me lose my mind and I'll want to fight some other guy to the finish for him. Today is not that day, and you are definitely not that man." I was pretty proud of my little speech until Gabe narrowed his eyes like I had just tossed out a challenge.

He grabbed two fistfuls of my coat and hauled me to him. Gabe lowered his head until his mouth hovered just above mine and said, "Bullshit." It was my only warning before he pressed his lips against mine and his eager tongue sought entrance into my mouth.

It was the surprise that had me parting my lips for him, not want. I did not want him and all the trouble he would bring. The nip I gave his tongue was more of a playful one than a warning. The growl emanating from his throat was a warning, but not one I heeded. I clutched to his strong biceps as he ravaged my mouth. I went from semi hard to capable of drilling concrete in seconds. I hated that I wanted him so much, but there was no point in lying to myself any longer. I just didn't know what I was willing to do about it.

At that moment, I was willing to rub my tongue against his before I sucked it into my mouth. I admitted to myself that I'd rather be sucking his cock, but I wasn't willing to jump back into bed with him. He was bad for me; I knew it with every fiber of my being. He would hurt me, probably worse than the others and then where would I be? I'd worked too hard to build a protective shield to keep guys like him away.

Gabe broke the kiss to get some air. I stood staring at him as our puffs of breath were visible in the cold night air. "Come to my house tonight after you drop off Chaz." It was more of a plea than a demand, which I appreciated, even though it didn't change anything.

I was tempted, good God was I tempted. "I can't." That was the only answer I was willing to give him, and I hoped he didn't ask for more.

"Aren't you at least a little tired of ignoring this thing," he gestured with his hand between us, "that we have going on? You want me, and I want you; so why the resistance?" Gabe turned his back on me and ran both hands angrily through his hair when I refused to answer him. "Look, I've apologized to you for my behavior that first night we met. I've gone out of my way to try and bridge this chasm between us, because I can't get you out of my mind, Josh. The reasons for it are unknown to me. You obviously want to pretend you don't feel it too, or something in your past is preventing you from taking a leap here. I can't fight what I don't know, so I'm just going to step back and let you decide what you want."

God, I wanted to be able to trust him. It was pathetic how much I wanted to believe him, but I just couldn't. I knew when he saw my decision in my eyes. He shook his head, more in resignation than disgust, and then walked around to the driver's door of his car.

"Josh, I won't bother you again. Just knock on my door if you change your mind. I won't need an explanation from you or a confession. I'll just open the door and let you in—no questions asked." He got in his car and drove away.

I tried to convince myself it was the sting of the wind that had my eyes tearing up, but I knew better. I returned to the waiting room and took a seat, feeling the eyes of the receptionist, Alyssa, on me the entire time. She had a front row seat to the kiss Detective Luscious Lips gave me through the big picture window. She was one of the biggest gossips in town, and by noon the next day, everyone would know that I locked lips with Gabe.

Of course, she'd probably hurt herself getting to Dr. Vaughn as soon as Chaz and I left. I ignored her intense focus on me and chose to read a magazine about cats instead. None of the cats featured were nearly as pretty as my Diva, and I took great pleasure in acknowledging it. Still, there was a lot of interesting information, and it helped me pass the time until Chaz and Harry returned, which seemed to take longer than it should. Chaz came out to the waiting room with flushed cheeks and glassy eyes. Hell, it looked like he'd just been kissed within an inch of death or gotten high.

"What's wrong with Harry?" I asked.

"Huh?" Chaz sat the carrier down then put on his coat.

"Harry," I said, pointing to the carrier. "I seem to remember a frantic call about how he was dying. What's wrong with him?"

"Urinary tract infection," Chaz said, finally shaking off his daze. "He has some medicine to take and will be right as rain in no time."

I rose from my seat as Chaz picked up the cat carrier. I looked over at the reception desk, and sure enough, that damned Alyssa was already bending the good doctor's ear. I saw his eyes widen before he turned his light blue gaze on me. I couldn't help but stiffen as I waited for a look of disbelief to cross his features. Instead, he sent a warm smile my way.

What the fuck was that about?"

After I had dropped off Chaz and Harry, I drove straight home, parked my car, and turned it off. I'd had a rough few days and a long work day ahead of me the following morning, if the clients didn't cancel their appointments when word got around that I was questioned by the police for Georgia's murder. Fuck, I hoped not. I knew in my heart that Georgia did not mean what she said about destroying my business, so I hoped like hell that my salon didn't turn out to be another casualty.

EIGHT

Gabe

"You doing okay, partner?"

I looked up from the Beaumont case file I'd been studying intently and gave Adrian a questioning look. "Yeah, why?"

Adrian narrowed his eyes and raked them over my face and upper body, grinning when he took in my clenched fists. Fine, I wasn't "okay," and I wouldn't be until after I got the shit with Josh straight in my head. He wanted me. I wanted him. Why weren't we seeing where this would go? Damn, I must've been clenching my jaw just as tightly as my fists because it began to ache and I felt a nasty headache brewing.

"Uh huh." Adrian reached into his desk and pulled out a bottle of ibuprofen and tossed it to me. "You want to tell me what's put that scowl on your face? And don't bother telling me it's the case either," he rushed to amend, taking away the avenue I had planned to use.

I swallowed two tablets of ibuprofen with coffee that was cold as an evil witch's heart. Yes, the Beaumont case bugged the hell out of me, but my condition had to do with one frustratingly beautiful and complicated man. I felt the way he responded to me the night before when we kissed. I saw all the signs of jealousy in his body language when he saw me with Kyle. I saw him stiffen out of the corner of my eye when Kyle reached over and touched my arm. Hell, I stiffened too. What the hell was Kyle doing? It would've been awkward *without* Josh being there, but it was so much worse with him watching.

I wasn't sure where Kyle had been heading with his touching and peering into my eyes bit. I suspected he was horny and looking to scratch an easy itch. That's what we *used* to be to one another after our breakup. The first time it had been awkward, but the few times after were very similar to any hookup. We got our fuck on then went our separate ways. I didn't want that with him anymore, and I wasn't sure how to approach the subject—not that I would have in his reception area with Alyssa watching us. Kyle had once said she was the biggest gossip in town and I didn't want to have people discussing my personal life at The Brew or Edson and Emma's Diner.

So, I *accidentally* let go of Buddy's leash, and he didn't let me down. He headed right for the one person I wanted to know better. I couldn't resist taunting Josh a little when I retrieved my dog and was completely ecstatic when he took the bait. I listened to his spiel about how it wasn't the day, and I wasn't the man he'd be willing to fight over. Blah. Blah. Blah. Josh's eyes told me differently so I called him on his bullshit and planted a fierce kiss on him. I had no intention of telling Adrian about my run-in with Josh the previous night.

Of course, when I looked back up at Adrian he wore a knowing smirk on his face. He knew the real source of my irritation. Luckily, he was a great friend and let it go. "What are you thinking?" he asked and then quickly added, "about the case."

"Josh isn't the killer. He has an alibi, and the motive was pretty thin," I told Adrian, trying to ignore the pinch in my heart when I thought about Josh's overnight guest. "There was no sign of forced entry or that the lock had been tampered with, so the perpetrator had a key or she let them in."

"Why would she let someone in and then get in the bathtub with a glass of wine and a romance novel?" Adrian asked. "That, plus the time of death, implies intimacy. My wife loves her friends, but she wouldn't invite them over after midnight then climb into a bathtub. That leaves us with someone entering the premises with a key given to them by Georgia or someone else who had access to them."

I rubbed the back of my neck while I listened to Adrian's thoughts that mirrored my own. "I've heard that Georgia wasn't a well-loved woman in the community, but that doesn't usually give someone a motive to kill. The two likeliest suspects are each other's alibis."

"Rocky and Nadine," Adrian said, nodding his head.

"Yep, unless there's an heir to her estate that was eager for their inheritance," I added. "That crime scene was too clean. We won't get reports back from the state lab in Columbus for weeks, or even months, but I'm not expecting any 'smoking gun' evidence when we lay eyes on them."

Adrian licked his bottom lip as he processed what I said. "Are you thinking someone hired it done?"

My theory sounded like some far-fetched TV drama, but in a way, it was the only thing that made sense to me. "Let's have a chat with her housekeeper to see just how many people had keys to that home and make sure they're all accounted for."

"That would be Mrs. Honeycutt," Adrian said as he rose to his feet and removed his jacket from the back of his chair. "She was my Sunday school teacher when I was a kid. I'm sure she's witnessed a lot of things at the Beaumont house over the years. Let's see what she has to say."

Wanda Honeycutt was seventy, but looked much younger, and had worked for Georgia Beaumont for more than two decades. When we arrived at her small ranch home at eleven thirty, she was still dressed in her bathrobe. Her eyes were red-rimmed and puffy, as was the petite nose that rested above trembling lips.

"Adrian," she said with a tearful voice. "It's good to see you." She turned to me then offered a weak smile. "I don't think we've had the pleasure of meeting yet." Wanda fell back on her good manners, regardless of how heartbroken she was over the loss of her long-time employer.

"Gabriel Wyatt," I said, extending my hand to her. Wanda's tiny hand trembled in mine when she shook my hand. It was obvious that Wanda was grieving over Georgia's death and I was grateful that she hadn't been the one to find her. I was thankful that Josh hadn't stumbled upon the scene either. He had been heading over to her house early that morning. What if he'd gone around back if Georgia hadn't answered the front door? I thought Josh had seen his quota of dead bodies and pushed the thought out of my mind to concentrate on the woman in front of me.

Wanda showed us to her kitchen and insisted on pouring us both a cup of coffee. She took a lid off a cookie jar then placed cookies on a plate before putting it on the table between Adrian and me. Adrian didn't hesitate to reach in for a cookie, but I held back a minute. I couldn't so much as think about a chocolate chip cookie, let alone eat one, without thinking about Josh. Adrian nodded for me to take one, but I didn't. I felt irritation building inside me for acting like a lovesick teenager rather than a grown-ass man. Was I going to ban chocolate chip cookies unless they came from Josh? Hell would freeze over before he baked me another fucking cookie. *Fuck it!* I grabbed two cookies from the plate and took a big bite out of the first one. They were really good, but not in the same ballpark as Josh's.

"I'm so sorry for your loss, Mrs. Honeycutt," Adrian said soothingly. "I know it must have been a terrible shock to you. If you don't mind, Gabe and I have some questions for you."

"Anything I can do to help you catch the despicable person who hurt Georgia. She was good to…" Mrs. Honeycutt choked up and couldn't finish her sentence. She wiped the new stream of tears that ran down pale cheeks with a wad of tissues. "Sorry," she said once she composed herself again. "Ask me anything."

I could see Adrian hesitate because he didn't want to upset Mrs. Honeycutt anymore, but I knew we had to start somewhere or we'd be there all day. "How long did you work for Mrs. Beaumont?" I liked to start all interviews with easy questions that I already knew the answers to for a few reasons. In some cases, I did it to see how honest the person was going to be, but in that case, I just wanted to ease her into the questions.

"Twenty-five years," she replied sadly. She looked down at a ring she wore on her right hand and began twisting it around her finger. "Georgia had just given me this ring in honor of all the years I worked for her." Mrs. Honeycutt extended her hand and showed us a gold band with a small emerald surrounded by diamonds. "It's my birthstone."

"That's very pretty," I replied. "You must've been very special to Georgia."

Mrs. Honeycutt nodded silently for a few moments and then

said, "Most people misunderstood her, but of course, she didn't do anything to change people's opinion about her. It was almost as if she liked to be disliked if that makes any sense." It didn't, but I had learned that people were complex and often didn't make sense to me.

"Can you think of anyone who disliked her enough to kill her?" Adrian asked.

"Besides Rocky and Nadine?" The scorn that dripped off her tongue when she spoke their names was almost comical. "Those two assholes are the only ones who'd want to hurt her. Certainly not Josh Roman!" She pinned Adrian and then me with a hard glare. "Why in the world would you have that sweet boy brought in for questioning? He loved Georgia as much as I did." Mrs. Honeycutt leaned forward, her complexion changing from pale to pink as ire built inside her. "Do you know that Josh came to her home to do her hair when Georgia was too mortified to step out in public after Rocky's affair was exposed? Hell, he was the one who convinced her to leave the house with her head held high, and a 'fuck them' attitude."

Adrian nearly choked on the sip of coffee he'd just taken, and I suspected it was because of Mrs. Honeycutt's bawdy language. I thought it was hilarious and couldn't keep the grin off my face.

"Josh was cleared, Mrs. Honeycutt," I assured her. "He has an alibi and no motive to hurt her, so that's why we're here talking to you today."

"Who all has keys to Georgia's house?" Adrian asked once he was done sputtering and coughing.

"Just Georgia and I. She had all of the locks changed once she tossed that cheating bastard out of her house." She shook her head in disgust and then blew out a frustrated breath. "It's against the Lord's teachings, but I hate that man." I assumed she was talking about Rocky and her next words made certain I didn't have to ask. "Georgia gave Rocky everything she had, and I mean she turned herself inside out for that man. She tried for years to get pregnant and couldn't; he was so cruel to her about it when he should've been loving." She pounded her tiny fists unexpectedly on the table hard enough to make both Adrian and me jump. "That bastard acted like he was royalty and he needed an heir or some shit. Georgia mentioned other means of having a family, but he wanted no part of it. He didn't want to adopt someone else's castoffs, as he called them, and refused to consider a surrogate."

I couldn't help but feel bad for Georgia and wondered if those were things Josh knew about her. He seemed to know her pretty well, and I wouldn't be surprised if she had told him personal things while he did her hair. It sounded like hair stylists and bartenders had a lot in common. They both had clients that wanted to divulge the personal details of their lives while they looked for something to make them feel better, whether it be a new hairstyle or a stiff drink.

"Rocky and Georgia have been divorced for about five or six years, right?" Adrian asked.

"That sounds right," Mrs. Honeycutt agreed.

Adrian followed up with, "Was Georgia seeing anyone?"

Mrs. Honeycutt harrumphed and crossed her arms over her chest. "Georgia thought she was damaged goods. *He* convinced her of that, and she thought no one could ever love her. All she wanted in the whole world was for someone to truly love her." Her words echoed what Josh spoke on more than one occasion. "I couldn't understand why she was letting him back in her bed." She shook her head in disappointment. "She tried to keep it from me, but I'd been around that man for two decades and could pick out his sleazy smell while wearing a blindfold in a room with a hundred men."

My heart rate kicked up when I realized what the hell she had said without *actually* saying it. However, we needed her to say the words, so I asked, "Were Georgia and Rocky seeing one another again?"

"Seeing?" she asked with a raised brow. "Yeah, I guess you could say they saw parts of each other up in her bedroom. Pecker tracks don't lie." They were words I never expected to hear from a woman her age and hoped never to hear again.

"Did CSU take the bedding from her room?" I asked Adrian.

"I'll find out." He rose from his chair and walked into Mrs. Honeycutt's living room to call the station.

"Was there a pattern to Rocky's visits, Mrs. Honeycutt?" If so, there had to be a witness to it or someone who knew about him sneaking around to see his first wife.

"He was coming over on Thursdays, which were my days off and his bowling league nights. I would find the *evidence* of his visits when I made her bed on Friday mornings. I changed bedding each week on Monday and would've offered to change the sheets on Fridays, but it was obvious to me that Georgia didn't want me to know about the development with Rocky. She knew I'd be angry about it. She thought because I was old that I didn't see what was going on in that house." Mrs. Honeycutt shook her head sadly. "Georgia deserved so much more than piddly handouts from him."

"How long would you say this had been going on between Rocky and Georgia?" I asked.

"Six months, maybe a little longer," she replied.

Adrian returned to the kitchen and gave me a quick nod, letting me know that the bedding was collected for processing. I rose from my chair because we got what we needed from Mrs. Honeycutt.

"Thank you for your help, Mrs. Honeycutt," I said, extending my hand to her.

"Promise me you'll nail someone's balls to the wall for what they did to her," she said, her eyes full of sorrow and misery.

I knew better than to make promises I couldn't keep, but that didn't stop me from saying, "I promise. I'll make them pay."

Adrian and I left her house and climbed into my car. I fired up the Charger and drove to the next logical destination—the mayor's office. We showed our badges to his secretary, although it probably wasn't necessary for a town our size. The young blonde woman wound her long hair around her finger as she peered at us nervously.

"Rocky... uh, I mean Mayor Beaumont, is in Columbus for the state's annual mayoral convention." Her worried blue eyes flitted back and forth between Adrian and me. "Can I give him a message or something?"

"Just tell the mayor we stopped by and would like to schedule a time to meet with him," I told her. "He can call the station and ask for either Detective Wyatt or Detective Goode, and they'll transfer his call to one of our cells."

"At his convenience," Adrian added to downplay our visit.

"Yes, sir. I will do that, sir." She began writing the message down on a pink pad. "Detective Goode and Wyatt." She said the words out loud as she wrote them. Once she finished, she made a point to check out my left hand before looking back at my face. "By the way, my name is Rebecca."

"Good to know," I replied politely. "We'll be on our way so you can get on with your work, Rebecca."

"Have a good day now," Adrian told her.

"Well, that's a letdown," I told Adrian once we were outside. "I was ready to ask him some tough questions."

Adrian had paused before he opened the passenger side door. "Let's head on back to the station and let the captain know what we learned. Rocky might be a small town mayor, but that's almost celebrity status around here."

"Agreed."

On the way back to the station, we passed Curl Up and Dye. There were cars parked on both sides of the street for practically the entire block. I had worried that Josh's trip to the station for questioning might damage his business, but it looked like it brought out the nosey Nans in spades.

"Smalltown, USA," Adrian said after he had a good chuckle. "Speaking of that, is Josh a good kisser?"

The question came out of the blue and caught me completely off guard. "What?"

"I heard you laid one on him in the veterinary hospital parking lot," he replied, not bothering to keep the humor out of his voice. "Hell, people were talking in the diner this morning like you were about to put a ring on it or something."

"Fuck me!" That was all I needed. If Josh were skittish before, he'd be doubly so after the rumors of our kiss spread like wildfire all over town.

"You're not my type." Adrian laughed hard at his snappy comeback.

I looked over at my friend and partner after we arrived back at the station. I wasn't a kiss and tell kind of guy, which he knew damn well. I didn't like people knowing my personal business, so it meant that Adrian only asked to get a rise out of me. Instead of taking the bait, I smiled wickedly then said, "He's a damn good kisser."

NINE

Josh

I HAD ERRONEOUSLY WORRIED THAT MY SALON WOULD SUFFER business once word got around that I was questioned by the police. I should've known that every Theresa, Debbie, and Harriet would be in my salon hoping to learn a juicy bit of gossip. The funniest part was the side eye they gave each other as if they were shocked to find out that other people came up with the same idea as them. On the bright side, I sold out of my hair care products, nail polish, and hair styling tools. The downside was that it left me feeling chaotic and out of control.

Which was why I was jogging on a Tuesday evening. I rarely ran on consecutive days, choosing to let my body recover and do yoga on my off days. Yoga, which normally helped me find balance and center myself, wasn't getting it done. So, I put on my running gear with the reflective stripes due to the late hour and set out to run the frustration out of my system.

I made it as far as Gabe's house, saw the kitchen light glowing through the windows in the rear of the house, and stopped. I clenched and unclenched my fists while shuffling my feet from side to side as I tried to talk myself out of making a huge mistake. *Again.*

"Fuck it." I let myself in through his gate. I quickly knocked on his door before I changed my mind. I heard Buddy barking ferociously and Gabe calming him down. Too bad his words did nothing to soothe the unrest I felt flowing through my body. "What the hell am I doing here?"

Gabe opened the door before I could change my mind and run away like a kid pulling a prank. I had seen the man wearing many different things—suits, casual clothes, and nothing but a "fuck me" smile. Somehow, seeing him in a t-shirt, flannel pajama pants, and bare feet felt more intimate to me. It was enough to scare the sense back into me, and I took a step back from the door.

"Oh, I don't think so." Gabe fisted my running jacket and pulled me inside his house. "I got you now." He shut the door soundly behind me, and I stared up into dark, lust-filled eyes.

"I'm not sure I even like you," I heard myself say to Gabe, earning a quick flash of a smile from him.

"That's okay because I'm not sure I like you either." He relaxed the fist that held my jacket and slid it around to cup my neck. "But I will respect you in the morning."

Then his mouth was on mine—hard and hungry. I opened to him automatically, as if it was what I wanted all along. My brain and my heart might've wanted to steer clear of Gabe, but my body knew what I wanted. His grip on my body was firm, but not hurtful, like he worried I might try to escape. He had nothing to worry about because I was his after the first tangle of tongues.

Like the first time we were together, flames engulfed my body. My hands wanted in on the action and were unwilling to lie idly against my body. I slipped them beneath the hem of Gabe's t-shirt and relished the way his muscles quivered beneath his skin at my touch. It was good to know I affected him as much as he did me. I let my hands roam all over the hard body that I thought about every time I closed my eyes.

I was honest about my uncertainty that I liked him, but I knew that I was safe and he wouldn't hurt me, at least not physically. He let me take control and set the pace the first time we were together, but that wasn't what I wanted, or needed, when I showed up on his doorstep.

Gabe's ravenous mouth consumed me, turned me inside out, and made me feel raw; like I exposed the most secret parts of me to his touch. I moaned when he slowed his kiss and finished with a few sweet pecks before he bit my bottom lip and gently tugged it. I felt that pull everywhere in my body, especially my dick who wanted a piece of the oral action.

"I've wanted to strip these things off you since the first time I saw you running in them," Gabe said, running his hands over the slick fabric that clung to my ass. "Jesus, you might as well run naked."

"Too much bounce," I said. Gabe answered my smart reply with an even smarter slap to my ass. I'd never given slap and tickle much thought before, but I had to say I liked the way my skin burned a bit beneath his hand. "So, you've been perving on me, huh?" I asked once the real meaning of what he said penetrated my mind. *Did I like that he watched me?*

Gabe's cheeks flushed a deeper shade of red than lust had brought out in his skin. "It's hard not to notice with those wild-ass colors you wear," he said, trying to deflect.

"Sure, blame it on my wardrobe." A month ago, his words would've made me think he was comparing me to a woman and would've pissed me off. I didn't know Gabe Wyatt, but I believed his apology and the erection straining his jammies told me just how much he wanted to be inside me. I reached down and stroked him through the soft flannel fabric. "Are you going to fuck me or not?"

Gabe's nostrils flared as he inhaled air deep into his lungs before releasing it slowly. "Hell yes." He let go of me long enough to turn off the stove before reaching for me again.

Nerves tried to flare up in the pit of my stomach as I followed him up the stairs to his bedroom. Even though I'd been there before, I didn't know a single thing about his space beyond the color of his comforter. I had focused on getting fucked, and later, sneaking out without waking him. I didn't stop to take inventory of the room on that visit either. I wanted to say it was because I only cared about getting fucked again, and I did, but another part of me didn't want to learn the personal details of the man that might endear him to my heart. I wasn't foolish enough to think something real would develop between us, no matter how badly we wanted each other. Lust didn't equal love and fucking didn't equal commitment.

I reached for Gabe's shirt and pulled it over his head to quiet my internal voices that made a last-ditch effort to convince me to run. It worked too. His naturally bronzed skin and perfectly toned torso distracted me. I kept my eyes away from his because I didn't want him to see just how much I enjoyed his body; his ego didn't need bolstering. I felt his eyes on my face as I watched my hand move over the smattering of dark hair that covered his pecs.

I risked looking into Gabe's eyes and was surprised to learn that mine weren't the only ones giving up secrets. Not only did I see the want in his eyes, I saw that he was going to make me pay for dragging this out longer and making him wait for what he wanted so badly. I also saw that he needed me to make the next move, to give a little bit more of myself so that I couldn't come back later and deny what happened between us. I pulled my jacket and shirt over my head and tossed them to the floor. I dropped my hands to the waist of my running tights, but Gabe stopped me.

"Let me," he said, lowering himself to his knees.

I expected him to pull my pants down right away so we could get to fucking, but that wasn't what happened. Gabe leaned in and kissed my stomach above my waistband while he stroked my erection through my pants. I could feel pre-cum seeping through the fabric as he continued to tease me. I lowered my head in time to see him run his tongue over the wet spot that betrayed how badly I wanted him.

I slid my hands into his hair and tugged on the silky, dark strands. I could feel the heat of his breath through the fabric and couldn't stop myself from pushing tighter against him. Gabe pulled my pants down just far enough to expose the head of my dick and teased the leaking slit with his tongue.

"Gabe." His name left my lips in a growl of need. I didn't have to tell him; he knew.

He yanked my pants to my knees and sucked my cock deep into his mouth. It was nirvana, pure and simple, the way Gabe worked my dick with his mouth. Foreplay had been nonexistent the first time we were together, and I hadn't expected that to change, but I sure as fuck wasn't complaining. Gabe nearly brought me to the brink of climax before he pulled off and rose to his feet so fast that he left me teetering. He grinned as he reached over and grabbed my arms to steady me.

"Jackass," I mumbled beneath my breath.

"What? Did you say that you want me to fuck your ass?" he asked.

"Actually, yes." I toed out of my running shoes then removed the rest of my clothes, including my socks. Sex and socks didn't go. "Your turn," I said, stepping around him on my way to the bed.

I had just put one knee on his bed when I felt his heated, bare skin against mine. His hands roamed all over my chest as he nibbled the side of my neck. I loved the feel of his strong, hard body against mine, but leaning on someone wasn't something that I did. I didn't want to become used to it, not even in the bedroom with him, so I pulled out of his arms and crawled onto the bed. I got on my hands and knees and waited to feel him crawl up behind me, but instead, he wrapped his hands around my ankles and pulled so that I fell onto my stomach.

"I don't think so," Gabe said roughly, as he rolled me over onto my back. Only then did he climb onto the bed and on top of me. "You came here because this was what you wanted, so there'll be no hiding. I want your eyes on me."

I opened my mouth to protest, but he silenced me with a searing kiss that made my toes curl. Damn, but the man could kiss like no one's business, and the fight left me as quickly as it flared up. I wrapped my arms around him and savored the feel of him against me.

I spread my legs in invitation and Gabe eagerly moved between them. He took both of our cocks in his hand and began stroking them together. He already had me close to coming once, and I knew if he kept it up I would spill all over his hand. I pulled back from our kiss and looked up at him. "Fuck. Me. Now."

Gabe broke away from my embrace to get a condom and lubricant from his bedside table. He returned to me quickly and began prepping me immediately. I loved the slight sting caused by the penetration of his fingers. My eyes started to close as I relished the push and drag of his fingers over my nerve-laden opening. Gabe's fingers pushed against my prostate, and I jerked my eyes open to look at him.

The smile Gabe wore told me he knew exactly which button he was pushing and just how much I enjoyed it. Like with our personalities, we seemed to be at an opposite end of a spectrum. He seemed to want to take his time stretching me open, and I wanted him to hurry up and fuck me. I could tell he enjoyed the way my body shook every time he lingered on my prostate. Well, two could play his sexy games. I spread my legs even further apart then reached down and began stroking my cock. It was my turn to smile wickedly at him when he growled hungrily.

"Quit toying around and fuck me," I demanded.

I could see the internal conflict in his eyes. He wanted to give in and fuck me, as I imagined his body was demanding, but he didn't want to give in to *me*. Making me wait was part of his plan to punish me for doing the same to him. Or, maybe he thought it would be the last time for us to be together and he wanted to make it last. I felt a sharp pang in my heart at the thought but refused to examine the reasons.

I could see the moment that I won; lust overrode any other plan he had for me that night. He made quick work of rolling the condom on his erection before I felt him pushing against my entrance. He pushed inside me with one, long stroke until his dick was buried to the hilt.

Gabe rested his forehead against mine as he waited for my body to adjust to his penetration. "You feel so fucking good; like you were made for me." His breath ghosted across my lips, and I tried not to be moved by his words. It was the sex talking; it always was.

I raised my mouth for a kiss because he couldn't talk if he were kissing me. He couldn't tell me meaningless words that my heart would choose to cling to; the stupid organ didn't know anything except a yearning to be loved and accepted. Gabe held my face between his large hands and kissed me; soft, slow, and long. I couldn't name the emotion I saw in his eyes when he pulled back and looked down at me. I just knew it was nothing I expected when I knocked on his door.

I grabbed two handfuls of Gabe's ass and urged him to move inside me, to finish what we started. I wanted to be fucked, but Gabe didn't seem to get the message. When he finally began to move, it was slow and deep like he was savoring every second he was inside my body. That wasn't what I came to his house for, yet, my body began to come alive in ways it never had before then.

I kept my gaze locked with his while our breathing synchronized as he rocked his body in and out of me. I felt him in every pore, every muscle, and every molecule as he gave me what I didn't know I needed. I resisted it; I tried to spur him on by digging my heels into his thighs and raising my hips up to meet his thrusts.

Gabe just kept the same steady pace that threatened to unravel my tightly coiled sanity. "This isn't what I came here for," I told him. I was desperate to hold onto the defenses I built up to protect myself while he seemed hell bent on tearing them down.

"I know." He swept his thumbs over my cheeks tenderly, and I had to turn my head and look away from him. Gabe turned my face until I was looking at him again. "No hiding," he reminded me. "You win, Josh. This time," he amended, right before he pulled back slow once more and then slammed inside me.

Gabe aimed his cock at my prostate with each hard thrust, giving me the fucking I needed. The only thing I could do was hold on for dear life as waves of pleasure rolled over me and threatened to drown me. My nails dug into his back, and I gasped into the mouth that captured mine in a devastating kiss. I knew I'd feel the way his mouth felt against mine long after the tremors of ecstasy left my body.

I felt my balls tighten and retract as my body shook from the strong orgasm building inside me like a fierce thunderstorm. Gabe was close too. We might've only been together once before, but I recognized the way his body tightened and the sexy growls that emanated from deep inside his chest.

I reached between our bodies and began stroking my cock furiously. It didn't take, but a few pulls before my body stiffened, and I shot all over my stomach and chest. Gabe captured my cries of pleasure with his mouth then pulled back. I opened my eyes to find him staring down at me as he fucked me mercilessly. The raw emotion I saw in his eyes looked suspiciously like tenderness. I wanted to look away from him again, but his dark gaze ensared me.

His powerful body glistened with sweat, and the sound of his body slapping against mine echoed throughout his room. Gabe buried his head between my neck and shoulder, holding me as tightly as he could while his orgasm ripped through him. I reveled in his shouts of pleasure that were muffled by my skin, the jerky way his body moved as he spilled himself in the condom, and the boneless way he melted against me when he had nothing left to give.

We held each other for a long time as we caught our breath. Gabe's weight made it harder for me, but I wouldn't have changed it for the world. Eventually, he rose and gingerly pulled out of me. I lay there sprawled on his bed while he went into the bathroom to discard the condom. When he returned, he brought a warm washcloth with him and attempted to wipe me clean. Of all the things we shared, that seemed too intimate for me to handle, so I took it from him and finished cleanup duty.

I started to rise from the bed when I finished so I could get dressed and do the run of shame back home. Gabe had other ideas. He took the washcloth from me and tossed it on the bedside table and then jerked the covers out from beneath my body before he slid in next to me. I wanted to protest, I honestly did, but that orgasm did a number on me. Running home after a short nap sounded more appealing right then.

"I didn't come here for this either," I said sleepily.

"Shut up," he groused. "Just rest a bit. I'll wake you up."

The next thing I knew, Gabe was standing beside the bed fully dressed in one of his detective suits extending a cup of coffee towards me. I lay there staring up at him in confusion until I realized that I saw sunlight creeping through his fucking curtains.

"Fuck!" I threw back the blankets and nearly knocked the

coffee out of his hand. Gabe wisely backed away from the bed as I made a mad dash for my clothes that were strewn all over his floor. "I thought you were going to wake me up," I said accusingly.

"I did," he replied, gesturing to the cup of coffee. "I just didn't say what time."

"You're such a fucking asshole." I pulled on my clothes and shoes as fast as I could. "Damn it." It didn't matter that it was still early morning. Some neighborhood busybody would see me leaving his house, and the whole goddamned town would be talking. It was probably his motherfucking plan all along.

"I made you coffee," he said as if that made up for it.

I took the coffee cup out of his hand and left his room with another "asshole" tossed over my shoulder.

Gabe called out, "You're not going to give me a goodbye kiss, honey?"

"Fuck you!"

His laughter echoed through his house as I practically stomped out. I couldn't resist slamming the back door hard enough to rattle the frame. Okay, my exit might've been a bit melodramatic, but I was good and pissed.

It turned out that I had every right to be because as soon as I exited his gate, I came face to face with Alyssa from the vet's office who was out walking her dog. Her eyes were huge as saucers as she looked me up and down, paying close attention to the cup of coffee I had in my hand.

"Good morning, Alyssa." My mother's teachings about good manners took over as we stared at one another.

"Hmmm, I imagine it is," she said cheekily before she continued her walk.

Well, at least one good thing would come of that little episode. Dr. Hot Eyes and Fast Hands would know that Gabe was no longer… Yeah, I put the screeching brakes on that shit! It was one night—okay, technically it was the second. I vowed to never do it again. I didn't even like that asshole, so Gabe was free to fuck whomever he wanted whenever he wanted.

I took a sip of the coffee Gabe made for me as I walked toward my house. Fuck him and his perfect coffee making skills. I glanced down at the cup and realized what held Alyssa's attention. There was a pair of handcuffs on the mug beside the words: **Some like it cuffed.** I was certain his choice of mug for me to take home wasn't accidental.

"Asshole," I muttered, but it was missing some of the venom from earlier.

TEN

Gabe

I SHOULDN'T HAVE LAUGHED AT JOSH'S REACTION, BUT I COULDN'T help myself. It was a much better alternative than the disappointment I felt when he was unhappy to wake up in my bed the next morning. Besides, the myriad of emotions that crossed his face was pretty damn funny. First, there was the adorable look of sleepy disorientation as he tried to figure out where he was and what the hell I was doing there. He blinked in confusion as he took in my wardrobe. Then there was a brief but definite look of pure bliss as he saw that I had a cup of coffee prepared for him. Finally, he must have seen the early morning dawn trying to creep in between the cracks in my curtains because his eyes got as round as saucers.

Josh jumped out of my bed and moved about my room like a whirling dervish as he quickly got dressed, grumbling beneath his breath the whole time. It sounded like he was cursing me, the day I was born, and every one of my living blood relatives on planet earth. His hair was sticking up every place, and he put his pants on inside out. Somehow, I didn't start laughing until after he snatched his cup of coffee out of my hand and stomped out of my room like an angry toddler.

He sure clung to me in his sleep for someone who professed not to like me much. Neither Kyle nor I had been cuddlers in our relationship, but then again it wasn't often we slept at the same time until we moved to Blissville. It hadn't been my intention to have Josh stay the entire night, but I didn't want to turn loose of him once I had him in my arms. The body heat generated between the two of us was hot enough to wake me up a few times in the night, but I held on tighter instead of pulling away.

I didn't bother examining the reasons or look for a deeper meaning because it didn't matter. Simply put, Josh Roman just did it for me. End of story. I *wasn't* sure we liked one another beyond the physical attraction we both clearly felt. It wouldn't have mattered to me ten years ago; I would've just enjoyed the ride and walked away when it was over. I felt differently about a lot of things at age thirty-five though. Starting something with Josh, that I knew would end badly, wasn't a good idea, especially living in a small town where we'd run into one another. Hell, I had that with Kyle and was fortunate enough that neither of us had bad feelings towards each other.

I would've made Josh breakfast had he bothered to stick around, but instead, I found myself making an omelet and toast for one. I couldn't help but wonder if I'd ever have the chance to cook him breakfast after a night of sex or would he always run off. I didn't doubt that there'd be another time because I instinctively knew we would find ourselves naked in each other's arms again. It was what came after that had me puzzled.

I pushed all thoughts of Josh away and focused on getting Buddy set for the day. He had adapted to our morning routine quickly, and I was ready to give him a shot at roaming the entire house, but not until he got over his disappointment at being shut out of my bedroom the previous night. I had a pissed off… Josh—for lack of knowing what to call him—and a pouting dog to contend with that morning. I hoped the rest of my day held less drama.

Adrian beat me to the station that morning and was at his desk when I walked in. His shrewd eyes looked me up and down before a knowing grin split his face. "You look… different," he said, pretending to puzzle over the changes. "Is that a new tie?"

"No," I replied calmly, refusing to take his bait. "I wear this about once a week. You know, maybe I should talk to the captain about getting a new partner since my current one isn't as observant as he used to be."

"Oh, I'm plenty observant, all right," Adrian disputed. "I'm observing that you look a lot more relaxed than you did yesterday. You must have had one hell of a night's sleep."

"Sure did," I said, sitting down at my desk and powering up my computer. "Good breakfast too."

"Yeah, I bet…"

Adrian wasn't able to finish his sentence because Officer Dooley stopped by our desks and said, "The captain wants to see you guys."

"I wonder what that's about?" I asked Adrian.

"I guess we'll find out," he responded as he rose from his chair.

Captain Shawn Reardon was a no-nonsense man in his late forties whose discipline was evident in the way he presented himself to the world. He walked tall, spoke precisely and said only what needed to be said, and ran our precinct like a well-oiled machine. Men respected him, ladies lusted after him, and he didn't seem to care about either. In fact, he cared about one thing and one thing only—justice. He didn't bat an eye when we told him what we had learned from Mrs. Honeycutt and informed him that we wanted to question the mayor.

"You don't need my permission to follow leads," he had told us. So, I wondered what new development happened that would prompt him to call us into his office. I suspected it had something to do with the case, specifically the mayor.

"I received a call from a man claiming to be the mayor's attorney," Captain Reardon told us once we were in his office. He sat back in his chair with his hands steepled in front of his chest. "He demanded to know why we wanted to speak to his client and I refused to go into details over the phone with a man from Dayton that I had never met before. I expressed to him my extreme disappointment that he would think I was so stupid." A lot of people made the mistake of treating small town Americans as if they were backward or stupid. "After I set him straight, he informed me that both he and his client would grace our presence tomorrow morning at nine."

"That's great news," I told the captain.

"We'll be ready," Adrian added.

"While the mayor's out of town, I think you should visit with the current Mrs. Beaumont. See if maybe things aren't as peachy as she'd like the town to believe. Maybe she knew that Rocky was fooling around. She might recognize the signs from when he had an affair with her."

"On it, sir."

As we were leaving the captain's office, Officer Dooley stopped us. "We just received a call of a possible break-in at Georgia Beaumont's house," he said. "A neighbor spotted the back door gaping open and called the station. I figured you'd want to know."

"Thanks, Dooley. Radio the officers and let them know we're on our way," Adrian said.

We grabbed our jackets and headed over to meet up with the

responding officers. Jones and Kasey were waiting for us on the back porch. We all entered with our guns out in case the perpetrator was still inside the house. The four of us split up and checked each and every room before we regrouped in the kitchen once we were sure the house was clear.

"Master bedroom and bathroom were completely trashed," I told the group. "I don't know if they were looking for something or just wanted to vandalize the rooms."

"Guest rooms are trashed too," Adrian said. "It looked like they were searching for something because all of the drawers in the dresser are open, the mattresses are pulled off the beds, and the box springs were cut open."

"That's what I found in the master too. It looked like they ripped all the clothes off the hangers and pulled every box down off the closet shelves and dumped it on the floor. The contents of her jewelry box were strewn across the top of her dresser." I let out a frustrated breath. "The only person who might know if there's anything missing is Mrs. Honeycutt. Adrian, why don't you give her a call and ask if she's willing to assist us."

He pointed a finger at his chest. "Me?"

"She knows you well. Use your charm," I teased Adrian as he left the room to place the call.

"Downstairs doesn't appear to be touched at all," Officer Kasey said. "I'm leaning more toward someone looking for something specific rather than vandalism, or even theft if her jewelry was still there."

"I agree," I told her. "If only we knew what they had been looking for."

Adrian returned to the kitchen and said, "Mrs. Honeycutt is on her way."

"Great," I replied then turned to address Officers Jones and Kasey. "Adrian and I have an interview to conduct so we're going to leave Mrs. Honeycutt in your capable hands. Call us if she thinks something has been taken or even suspects what the perp was looking for."

"Will do," Officer Jones replied.

Rocky Beaumont's new residence wasn't quite as grand and glamorous as his first. I wondered if that bothered Nadine Beaumont that her predecessor got to keep the mini mansion in the divorce settlement while she got stuck with a house that would fit on Georgia's first floor.

The door wasn't answered right away when we rang. I could hear the sound of kids romping inside the house, so I knew that someone was at home. When Nadine Beaumont answered the door, she looked like she hadn't showered or dressed in days. Her hair looked like a rat had made a nest in it, she had a swollen nose, and dark circles under her eyes from her broken nose. She wore stained pajamas and an ancient looking robe.

"I've been expecting you." She opened the door for us to come inside.

We followed her into a living room that was in just as bad a shape as Georgia's ransacked bedrooms. There were toys tossed all over the room and dirty dishes on every available surface. It would seem that, not only did Nadine get the smaller house, it also didn't come with a Mrs. Honeycutt. Adrian and I exchanged quick looks that said something wasn't right about the situation.

Two small children ran into the room whooping and shouting as they chased one another until they saw that strangers were present. The boy and girl screeched to a halt and stared up at us with matching sets of big brown eyes. As unkempt as Nadine was, I had expected the kids to be in similar shape, but I was wrong. They were clean, dressed, and appeared to be very happy children. I couldn't say that about their mother.

"Have a seat," Nadine said dispassionately, gesturing to the sofa covered in toys. "I'm going to take the kids in the other room and put in a movie for them."

I picked up a stuffed dinosaur off the couch and set it on the coffee table next to a plate with a half-eaten peanut butter and jelly sandwich before I sat down. I had conducted some strange interviews before, but I had a feeling this one would take the cake. I looked over at Adrian, and he wore a similar expression of disbelief on his face.

Before I could say anything to him, Nadine returned to the living room. "Sorry about that," she said, smoothing down the front of her robe nervously with her hands. She sat on the love seat across from us and offered a weak smile. "What can I do for you, Detectives?"

I was wondering just how to approach the situation with her. Adrian and I didn't have time to discuss a game plan before we came over because of the situation with Georgia's house. She had already given her alibi for the night that Georgia died, which happened to be her husband. As alibis went, it was a weak one; besides, we were going on a theory that someone hired a killer since the crime scene was immaculate.

"I know what you want to ask," Nadine said as if she was reading my mind. "You want to know if I'm covering for Rocky by saying he was home with me the night Georgia died." Close, but I wasn't about to correct her; I wanted to see what she said voluntarily. "Look, Rocky is many things, but a killer isn't one of them. I wouldn't be here if I thought him capable of hurting someone like that."

"What about you?" Adrian asked, not hesitating to ask the tough question. "There was no love lost between you and Georgia Beaumont."

The question didn't faze Nadine one bit. She let out an unladylike snort before she said, "I once loved Georgia a lot, and she loved me too. I let greed and my desire for a better life override my moral code and ruined our friendship." Her voice cracked at the last part and, if possible, her posture crumpled even more. She stared down at her feet for a very long time before she looked back at Adrian. "The things I said to her in the salon were terrible, and I have to live with that for the rest of my life."

"Yet, you came to the station that night to press charges against her," I reminded Nadine. "That doesn't sound very remorseful." I was hoping to get a rise from her because anger often brought out truths people didn't want to reveal.

"It was foolish pride. I was embarrassed that Georgia broke my nose and pissed that we had to cancel our anniversary dinner plans because of it," Nadine replied while looking me straight in the eye as if she had nothing to hide. "I do regret the way I acted in the salon, at the station, and a lot of other things."

"Nadine, you said you were once close to Georgia, so can you tell us if there was anyone in her past that would want to hurt her?" Adrian asked.

"No one from her past that I could think of," she replied after several moments of contemplation. "I think she was seeing someone though."

"What makes you say that?" I asked, wondering if she suspected it was her husband.

"The gossip hags made it known that she'd ordered some new lingerie from the boutique in town. Why would a single woman order lingerie?" Nadine asked.

I could only shrug because I didn't have an answer, although I suspected she was right. I mean, I knew next to nothing about women and thought it could be possible that wearing pretty things might just make them feel better about themselves, but I didn't know.

Well, we wanted to get an idea on whether Nadine suspected her husband was cheating on her with his first wife. Either she didn't know, or she was a brilliant actress. It was still supposition at that point, as we had no physical evidence to prove that Rocky and

Georgia were sleeping together; only the word of a bereaved woman who disliked Rocky immensely—okay, she hated his fucking guts.

I looked over at Adrian to see if he had any more questions for her and he shook his head slightly indicating that he didn't. We rose to our feet at the same time. "Thanks for your time, Mrs. Beaumont," I said politely.

"You're welcome," Nadine replied. "I suppose you'll be wanting to talk with Rocky when he returns from his hunting trip in Tennessee."

Her surprising words almost made me turn around and ask her to repeat herself, but I could tell by Adrian's posture that I heard her correctly. Rocky's secretary said he was in Columbus at a mayoral convention and his wife said he was hunting in Tennessee. Furthermore, Rocky had already scheduled an appointment to speak with us, but didn't tell his wife. Either she was a good liar, or she was fucking clueless. From what I was learning about the *good* mayor, I was betting on the latter.

"We sure do, Mrs. Beaumont."

ELEVEN

Josh

WEDNESDAYS WERE USUALLY SLOWER DAYS AT THE SALON WITH A more laid-back vibe, but not that week. Everyone who wanted to come in the day before to stick their nose in my business, but couldn't, showed up. Included in the mix were a few hair emergencies that needed my immediate attention, like the four-year-old girl who cut her own hair with a pair of scissors or the client who was too impatient to wait for her appointment and took the hair color dye into her own hands. Praise Jesus she didn't use a permanent color because five hours and $250 later, she looked like a brand new woman. The mother of the little girl had fared much better than my DIY client. The little girl stopped before she got to her bangs, so I was able to give her a cute inverted bob that mom adored and wanted for herself on her next visit.

I was pleased with the success I achieved, but it also meant that I got very hangry when I worked long past my lunch break. I wasn't one to use annoying hip terms like bae or fleek, but I loved the word hangry because it properly expressed how grouchy I became when I let my blood sugar get too low. I didn't eat after I fled from Gabe's house and I missed lunch because of the two emergencies I handled back-to-back. It was well after two in the afternoon by the time I made a quick escape to Edson and Emma's Diner. Luckily for me, the place had thinned out pretty good that late in the afternoon.

My waitress, Daniella, stopped by my table with a tall glass of sweet tea. She didn't need to ask what I wanted to drink. "A little late for lunch today, aren't you, Josh?"

"Hair emergencies," I said like that explained it all.

"Ahhh," she replied. "Chicken salad on a croissant, potato chips, and a pickle, right?"

It was what I normally ate on Wednesday, but a little voice in the back of my head told me to shake things up a little and go outside my comfort zone. "I think I'll take a grilled cheese sandwich and a bowl of vegetable beef soup instead." Daniella narrowed her eyes, assessing to see if I was joking. "For real," I told her. "Soup sounds amazing, and no one makes a better grilled cheese than Emma."

"Oookay," Daniella said slowly. She looked at me as if I had just told her that I was a straight man after all. She finally walked to the kitchen to give my order.

Emma peeked out the window between the kitchen and dining room. "Are you feeling all right, Josh?"

"Perfectly fine, Em," I replied, although I was anything but fine. I had to play it cool though, or she'd call my mom in Boca Raton and get her all riled up.

Nothing about the situation with Gabe was fine, and I wasn't sure what to do about it. I had forced thoughts of him out of my mind all day long and focused on work. Unfortunately, I had nothing to keep my mind occupied while I was waiting for my food, so naturally, Gabe was the only thing it wanted to concentrate on.

The first thing my brain wanted me to admit, but I refused, was how well-rested I felt that morning. I hadn't slept well since Bianca's killer attacked me in my bedroom. I kept referring to him as "the man" because I didn't want to know his name or anything about him. It was hard enough getting past what happened when I didn't know a single detail about him; I feared he'd haunt me forever if I knew even the slightest thing about him.

I wasn't about to give Gabriel Wyatt credit for my good night's sleep. Nope. I was exhausted after a chaotic day that wore me out. I blamed the exhaustion for the reason why I showed up on his doorstep in the first place. I would've run right on past his house had I been functioning on full steam. I knew the feeble-ass excuses were lies, but I'd never admit that to anyone, let alone Gabe. I couldn't let that man have the upper hand in whatever was happening between us.

I decided to lose myself in trivial shit on Facebook while I waited for my sandwich. I looked at the time on my phone and realized I'd already been there for ten minutes. How the fuck long did it take to scoop chicken salad onto a plate and add chips? Shit! I remembered that I ordered a grilled cheese sandwich and soup instead. I had an appointment soon, and I didn't want to be late. I loathed running late. I looked suspiciously at the kitchen window and noticed it was pretty damn quiet in there. I had a sneaky suspicion that Emma was up to no good and was about to get up and investigate when I saw Daniella walk by the kitchen window with my lunch.

"Here you go, honey," Daniella said. "I'm sorry it took so long. I had to take a few carryout orders."

That was a relief because I had convinced myself that Emma had snuck outside on her cell phone to call my mom, who just happened to be her best friend since kindergarten. The last thing I needed was Roberta "Bertie" Roman dialing me up and threatening to come back to Ohio to fix whatever was bothering me. She might've been over a thousand miles away, but she was still my mom, and I was her only child. I was on the receiving end of *all* her maternal focus and attention, and it got to be a little much at times.

I bit into my grilled cheese, and all my cares momentarily faded away. My only thoughts were of buttery toasted bread and the cheesy goodness in the middle. I must've moaned my appreciation out loud because I heard a male chuckle coming from behind me.

"Good stuff, huh?"

I wanted to hang my head in resignation or perhaps crawl beneath the table to avoid the conversation that I knew was about to take place. How the hell did I miss the big hulking figure of the hunky town vet when I walked into the diner? I blamed Gabe for that too—for everything odd that happened in my life since the moment we first spoke.

Sure enough, I heard the scraping sound of someone scooting their chair back from a table followed by footsteps that got louder as they approached me. Finally, Dr. Studly stood in front of my table smiling down at me. "May I?" He gestured to the empty booth across from me with his hand.

I wanted to say no, I wanted to stretch my feet beneath the table and prop them up on the other bench seat to block him from sitting down, but instead, I acted like a mature adult. "Sure." I glanced at the clock on the wall and amended, "But I don't have long."

"Fair enough," Kyle said amicably as he slid into the booth across me. "I won't keep you." He offered me a friendly smile before he said, "So, you and Gabe, huh?"

"Nope." It was true; there was no me and Gabe. I didn't know what someone would call us. We weren't fuck buddies because we weren't buddies. I knew virtually nothing about the man except that I liked to climb all over him like a human jungle gym. We certainly weren't in a relationship. Just thinking the word gave me the heebie-jeebies.

"That's too bad," Kyle said, surprising the hell out of me. "I think you'd be really good for him."

"You do?" I couldn't help but ask.

"I do," he said, nodding his head. "Gabe is a good man—a great man, really, but he could stand to shake things up a bit." I knew that people probably said the same about me. It sounded like that was the one thing that Gabe and I might have in common besides sex. "I want Gabe to be happy."

"And you think I could do that?" The scoff he heard in my voice made him smile. "I'm not the person he's looking for in life," I said with a shake of my head.

"Don't be so certain, Josh." Kyle slid out of the booth and patted me on the shoulder. "I don't think you should be so quick to dismiss the idea that the two of you are well suited for one another."

I could do nothing but stare at him with my mouth open. *He had to be joking, right?* What did Kyle know, or think he knew, that I didn't?

"I'll see you around," Kyle said. He turned and walked to the register to pay his bill.

"Later," I said in a quiet, awed voice.

I snapped out of my stunned stupor and concentrated on eating my lunch so I could get back to work. It was safe there; everything had its place and purpose. I was in control, and there was no guess work, no uncertainty.

"How was your chicken salad and potato chips?" Chaz asked when I returned to the salon.

"I had grilled cheese and veggie beef soup," I replied, absently. Then I realized that all the noise in the salon stopped. I looked up, and all the stylists, their clients, and Chaz were looking at me funny. "What?"

My newest stylist, Marci, turned to look at her mentor, and fellow stylist, Heather. "What day is this?"

"Wednesday," Heather said in shock like I'd just squatted in the middle of the floor and took a shit.

"Oh, come on, guys," I said in exasperation. "I just wanted to try something a little different."

"So we've heard," said Janet Wiseman, the client in Marci's chair. "Seems like a little romance is brewing between you and that sexy detective."

"Damn that man is fine," Marci said.

"Pin me down and do me, baby," I heard Savage call out from the other room. "Uh, yeah." Thank God for small favors, because the blue bird figuratively swooped in and pulled the focus off me. I decided I would give him an extra treat later after I closed the salon for the day.

"Sounds like your bird wants to take your man, Josh," said Brenda Calhoun, who was sitting beneath the dryers. I had no idea how she heard anything under that hood.

"He's not my man," I said between gritted teeth.

The bells above the door chimed, and a tall blonde woman walked in and gave her name to Chaz. He pointed over to me, and she looked in my direction. I didn't connect the name to a face when I saw it on my list of appointments for the day, but I realized who she was the second I laid eyes on her. Sally Ann Goode, the wife of Gabe's partner. I had to wonder if this was a coincidence or if she was another busybody.

Sally Ann hung her coat on the rack and then began walking to my station. The smile she gave me was warm and friendly, not at all conniving. "Hi, I'm Sally Ann," she said, extending her hand to me.

"Josh Roman." I shook her hand. "Why don't you have a seat so we can get started." Sally Ann sat in my chair, and I draped a cape over her body, securing it behind her neck. I ran my fingers through her hair and pulled it back from her heart-shaped face. I looked into the mirror and caught her eyes. "What did you have in mind today?"

"I want a big change," she said, her eyes shining with excitement. "I want to cut off enough hair to donate it to an organization who makes wigs for children with cancer. Can you help me with that?"

"Absolutely," I replied. "How short are we talking? Do you have a picture of a particular cut you like?"

Sally Ann reached beneath the cape and pulled out her cell phone. She swiped it on and said, "I have a few ideas. Maybe you can help me figure out which one looks better with the shape of my face."

She showed me a few different hairstyles that varied from shoulder to chin length. "They'd all look really good on you, so it's just a matter of how much hair you want to cut."

She chewed on her lips for a second and then went with the shortest of them all, just as I expected she would. I had learned a long time ago that women took great pride in their hair. They would often feel negative about their bodies or maybe their looks but would take comfort in the fact that they had long, lush hair.

"Are you sure?" I asked.

She thought quietly for a few seconds and then nodded her head rapidly. "Let's do it."

I pulled her hair back into a rubber band where I needed to make my initial cut. I looked at her in the mirror and raised my brows in question while holding the scissors up for her to see. Her answer was an emphatic nod, so I made the first cut fast then held up the long ponytail of hair for her to see.

She squealed and covered her mouth in what appeared to be nerves and excitement. Of course, the hair left on her head looked all jagged and uneven—not at all what she envisioned. "It's going to look great," I said confidently.

"I believe you," she replied with a smile.

I guided Sally Ann back to the sinks and made sure she was comfortable before I tipped her head back into the groove made to support her neck. I started washing her hair and smiled when happy purrs escaped her.

"I could hire you to wash my hair every day," she said, as I massaged her scalp all over. "This is almost better than sex."

I couldn't help but laugh at her comparison, although I imagined it was quite an exaggeration. Surely Adrian Goode's bedroom skills were better than a scalp massage. His partner's sure… I wouldn't allow myself to complete that thought. *Nope. Not going there.*

Once I finished washing and conditioning Sally Ann's hair, we moved back to my station. "This is when the magic happens, right?" she asked.

"Oh yeah," I said brashly, parting her hair in segments. "You'll feel like a new person when you leave."

"I'm counting on it."

I expected her to mention Gabe at least once in conversation while I cut her hair, but she never did. She talked about meeting Adrian a few years ago and falling in love. She laughed as she told me how different her life became when she moved to a small town. She even talked about teaching school and how much she loved working with kids. Not one time did she bring up Gabe.

I turned her away from the mirror while I dried and styled her hair. I loved seeing the expressions on my clients' faces when I spun the chair around, and they saw their reflections for the first time. I adored how Sally Ann's hair was turning out, and it looked even better than the picture she showed me.

"Are you ready?" I asked her.

"Yes!" Her eyes grew as big as wagon wheels when she saw her reflection in the mirror. "Oh, my!" She covered her mouth and blinked several times before she smoothed her hands over her sleek new style. "Oh, Josh, it's perfect. It's even better than I imagined." She stood up quickly from her chair and turned to hug me. "Thank you so much."

"You're welcome." I patted her back. "You do look amazing."

"Adrian is going to love it," she said, but I wasn't convinced. It seemed like most straight men loved long hair on women and I hoped he wouldn't be gunning for me later that night.

"What matters is how much you love it," I replied, and I meant it.

"Thank you so much." She threw her arms around me once more. I couldn't help but laugh at her exuberance. Sally Ann practically floated over to the register where Chaz waited to ring her up. She returned several minutes later while I was sweeping up the hair mess off the floor. "Here you go," she said, handing me a very generous tip. "I didn't know you offered massage services here too. I bought a gift certificate for my husband's partner. His birthday is on Sunday, and I think a good massage would be a great way for him to get rid of some tension."

"Um, yeah. Massages are great for that." So are mind-blowing orgasms, but I didn't think Sally Ann wanted to hear that.

"I'll see you in about a month to get my hair trimmed," she said, sliding on her coat.

"I look forward to it," I said and meant it. She was an easy person to be around who didn't even attempt to pry into my life.

The rest of my workday went relatively fast for which I was grateful. I made sure to push every image of Gabe wearing nothing but a white sheet in my massage room out of my mind. I ignored the unsettled feelings I had when I pictured Josi's hands all over Gabe's body as she worked the tension out of his muscles. I refused to even think about the implication of what that feeling in the pit of my stomach meant. Gabe meant nothing to me. His body was free to be touched by someone—anyone—other than me.

I had just made it upstairs to fix myself some dinner when my cell phone rang. I thought about ignoring it but figured whoever it was would just call right back. I looked at the caller ID and saw that it was my mom, and I silently cursed Emma and her busybody ways.

"Hi, Mama," I said in greeting.

"Baby, what's wrong?" Mom asked. "Tell Mama."

"Nothing is wrong." I tried to assure her, but I knew it was going to take more than a few words to make Bertie Roman believe me.

TWELVE

Gabe

I ARRIVED AT THE PRECINCT A LITTLE EARLIER THAN NORMAL SO that I was primed and ready for our interview with the mayor. Adrian was already at his desk when I arrived, whistling and looking livelier than normal.

"Morning." I sat down and powered up my computer. "How's Sally Ann feeling?"

"She's doing great, partner. She's feeling less nauseous as she approaches the twelve-week mark and starting to have more energy."

A sly smile slid across my partner's face, and then he said, "She met your guy yesterday afternoon when he cut her hair. He made her very, very happy and I reaped the benefits." Adrian winked playfully, and I just shook my head.

"He's not *my* guy," I argued, but I noticed there wasn't a lot of conviction behind my words. I didn't even sound convincing to my own ears so how did I expect others to believe me? I didn't know what was going on with Josh; he was a complete mystery to me. He played things extremely close to the vest and didn't seem like he wanted me to know anything personal about him. Well, beyond finding his prostate and making him moan with pleasure anyway.

"Yet," Adrian said with confidence that I didn't feel.

I wasn't even sure I wanted Josh to be *my* guy. We were both honest when we said that we weren't sure we liked one another. It all went back to not knowing enough about him. I mean, what if he was one of those people who talked throughout a movie or made a lot of noise when he ate? Worse, what if he wore socks during sex or to bed? I watched as he removed them the last time, but I had no idea if that was a fluke on his part. Those were important things to know.

I opened my mouth to respond, but Rocky Beaumont showed up with his slick-as-fuck lawyer just then. The lawyer stood in his pristine suit that probably cost more than my monthly salary, looking around the precinct like every single one of us was beneath him. I hated him upon first sight.

Then I took in the sight of Rocky, who attempted to stand all big and bad next to his overpriced mouthpiece. He reminded me of a bulldog with his smashed-in face and short, stocky build. That smashed face was cute on a dog, but not so much on a human. I didn't know if Rocky was a killer, but I knew without a doubt that he was a poor excuse for a human being. He sure as hell was a pathetic excuse for a husband and I doubted his parenting skills were much better.

Adrian and I rose from our chairs and walked over to greet the pair. "Mr. Mayor," I said respectfully, "my name is Detective Wyatt, and this is Detective Goode. Thank you for coming in today and speaking with us."

"Were you the same men who went to my home yesterday and harassed my wife?" he demanded to know.

"Is that what Mrs. Beaumont said?" Adrian asked him doubtfully.

"You had no business speaking to my client's wife in an attempt to get information out of her to use against him," the pompous windbag lawyer said.

The captain approached our small group. "I think we should take this to an interview room." Once inside the interview room, the captain turned to the lawyer and held out his hand. "Captain Shawn Reardon," he said, introducing himself and gesturing with his hands for us all to have a seat at the table.

"Nash Carrington *the third*," replied the slick bastard. "I was just telling your detectives that they had no business interviewing Nadine Beaumont without me being present."

"I don't agree," the captain said in a clipped tone. "Quite frankly, you said that you represented Rocky Beaumont, not Rocky and Nadine Beaumont. Someone as smart as you surely are should know that we'd want to talk to Georgia Beaumont's former assistant about people who might potentially want to hurt Georgia and then ransack her house looking for something."

"We didn't ask a single question about Rocky, his whereabouts, or their relationship," I told the lawyer. "However, Nadine voluntarily told us that Rocky was in Tennessee on a hunting trip when we were leaving her home. We were shocked to hear that from her because Mr. Beaumont's secretary stated that he was in Columbus at a mayoral convention." I pinned Rocky with a look that told him I wasn't fucking around. "Where were you really, sir?"

Rocky looked at his lawyer for guidance on whether or not he should answer the question. Mr. Fancy Pants City Slicker didn't look too happy with his client at the moment. He probably could have cared less if Rocky was a killer, but he did care if he was made to look a fool in front of us low life hicks. Carrington *the third* nodded at Rocky to answer the question.

"Um, I was at the cabin in Tennessee," Rocky answered reluctantly.

"Alone?" Adrian asked.

"No," Rocky replied, but offered nothing further.

"We're going to need the name of who you were with to corroborate your story," I told Rocky. I could tell by the guilty look on his face that whoever he was with was not a cousin unless it was of the kissing variety.

"Look," Windbag *the third* said in a lowered voice. "My client doesn't want this to get back to his wife. What he's about to tell you has nothing at all to do with the death of Georgia Beaumont, and I'd appreciate it if this could stay private."

"Let us be the ones to decide if this is relevant to our homicide investigation," I said hotly. I had no use for his bullshit. "We're not in the business of destroying marriages," I told the two men sitting across from me.

"I was with someone that I don't want my wife to know about," Rocky said, obviously not concerned about wasting our time as he doled out one little tidbit after the other.

"Did your wife and Georgia know that you were sleeping with *someone* other than them?" I asked, no longer willing to beat around Rocky's bushes.

Rocky's mouth fell open in shock, and he audibly gasped. "I-I don't know what you're talking about." The sweat that popped out on his forehead and the way he averted his gaze from me, were classic signs that he was guilty as charged.

"Rocky, this is a very small town," Adrian said as if he wasn't talking to the mayor. "You have to know that there are no such things as secrets." Rocky's eyes darted up to meet Adrian's then returned to the table in front of him. "Surely you realize that someone has seen you coming and going from Georgia's house on Thursdays."

"Don't forget the biological evidence left behind on the sheets," I added and enjoyed the way Rocky flinched.

"You don't have to answer them," Carrington told his client.

"We haven't asked a question yet," I told the attorney. *Arrogant prick.* "Right now we're telling you that we have witnesses that have seen your client enter and exit Georgia Beaumont's residence on Thursdays." I stretched the truth to suit me. "We also know emphatically that the biological evidence is only present after he leaves. Now, it's in your client's best interest, to be honest with us from this point on." I turned to look at Rocky. "How long had your affair been going on with Georgia? Or the person you took to the cabin with you?"

"How is any of that relevant?" Carrington asked. "My client has an alibi for the night of the homicide and the break-in. What would be his motive for harming Georgia Beaumont?"

"Maybe she was about to ruin his marriage by telling Nadine about their affair. I find the timing of her death to be rather convenient," Adrian replied to Carrington. "Nadine and Georgia had a big fight, and Georgia is killed later that same night."

"The alibi for the night of the homicide is a bit shaky," I told the attorney. "We're not going to just accept what Nadine tells us. Georgia might not have gotten along with a lot of folks, but none of them had a motive to kill her. Besides, it doesn't mean that he didn't hire it done."

"I would never hurt Georgia," Rocky said emphatically. "I was—*am*—a bad husband with a wandering eye," *and dick,* "but that doesn't mean I didn't care for her. I loved Georgia; I always have and always will. I fucked up with her, but I can't regret my kids, Detectives." He took a resigned breath and said what we both already knew was true. "I had been sleeping with Georgia for a few months. I'm not even sure how it happened. I just showed up randomly at her house, and one thing led to another."

I just stared at the philandering man sitting across from me who acted like cheating on his wife was no big deal. "It just happened. One thing led to another." Affairs didn't just happen, and a person could easily prevent one thing from leading to another by never putting themselves in that position in the first place. I didn't believe for five seconds that he just showed up at Georgia's without ulterior motives. He knew that Georgia was lonely and he took advantage of her. Did he tell her that he loved her to get back in her bed? Did Rocky tell her he was leaving Nadine? He must've told her something to keep her quiet because only the housekeeper knew about the affair. Of course, I wasn't about to tell him that. Let him think multiple people saw him sneaking in and out of Georgia's house.

"You weren't worried that she'd tell Nadine? Surely she hated Nadine's guts after she stabbed her in the back and had an affair with you," Adrian told Rocky. "You'd think she'd jump at the chance to get even with Nadine."

"Georgia didn't want me back," Rocky said softly. "She told me so after the last time we were together. She was happy with how things were between us."

What he said didn't jive with what Josh and Wanda Honeycutt said. Both of them emphatically said that Georgia wanted to be loved and sex without strings was the furthest thing from being loved. Was it possible she was playing Rocky's ego, making him think she didn't want him so that he'd work harder to get her?

"We'll ask you what we've asked everyone so far. Who would want to hurt Georgia?" I asked him.

"I honestly can't think of anyone who'd want to hurt her. I mean, she was kind of bitchy to just about everyone, but still..." Rocky shook his head.

"Who stands to inherit her estate?" Adrian asked. We were still waiting for her attorney to provide us with a copy of her estate, including her will. He had asked for a little bit of time since he needed to make final arrangements for his client.

"I don't know," Rocky replied. "I'm sure she changed her will after our divorce, but I've never seen a copy of it. She didn't have any siblings and both her parents are deceased. I was her only family once upon a time." Once upon a time were words associated with fairy tales. Being married to Rocky was more like a Grimm fairy tale rather than Disney.

How fucking pitiful was it that Rocky had been her only family? It made the sadness I had felt listening to Josh speak about Georgia even stronger. I was even more determined to give Georgia justice. "We're going to need the name and phone number of the lady friend you spent time with in Tennessee to verify your alibi for the time of the vandalism yesterday," I told Rocky, sliding a pad of paper and a pen to him.

"No," he said, sliding it back across the table. "I have a gas receipt that is time stamped and has the address of the gas station in Tennessee from yesterday. That's going to have to be enough, fellas." He reached into his pocket and pulled out a gas receipt confirming just what he said.

"We're done here anyway," Carrington said. I had almost forgotten the pompous asswipe was in the room. "This has been a complete waste of time for us both," he told Rocky. He then turned to the captain, choosing to ignore Adrian and me, and said, "You'll need to call me if you want to speak with Rocky *or* Nadine Beaumont again." He put his hand on Rocky's shoulder and said, "Let's go."

Rocky and *The Third* left our station without so much as another word to us. The captain looked at Adrian and me then said, "Well, what do you guys think? Did he hire someone to kill Georgia?"

"What would be his motive?" Adrian asked. "He seemed to be telling the truth when he said Georgia didn't want him back and was happy with keeping their relationship as it was."

"Maybe," I said. "Rocky's such a sleazebag politician that it's impossible to know when he's selling you something or telling the truth."

"I wonder if he even knows what the truth is anymore?" Captain Reardon puzzled out loud. He shrugged his shoulder and added, "He sure doesn't want us knowing who he was with in Tennessee."

"That's for sure," Adrian replied.

"It could be important to the case to find out her identity." I held up the receipt and added, "I wonder if this gas station has cameras aimed at their pumps to ward against theft."

"I like the way you think, partner," Adrian said, slapping me on the back.

"Call the gas station and ask. Let them know it's for an official investigation and ask them to email the footage to us ASAP." He rose from his chair, signaling that our discussion was over. "Good work, guys."

"Now what?" Adrian asked me once the captain left the room.

"Well, Mrs. Honeycutt couldn't tell if anything was missing, so I think we can rule out theft," I replied. "Someone was looking for something that might've had personal value instead of financial."

"Maybe we're asking the wrong people about Georgia," Adrian said. "Maybe we need to talk to someone who didn't like her so much. I think we can learn a lot from the people who considered her an enemy rather than a friend."

"Like who?"

"Pastor Harrison's wife, Darlene," Adrian said.

I didn't attend any of the local churches, but I knew who he meant. I pictured the short, quiet lady with mousy brown hair and pale blue eyes who was the exact opposite of her boisterous husband. "Why her?" I couldn't imagine she was anyone's enemy.

"According to gossip, she was engaged to Rocky when Georgia moved to town. Rumor has it that he took one look at the young blonde and Darlene was a distant memory."

"Is there anyone in this town that Rocky hasn't dated or slept with?" I asked facetiously.

"Me," Adrian replied with a grin that made me laugh.

"I mean, seriously. The man must be hung like a horse to get all the action he does, because it sure as hell isn't his looks or his personality," I told Adrian.

"He must know how to use it like a porn star," Adrian remarked and then chuckled. "I hope he's keeping their names straight."

We had a good laugh at Rocky's expense because the guy was a complete asshole and deserved it. "Okay," I said, trying to get us back on track, "let's go have a talk with Darlene Harrison then. I'm sure church ladies are full of information."

"You know what they say," Adrian said as we left the interview room. "The biggest sinners sit in the front pew."

I'd have to take his word for it because I didn't have firsthand experience. I'd heard enough bullshit talk about same-sex love being sinful, so going to church wasn't something that interested me. I had heard that open-minded churches existed, but I had never encountered one. I didn't have a problem with God; it was organized religion that angered me beyond reason. How many wars were fought in the name of religion? Too many to count, so I decided a long time ago that I would choose to do good things in my life and be a good person. It would have to be enough.

"I think it's time to talk to Georgia's attorney again. I understand he wanted to make arrangements for her funeral, but he's already made them. He should be able to put his hands on Georgia's file quickly and make a copy for us." I said.

"Good point," Adrian agreed. "Church, lawyer, and then lunch."

I looked at my watch and noticed it was only ten in the morning. I didn't anticipate that either stop would take very long. "A bit early for lunch, isn't it?"

"Some of us worked up an appetite last night," Adrian said. "I haven't been the only ravenous person this week. I do recall someone eager to eat lunch early yesterday."

He had a point. "I'm good with an early lunch."

THIRTEEN

Josh

FUNERALS SUCKED—PLAIN AND SIMPLE. THEY BROUGHT OUT THE best and worst in people. I stood in the back of the funeral home with my entire staff from the salon to pay our respects to Georgia on Thursday evening and shook my head at the spectacle in front of me. The place was jam packed wall-to-wall with people who supposedly stopped in to pay respects to her, our town's former first lady. What I saw was a bunch of harpies and gossipmongers who were looking for a juicy story.

I wondered what Georgia would think about the circus her viewing had become. The funeral was scheduled for the following morning at Sugar Grove Cemetery, and I asked myself how many of her *friends* would brave the blistering weather that was anticipated to say goodbye to her. I suspected not many. Well, one thing I knew for sure was that no one could find fault with her hair or makeup. I made damn sure of that when I prepared her for her big night.

I didn't do hair and makeup on deceased people very often because the funeral home had professionals on their staff who did that, but occasionally, someone requested my services, and I always obliged them. Oddly enough, spending time around deceased people didn't creep me out; it was the living ones that often made my skin crawl.

Georgia wasn't just someone to me, so I called the owner of the funeral home and told them that I wanted to do her hair and makeup one last time. I just couldn't let her go into the afterlife with helmet hair and the wrong shade of lipstick. Georgia detested pastels, and I knew she'd be very unhappy if she was stuck with pale pink lips for eternity. So, I used her favorite shade of ruby red and dared anyone to remark upon it.

My staff and I had finally made it to the front of the line to pay our respects when the muted whispers stopped, and a hushed stillness spread over the room. I turned to see what was going on when I spotted Rocky and Nadine standing in the archway to the viewing room chosen for Georgia. I felt my jaw clench in anger, and I had to wonder just how big were their balls? I couldn't believe that they had the nerve to show up after what they'd done to Georgia. In my mind, they could go to church and ask for absolution; her visitation wasn't the place to cleanse their souls.

At least Nadine had the grace to look both uncomfortable and sad as the crowd parted for them like the Red Sea did for Moses. In my opinion, it was because of the gatherings' eagerness to witness the spectacle rather than any respect felt for the mayor. Rocky placed his arm on his young wife's elbow and guided her straight to the front of the room where Georgia lay in her coffin. I had the irrational notion of shutting the coffin lid so that the two people who hurt her the most in the world couldn't see her. They shouldn't have been there at all.

Then my eyes landed on a gorgeous man in a dark suit standing in the back of the room who appeared to only have eyes for me. I got caught up in Gabe's intense stare and found myself feeling centered again. I felt like I'd been in a constant tailspin since learning that Georgia had died. I desperately wanted to get my life back to normal, but my brain cautioned me that relying on another person to help me find my balance always ended badly. I broke my connection with Gabe and stepped aside so that Rocky and Nadine could pay their respects and get the fuck out.

Of course, Rocky was in no hurry to shed the attention that was bestowed upon him right then. He stood looking down at his first wife and shook his head sadly as if he had so many regrets. I didn't consider myself a violent man, but I wanted to drive my knee into his ball sac and laugh as he collapsed on the ground, gasping for air. It was a lovely image.

Meredith must've sensed the path my thoughts were heading because I felt her small hand on my forearm as if she was stopping me from going through with my evil plan. Who knows, maybe I would have, but Meredith was a reminder of the good things in my life that I'd miss if I went to jail for assault. She wasn't the only person in the room I'd miss; I adored my staff and my clients. There was someone else in the room that I'd sort of miss seeing around, but I'd be damned if I'd admit that to him.

I turned back to look at Gabe and saw that Adrian and Sally Ann had joined him in the back of the room, but I wasn't sure he was aware of their presence because he still had his eyes locked on me. I tried sending him a silent signal to quit it before the entire town added the two of us into their tongue-wagging stories.

"You did good, Josh," Nadine said softly, pulling my attention away from the detective in the back of the room. I saw so much regret in her eyes and the sad smile she gave me. "She would've hated to wear a pastel or neutral color."

"She would've haunted me for the rest of my life," I replied.

Rocky looked at us like we were mad and it didn't surprise me that he didn't know anything about his first wife's preferences after being married to her for more than two decades. Rocky cared about one thing only—himself. "Let's get going, honey," he said to his wife. Nadine stiffened at hearing the endearment roll off his lips. It looked to me that there was trouble in paradise.

My staff and I paid our respects and then moved out of the way so that others could do the same. I tried not to look at Gabe as we walked in his direction, but it seemed someone on my staff had an altogether different idea because one of them tripped me from behind just as we came up on him.

"Whoa there," Gabe said, throwing his arms out to catch me.

I immediately pulled myself out of his arms when I got my equilibrium back even though I really wanted to remain pressed against him and sniff his aftershave, cologne, or whatever he used to make himself smell like sex on legs. I turned and pinned my staff, who I also erroneously considered my friends, with a death glare. They all wore an innocent expression on their faces and gave nothing away.

I turned back to Gabe and mumbled, "Thank you," before I resumed walking toward the exit.

We all decided to head over to the diner to eat together before we went home. The diner was practically empty with most the town crammed inside the funeral home looking for a cheap show. I figured that a lot of them would be heading to the diner afterward, so I was happy to beat the crowd and get back home before I had to witness any more pathetic behavior.

Daniella brought us menus as if we didn't have the damn thing memorized after eating there our entire lives. Much like the town of

Blissville, the menu never changed. We gave our orders to Daniella without even glancing at them.

I ignored the stares I was getting from everyone at the table. "So what, I ordered the fucking beef stew," I exclaimed after several awkward moments of quiet. "I don't care what day of the week it is; I wanted some motherfucking beef stew." I might've said that a bit too loud because Emma poked her head out of the kitchen window. Just great! I'd be getting another call from my mom, or worse—an emergency visit home.

"Yeah, Meredith," Chaz said as if she'd spoken up. "He wants some motherfucking beef stew."

"Well, okay then," Meredith replied.

The exchange was just what we needed to break the odd tension that had formed. Yes, I was doing things out of my normal order, and I wasn't sure why, but I didn't feel my actions warranted such scrutiny and worried reactions from the people who knew me best. I felt like I needed to shake things up a bit and food choices were safer than bed partners.

Talk turned to normal things like dates, clients, and weekend plans. Daniella brought our food, and we all made the best of a sad evening because life went on regardless of loss. Going to pay final respects at a viewing drove home just how fragile life was, so it was good to be reminded of the blessings we had in our lives. Each and every person at that table enriched my life, and I felt lucky to know them.

That night as I lay in bed alone, listening to the wind whipping through the barren trees, I couldn't help but remember the last time someone was killed in our sleepy town and the scary ramifications it had on my life.

The morning of Georgia's burial was as frigid as the forecasters said it would be. I stood atop the hill in the Sugar Grove cemetery with only a handful of people. I had canceled my appointments for the day, which was something I had never done in all the years I had been styling hair.

I wasn't surprised to see Georgia's longtime attorney and housekeeper at the cemetery, but Nadine's arrival shocked me. Her eyes were red-rimmed and swollen; she looked legitimately devastated. I wasn't quite sure what to make of her being there, so I steered clear of her, hoping to avoid any drama. Apparently, Nadine was of a different mind because she sought me out as soon as the graveside service ended. By that time, I felt like a popsicle and just wanted to go home.

"Josh, wait," she called out after me. I stopped and let her catch up to me. "Look, I just want you to know that I'm very sorry about what happened with Georgia. She deserved better than what she got." I wasn't sure what she was apologizing for—sleeping with Georgia's husband or the hateful things she said the day she died—nor could I figure out why she was apologizing to me. "I'm sorry for everything," Nadine said as if she could read my mind. "I don't like myself very much right now."

I wasn't exactly sure what to say to her. She looked sincere, but would she be saying any of it if Georgia was alive? She sure as hell didn't look sorry when she was doing her damned best to eviscerate Georgia in my salon, nor did she look sorry when she was rolling all over the floor trying to scratch her eyes out. All of it just made me sad, and I didn't have the energy to dole out forgiveness, even if I had the ability to give it out. I wasn't the one she should be apologizing to, but for some reason, she thought I was the next best thing.

"I'm not quite sure what you expect of me, Nadine," I said honestly, but without animosity. "I can't give you the absolution you're seeking."

"I think I'm just looking for someone to listen," she said sadly. Nadine had always put on such a happy face for the town, but between the night of the viewing and the morning at the cemetery, I was starting to believe it had all been an act. “I don't have any friends, Josh.”

I did feel sorry for her then because I couldn't imagine my life without my friends, especially Meredith and Chaz. We had been through so much together and came out on the other side stronger than before because we always had one another. Regardless of the mistakes, she had made, I wouldn't wish loneliness and misery on her or anyone.

“Never mind. It's not your problem, Josh. I'm sorry for dumping this on you.” Nadine spun around and walked off before I could respond.

I blew out a frustrated breath and headed for my car. I felt anxious and restless as I drove away from the cemetery. I didn't want to go back to the salon because I wanted some quiet and time to regroup. I briefly thought about going to Gabe's and stomped that notion down as soon as it formed. I decided to enter the back door of my salon and take the back stairs up to my living quarters so I could avoid the salon clients. My staff would see my car parked behind the house, but they'd respect my privacy.

I curled up on the couch with Diva, my Siamese cat, whose personality matched her name perfectly. Normally, Diva was all about herself. She must have sensed my somber mood because she tucked herself under my chin and purred in what seemed like an attempt to comfort me. Diva's ministrations worked too. The chill that had permeated my body disappeared and I could feel myself relax on the couch until I eventually fell asleep.

My ringing phone woke me up. I was disoriented because it had grown dark while I napped on the couch with Diva and I momentarily forgot what day it was. I looked at the caller ID and was shocked to see who was calling me. I debated on letting it go to voicemail for about two seconds before I answered it.

“Hello?”

"How are you doing?" Gabe's deep voice warmed parts of me that no amount of purring from a cat could affect.

"I'm doing okay," I replied. *Was I?*

"You feel like having company?" I heard the slight hesitation in his voice as if he wasn't sure how well his question would be received.

I knew what happened almost every single time that we were alone together. Was that what I wanted right then? "Yes," I said answering both of our questions.

"Good," he said, his voice deepening because he also knew what would happen. "Come down and let me in."

"You're here now?" I stood up and ran my free hand through my hair in an attempt to smooth it into place.

"Yes. Come down here and let me in. I'm freezing my nuts off," Gabe groused.

"Give me a few minutes," I said and then hung up. I flipped on a few lights on my way to the bathroom to brush my teeth. I rushed through my routine so that I didn't keep him waiting long. It was freezing outside, and I didn't want his balls to freeze. I was pretty fond of them, even if I was unsure of the man they were attached to.

"It's about time," he said when I opened the door to him. "What the hell took so long?"

I grabbed him by the coat and pulled him into me, pressing my lips against his. Gabe parted his cold lips, and I slid my tongue inside to explore his warm mouth in a languid kiss. For once, I didn't want to rush him into bed. I wanted to take my time and get to know his body better. Hell, I hadn't even wrapped my lips around his big cock yet; a mistake I planned to rectify immediately.

"Minty fresh," Gabe said when our kiss ended. "You're forgiven for making me wait."

"Come upstairs with me, and I'll show you other things I can do with my minty fresh mouth." I laughed when Gabe growled playfully. I needed to be careful, or else I'd start liking the detective and the things he made me feel.

FOURTEEN

Gabe

THERE WAS SOMETHING COMPLETELY DIFFERENT ABOUT JOSH when he took my hand and led me up the stairs to his living space. He almost seemed happy to see me, and that wasn't something I associated with Josh. There was a flirty lightness to him that I had never seen before and it was a welcome change over the sadness I saw etched on his face at the funeral home. My desire to drive away his sadness may have overridden my common sense.

Of course, my dick focused solely on what he planned to do

with his mouth. I adored his mouth and not just the sheer beauty of his full lips and the oral delights they offered. It was his smart, snarky words that held my attention or the vulnerability that he accidentally let slide out on occasion. He was a mystery that I longed to solve, but I wasn't sure the result would make me happy. I could wind up falling for a guy who might never feel the same.

Josh turned to face me once we reached the top of his stairs. "You're thinking too hard," he said, a sly grin spreading across his face. "We can't have that, now can we?" He reached down and cupped my growing erection through my jeans.

"No, we can't." I always felt like I was tiptoeing around him, even when it came to sex. I felt like he held back pieces of himself in reserve too. That just wouldn't do. I reached down and stroked him through the dress pants he was still wearing from the funeral that morning. I felt his reaction to my touch as he hardened and lengthened against my hand. "Part of you likes me."

"That's some good sleuthing you've done there, Detective." Josh released my cock and started walking backward, crooking his finger as he went so that I would follow.

"Some clues are more obvious than others," I gestured to the way he strained against his pants. "Others are subtle, like the way your nostrils flare when I'm near you, or the slight pink flush of your skin. The smell of your soap gets stronger when your body heats up." Josh stood in the middle of his bedroom looking at me with dazed eyes. I advanced on him, pressing my body flush against his. "Your body tells me just how much you want me, even if you don't like me."

Instead of crushing my mouth against his like I normally would, I cupped his face in my hands and slowly lowered my mouth to his. I was grateful that I did because I felt the slight tremble of his lips as our flesh met. It was another sign of how badly he wanted, or even needed, what I offered him. I wasn't foolish enough to think it was *me* he wanted. *Not yet,* a hopeful voice inside my head whispered.

Josh gripped my biceps tightly, and I couldn't tell if it was to hold me there or hold himself up. Either way, I liked what it symbolized. I took my time swirling my tongue around his and pulled back slightly each time he tried to take over the kiss. I knew he wanted to speed things up and get to fucking so he could throw me out, but I wanted to savor this side of him.

I kissed him with every ounce of longing and passion he made me feel as I maneuvered us toward his bed. Every time we were together, I expected the sexual intensity to fade a little bit, but instead, it seemed to grow in leaps and bounds. I started to worry that I might become addicted to the things he made me feel.

I made no move to lower him to the bed once I had him pressed up against it. I was plenty happy to keep kissing him longer, but Josh had other plans. He dropped his hands to my waist and began unbuckling my belt before he slowly worked each button out of their hole. Once he had my fly open, he teased the length of my erection with the back of his hand. Suddenly, all I could think about was his mouth wrapped around my cock, but I wasn't the kind of guy who just shoved a man to his knees and started fucking his mouth.

I reluctantly broke our kiss so I could pull my shirt over my head then I reached over and began loosening Josh's tie. Once I removed it, I held it in my hands between our bodies and pulled it tight a few times, as if I was testing the strength. Josh took the tie from my hands and tossed it to the floor.

"Not tonight," he said. His words caused the breath to catch in my throat. I couldn't keep the image of him lying prone on his bed with his hands tied above his head out of my mind. *Was that something I even wanted?* I never had before, but I was in unchartered territory with Josh. "Ahh, I can see that I lost you again. That's terrible for my ego, so I need to correct it immediately."

My heart rate tripled as Josh lowered himself to his knees. I felt the heat of his breath through the fabric of my boxers as he placed kisses on my hardened dick. I told myself to be patient, to not be a jerk and press my cock against his mouth, but he made it so hard to be good. I felt my abdominal muscles tremble beneath the skin when Josh pressed his lips to my bare flesh just above my waistband. I clenched my fists to keep from grabbing him then I closed my eyes, tilted my head back, and fought for control over my rioting body.

Something about Josh brought out a primal need to claim and possess, to mark him as mine. The feelings were new and almost startling at times because of their intensity. I didn't take Josh to be the kind of guy who liked the caveman routine, so I struggled to contain it. Once I had myself under control, I looked back down at the beautiful man in front of me; I didn't want to miss a second of the pleasure I knew he was going to give me.

Josh seemed happy to torment me by delaying the moment his lips wrapped around my cock. He ran his fingers through my happy trail, dipped one inside my waistband to spread my pre-cum around the flared head of my dick, and then sucked that finger into his mouth. The happy little sound he made in the back of his throat told me he liked the way I tasted on his tongue.

Finally, my little tormentor eased my jeans and briefs down my legs until they hung around my ankles. I was fully exposed to him while he remained fully dressed; I found the contrast to be outrageously sexy. My hands twitched with the need to touch him, but I was letting him set the pace. Josh did something I didn't expect from him; he looked into my eyes as he fisted my cock and guided it toward his mouth.

Eye contact during oral sex was extremely intimate; hell, not even Kyle did that during the years we were together. Josh was a guy who said he might not even like me, but he chose to lock his gaze with mine while he gave me head. My thoughts were befuddled as I tried to figure out if perhaps there was more behind his gesture, but then all thoughts disappeared when his mouth drew closer.

Josh slowly parted his lips, prolonging my torture as I waited for him to take me into his mouth. Instead, his tongue snaked out and licked all around the head of my dick and dipped into my slit to capture more of my essence.

It was all I could do not to push my dick inside his mouth because waiting to be inside him felt like a form of cruel punishment. My legs began to tremble with excitement and need. I nearly shouted with pleasure once he took pity on me and wrapped his lips around my dick then sucked it into the wet heat of his mouth. I couldn't keep my hands to myself any longer. I placed both hands on the side of his face and caressed the skin around his mouth with my thumbs, feeling the way he stretched to accommodate my girth.

Josh took his time acquainting himself with my dick by slowly working it in and out of his mouth. It was a great testament to my patience to let him when what I wanted to do was take control. I didn't want it to end too soon so I let him set the pace that he wanted, knowing that I'd take control once I had him pinned beneath me on his bed.

Josh's mouth felt so damn good on my cock. He used the perfect amount of suction and the right pace as he took me to the back of his throat over and over. He changed up the pace every few passes and even stopped to tease my head with his tongue. Josh released my cock with a wet popping sound then moved lower to suck one of my balls into his mouth, then the other. When I felt the wet rasp of his tongue on my taint, I knew it was time for him to quit before I passed the point of no return.

I slid my hands beneath his arms and hoisted him to his feet before I grabbed the top of his dress shirt and yanked hard, rending the material, and sent buttons scattering to the floor. The look of shock that crossed his face was almost comical. Did he find it that hard to believe that I could want him that much? I wrapped one hand around his neck and pulled him into me for another searing kiss while I worked his pants open with my other hand. I couldn't ever get enough of his mouth when we were together. I only broke the kiss so we could divest the rest of our clothes before we got on his bed.

I slid between his parted thighs and pinned his hands above his head, holding him hostage, as I devoured his lips. I loved the feel of his bare cock against mine and began to thrust my hips, building up a delicious friction aided by the copious amount of pre-cum seeping from my slit. I didn't know what it was about Josh that made me want him so badly and I didn't care. What I did care about was making our time together count; I wanted him to crave more of us. I wanted to leave a lasting impression on his soul.

Josh pulled back from our kiss and looked into my eyes. I saw a myriad of emotions there, but the one that struck me the most was fear. I knew he wasn't afraid that I would hurt him physically, I'd rather die first than betray the trust he showed me. The fear told me that he liked me more than he wanted to and it worried him; I worried him. I didn't know many things about Josh Roman, but I instinctively knew that he would require action from me to prove my worth, not talk. And damn if I didn't want to be worthy of his trust in all aspects of his life.

I released one of his hands so that I could cup his face with all the tenderness he made me feel in my heart. He wasn't the only one floundering around with new feelings. I saw him struggle to accept my gesture and could almost see the wheels in his brain turning as he tried to guide us back into more comfortable territory for him. I knew that I should let him, but I didn't.

Instead, I kissed a path from his ear to his jaw then nibbled the sensitive flesh there just beneath the jawbone and relished the way he shivered. I began placing kisses down his neck to his collarbone with the intention of making my way to his cock. I loved the taste of him on my tongue and wanted to experience it again, but Josh wasn't feeling very patient with me.

He snaked his fist through my hair and yanked my head up hard. "I want to feel you inside me. Now." I saw in his eyes that his tolerance for tenderness had passed. He slid out from beneath me so that he could open the drawer of his nightstand and remove the items we needed.

I poured the lubricant on my fingers and teased his pucker, watching his frustration grow as I didn't do exactly what he commanded. I anticipated the exact moment he was going to make more of his demands and slid my finger inside of him at the same time he opened his mouth. "I… oh, fuck!"

I kept the pad of my middle finger on his prostate, working it in circles to stimulate him and drive him wild. He wasn't always in control, and he needed to know that starting right then. Not one to give up easily, he began thrusting his hips trying to get more penetration from me, so I removed my finger from his tight clench. Josh's lips curled up in a frustrated snarl that I longed to kiss off his face, but I was too focused on getting him ready for the fucking he wanted so badly.

Again, I waited until he was ready to blast me verbally before I penetrated him again, but with two fingers that time. "Damn you," was all he said before his eyes nearly rolled up in his head. "I can't stand you."

I couldn't help myself; I had to chuckle just a little bit about that one. Josh might've been more convincing had he not been grinding himself on my fingers and gripping my biceps so hard that I would wear his fingernail scores on my skin for days.

"Asshole," he sneered, but his lips quipped up in a quick half-smile.

"I'm all up in there," I said, purposely misunderstanding what he said. I emphasized my physical location in his body by pressing against his prostate with both fingers, causing his back to bow off the bed. He was so fucking responsive to my touch, and it made me want him that much more.

I removed my fingers from his ass, earning a snarly growl from him so that I could suit up. Josh snatched the condom packet out of my hand and ripped it open with his teeth before he sat up and reached for my cock. Once he had the condom rolled on so that it snugly gripped the base of my cock, he smeared more lube up and down the length of my erection.

"I like it hard and wet." Josh climbed out from beneath me and got to his hands and knees so that his ass was up in the air invitingly.

Whether it was another attempt to avoid intimacy or not, it was a temptation that I couldn't ignore. Josh wanted it hard, so I decided to give it to him harder than he'd ever had before and would not stop until he lay beneath me in a boneless heap. Hard, however, didn't mean cruel, so I allowed time for him to adjust to my penetration before I set out to give him what he had demanded of me with his body and words.

I gripped his hips tight and pounded in and out of him, the sound of our skin slapping together was music to my ears. The needy moans coming from Josh spurred me on, and I thrust hard enough to push him down flat on the bed. I followed him down and covered his body with my own, careful to keep most of my weight on my forearms as I kept up the furious pace of my fucking.

"Do you feel me everywhere?" I asked Josh. I didn't want to be the only one who felt that way. When I was inside him, it felt like he was a permanent part of my body; an inked tattoo on my soul that marked me for life.

"Y-y-yes," he confessed in a pleasure induced stutter. "E-everywhere," he echoed.

I rode him hard, tagging his prostate with every slam home. "You're going to come so hard for me, Josh." I knew the added friction of the comforter against his cock, as I thrust long and deep inside him, was driving him out of his mind.

"So hard." His words sounded slurred as if he was drunk on the pleasure I gave him.

I gripped his hair and turned his head, exposing his neck for my lips. I needed to have them on his body as I felt him coming apart beneath me. I felt my climax begin to build and burn inside me. Sometimes my orgasm would come on fast and would end just as quickly, while others would build slowly and roll through me languidly. That night was a slow burn that began at the base of my spine and spread throughout my entire body. I savored each second of nearly painful pleasure as I felt Josh begin to unravel beneath me.

His breathing became choppy as he worked to pull air into his lungs, his fingers had a white-knuckled grip on the comforter, and his ass had a stranglehold on my cock. "Come for me, Josh," I commanded as I loomed closer to an orgasm. "Give me everything."

"Greedy bastard," he gritted out, but there was no heat to his words—just intense pleasure.

I could tell he was trying to hold back, probably out of spite. "Stop fighting me," I growled in his ear. "Come." Josh's body had stiffened beneath me before he came with a shout. "That's right. I want all of it." I fucked him until there was no fight left in his body and pleasured purrs were the only sounds he made.

I slid my arms beneath his chest and held him even tighter to my body, as I became a rutting beast, pistoning in and out of him. The pressure built inside me until I felt like I was going to implode. The pleasure released throughout my entire body as I flooded the condom I wore. I kept working my cock in and out of him as my orgasm rolled through me and only stopped when the last tremor faded from my body.

I knew that I was too heavy to collapse on him like I wanted to, so I gently pulled out then rolled off him and onto my back beside him. I turned my head and looked over at him to find him watching me through hooded eyes. I wanted to close mine and rest a minute, but I was pretty certain that staying wasn't something he wanted me to do.

"Are you hungry?" I asked, scrambling to find a way to spend more time with him.

"I could eat," he replied, but then narrowed his eyes as if a thought just struck him. "You mean here, right? Like you were going to get up and cook something you found in my refrigerator and cabinets." Panic was starting to creep into his voice, and I hated that I made him feel that way, but I found myself wanting to push him a little more.

"I was thinking the diner," I answered casually like it was no big deal.

"But people will see us and start talking," he replied, trying so hard to rein himself in.

"Are you ashamed of me?" I tried to keep a light tone in my voice, even though I wasn't joking. I needed to know if clandestine fucks were all I'd ever be to him. If so, I needed to decide if that was something that interested me.

"It's not a matter of being ashamed of you," Josh replied seriously. "It's a matter of the gossip and bullshit that will be flung around like manure behind our backs. I've had enough of that lately, and I don't want any more."

"They're going to talk anyway, so why not give them something real to blab about rather than let them speculate and make shit up." I was probably going to lose the battle, but I wanted to give it one last shot.

Josh closed his eyes and became so still and quiet that I wondered if he had fallen asleep. After a few long moments, he opened his eyes and the regret I saw in his eyes negated the need for more words. I reached over and ran the back of my hand down the side of his face in an attempt to comfort him, even though I was the one who felt burned by his rejection. I tamped my feelings down so that I wouldn't show him just how much I was disappointed.

"It's okay," I told him, even though it wasn't.

I leaned over and kissed his cheek before I rolled out of his bed then went into the bathroom to throw out the condom and clean up. He was still in the same spot that I left him in, and he didn't turn or acknowledge me in any way as I got dressed, or when I left.

My heart pinched painfully in my chest as I walked down the stairs and let myself out through the back door. I loved the way I felt when he was in my arms but hated the way I felt afterward. I decided then and there that I wouldn't let myself fall into his bed or him into mine anymore. There was only so much rejection a guy could take, and I had reached my limit.

FIFTEEN

Josh

THE SMALL PART OF ME THAT WANTED TO BELIEVE IN EVERLASTING love and happily ever afters wanted to say yes to Gabe. That part of me wanted to sit proudly across from Gabe and get to know him better over a shared meal. I could learn about his favorite music or movies; I could learn about his family and life before he moved to Blissville. But that part was so small that common sense easily overruled it. Sure, I knew on some level that I could be pushing away one of the best things to happen to me, but I couldn't put myself out there again.

Practical Josh, who liked routines and consistency, outshouted Feisty Josh, who dared to take risks and chances. Being a Gemini was tough work; it wasn't easy keeping the twins balanced and happy. Feisty Josh felt slighted because I only let him out to choose clothes and brightly colored underwear. Oh, and he picked out my convertible Mini Cooper because no way in hell Practical Josh would've picked out that bright teal color.

But he asked you out to dinner in a public diner. He's not trying to keep you a secret. That was all I had ever wanted with some of the guys I "dated," but I was no longer happy with just that. *It's a step in the right direction though. How can he prove himself to you if you won't give him a chance?* That was true, but I felt a pull to Gabe like I had never experienced before I met him. Everything was more intense with him, including my mistrust. I knew that, if given a chance, he could hurt me far worse than those from my past. I did what I thought was best for me and pushed him away.

I acted like a complete asshole to Gabe, and he didn't deserve that from me. I felt horrible about the way I reacted to his question, but there wasn't anything I was willing to do about it. Besides, I was pretty sure I saw the last of him unless we met in an official capacity. I felt a new tension in the air when he left that had never been present between us, not even when I confronted him when he was about to say that I was too feminine for his taste.

I kept reminding myself that night, and the many days that followed without a glimpse of him, that it was for the best. Truthfully, I missed bantering with him back and forth, and I couldn't help but wonder what he was up to. Was he getting anywhere with Georgia's case? How were he and Buddy getting along? Did he think about me half as much as I thought about him? I couldn't help but wonder if he still watched me as I jogged by his house.

I felt my resolve getting weaker as the desire to see him grew stronger. I needed to stay busy in my downtime, learn how to knit or something so that I didn't go over to his home and beg to have a go at his cock again. I was starting to feel and sound like a cock whore, and I didn't like it. Hell, I had a right hand—and a left if I wanted to shake things up. Maybe I needed to jerk off more and think about Gabe less.

My desperation to get over my self-inflicted misery led me to accept an invitation to go dancing from Merrick. He wanted to celebrate his new place and return to single life, which he claimed was better once he and Kevin broke up. Who was I to argue with him? I had never been in a real relationship before, so I couldn't say which was better. The only thing I did know was that I slept much better in Gabe's arms than I did alone. I chalked it up to remaining jitters and trauma from the shooting in my bedroom, but I suspected there was more to it than I wanted to admit.

"You know that Merrick's going to want to pick up where he left off, right?" Meredith maneuvered around vehicles she felt were driving too slow when they were only speeding ten miles over the posted limit rather than the fifteen or twenty over that she preferred. "Are you going to tell him that you're taken?"

"Taken? What the hell are you talking about, Mere?" Perhaps I shouldn't have asked Meredith to come along as the designated driver, but she was right about Merrick and his probable intentions. I wasn't interested in hooking up with him again, but not for the reason she mentioned. I wanted her along so that I would be able to have a few drinks and get home safely without having to spend the night at his place, which was what I suspected Merrick would suggest.

She snorted and shook her head like I was a complete idiot. "Sugar, you might be able to fool yourself, but you sure won't fool Meredith."

"Ew, don't talk about yourself in the third person. You know that creeps me out." I looked over at her, grinning from ear to ear. "Remember Travis Southerland?"

"Travis is hungry." Meredith's voice had dropped low to mimic our former classmate's. "Travis is the best quarterback in the state of Ohio." We burst into laughter. "Thank goodness he outgrew that habit."

"He sure was a hottie back in the day," I told Meredith. Travis was one of the few kids that went to college and never returned to Blissville after graduation. Last I heard, he was living in Dallas and owned a large insurance agency.

"I prefer brains over brawn," she replied.

"Uh-huh," I said disbelievingly. "You forget that I know every single guy you've dated since high school."

"It was a recent revelation," she said in a moderately defensive tone. "It's taken me a while to figure out where I've gone wrong in the past."

"Yeah, you've chosen guys who aren't good enough for you. I think it's more that they lacked balls and not a matter of brains or brawn." I looked over at Meredith and marveled for the millionth time in my life that her inner beauty rivaled her exterior perfection. Someday the right guy would come along and snatch her up, and I couldn't wait for the moment that he appeared in her life. "Aim high, baby."

"I'll do my best." Meredith saluted me playfully. "So, why couldn't Chaz come with us tonight?"

"All he said was that he had plans. He didn't say who or what he was doing," I added with a shrug. Chaz never missed an opportunity to dance the night away, and I was a little bit worried about him. I knew he'd come to me if something serious was going on. Therefore I chose to respect his privacy and not press him for information.

"I guess we'll just have to dance and live it up without him."

Vibe was the closest gay club, and it was nearly an hour away. The bottom level housed the dance floor while the second floor sported pool tables, dart boards, and other sporty things. I rarely went upstairs because dancing was my sport.

The club was hopping when we arrived, and it took us several minutes to find Merrick. He was pressed up against the bar by some tall, burly looking dude and didn't look in a hurry to leave him. It appeared that I would be avoiding any awkward rejection of his advances that night. *You didn't have any problems rejecting Gabe.* No! I would not be going back there again. I gave Meredith a relieved smile before I tugged her hand and pulled her into the crowd of dancers so we could get our groove on.

I let the music flow through me and became one with the beat. Music had always been my safe place to escape to when I needed relief from both the external pressures in the world and the ones I created in my mind. I threw my hands up in the air and focused on having a good time with my best friend.

It didn't take long for my clothes to become damp and stick to my body. I was starting to get thirsty, but I was having too much fun to stop. Mere was having a great time too, swaying with the music with her arms in the air and her eyes closed. After what seemed like hours of dancing, Mere stopped and gestured drinking with her hands. I nodded, and we both left the dance floor in search of a cold drink, or two.

Out of the corner of my eye, I saw the owner of the club, Nate Turner, approach the bar. He was a very sexy man, who rarely came out of his office to socialize with the patrons. I knew whoever had his attention must've been special. I turned my head to watch him, as did nearly everyone else at, or near, the bar. There were too many people blocking my view, so I had to lean forward over the bar to see who was sitting on the stool talking to Nate.

"I don't fucking believe it," I said loud enough to be heard over the thumping music.

"What, honey?" Meredith looked in the direction that I had been staring, and I heard her gasp. "It's probably nothing."

I told myself it didn't matter that Gabe was at the bar talking to Nate and looking all kinds of chummy. I freaked out when I fell asleep in his bed. I outright rejected any offer that he made other than sex. He was done and had moved on. I knew that, so why did it bother me to see it with my own eyes? I told myself not to look down in their direction again, but it was like my eyes had a mind of their own.

I watched as Nate placed his hand on Gabe's shoulder and nodded his head in the direction of his office. I had heard from some of the guys that worked at the club that Nate liked to invite someone who'd caught his eye on the monitors back to his office to fuck. It didn't often happen, which was why almost every eye at the bar was on the two men.

Of course, Nate noticed Gabe; who wouldn't? In all honesty, it looked like the little meet and greet had happened on more than one occasion. As if Gabe sensed my eyes on him, he turned his head and looked down the length of the bar in my direction. I had just enough time to duck back and hide behind the guy standing next to me, taking Meredith with me so that Gabe didn't see her either.

"Things aren't always how they appear." Meredith's eyes were filled with sympathy as she reached out and clasped my hand. "Go talk to him, Jazz. If you really want him then don't let him get away."

I didn't want him. I didn't want him. I... oh, fuck it! I pulled back from Meredith and headed down to the end of the bar where Gabe had sat to find someone else was already sitting there. I looked over toward the hallway leading back to Nate's office in time to see the two of them approaching it. Nate had his hand at the small of Gabe's back and the sight was enough to make me sick. My stomach pitched and rolled as if it was the morning after a total bender.

I pivoted on my heels and headed back to Meredith. I shook my head in answer to the silent question I read in her eyes. The music switched over to one of my favorite songs, but my mood to dance and be social had passed. The only thing I wanted to do right then was go home and curl up with my pets.

"Let's go, sugar," Meredith said, reaching for my hand.

I followed her silently to her car, trying hard to push the hurt and disappointment I felt out of my mind. I wasn't mad at Gabe because I had no right to be. I guess what upset me was that I had hoped he would try harder to make something between us work and that was so unfair to him. I mean, how many cold shoulders and rejections was he supposed to take before he moved on to someone who obviously wanted to be with him?

Still, as disappointed as I was, I almost felt better because I had been right. Gabe wasn't for me. I mean, there was nothing similar between Nate Turner and me. I was convinced that nothing real would happen between us and I was glad that I stuck to my guns, even if a part of me wanted him to prove me wrong.

We drove home in complete silence, which never happened when Mere and I were together. We often talked at the same time or completed one another's sentences. We never just sat in silence, but that was what I needed, and she was kind enough to give it to me.

Meredith pulled in the driveway behind my house and put the car in park. "You want me to come inside for a little bit?"

"Nah," I replied, "I'm okay. Thank you, Mere."

"Anytime." She leaned over and kissed my cheek before I got out of her car.

Once inside the warmth of my house, I collapsed on my couch and put my feet up on the coffee table "Well, fuck." There wasn't anything else to say on the matter.

"Blow me, baby," Savage said from his cage, making me laugh.

"Dirty bird," I told him.

"Dirty bird," he repeated.

Diva jumped up on my lap and head-butted my chin before she started to purr. I stood up from the couch and took the cat with me to let Jazzy the ferret out of her cage. No matter what went on in my life, I knew I could count on my friends and my pets to perk me up.

An image of Gabe lying naked in my bed came to mind, and I hated the way my traitorous body reacted because that wasn't the kind of perking up I had been thinking about. What Gabe and I briefly shared was over, and the sooner I accepted that, the sooner my life would return to normal. I wanted routine and structure back, even if others thought it boring. The opinions of others didn't matter because I had been happy before Gabriel Wyatt came into my life.

Liar.

SIXTEEN

Gabe

FRUSTRATION AND LONELINESS WERE NOT GOOD BEDFELLOWS, AND I was ready to kick them out of my bed so I could get some sleep, but there was one problem. Josh. Okay, the unsolved homicide of Georgia Beaumont was driving me crazy too, but he was the primary source of both of those feelings. I desperately wanted to shake him out of my system but found that I couldn't. I received an offer to solve my loneliness momentarily, but I wasn't interested in what Nate Turner had to offer me.

I'd hooked up with Nate the first night I went to his club when I was fresh off my breakup with Kyle. I'd heard about Vibe, but clubbing wasn't something that Kyle and I had done together. Needless to say, I was beyond flattered when the sexy club owner walked up to the bar and introduced himself to me. I saw the invitation in his eyes long before he verbalized it. We had a hot, hard fuck and one that I was happy to repeat at the time. I handed him my business card with my phone number on it after we were through and Nate just stared at it for a long time before he looked back into my eyes.

"I don't do repeats." He tossed the card in the trash can without regard for my feelings. "Although, with you, I'd be tempted."

"Don't do me any favors," I replied on my way out the door.

I had been to Vibe a few more times since then and had never run into Nate nor had I seen him select a plaything from the bar. I was shocked when he called me out of the blue the past weekend and said he needed my help with a delicate situation.

"How'd you get my number?" I asked him once I got past my surprise.

"You gave it to me, and I kept it all this time," he said, meaning that he had pulled my card out of his trash can after I had left. The tone of voice he used implied that I should've been flattered.

"Look, I'm not interested in hooking up with you if that's why you're calling me," I said. Nate inhaled sharply on the other end of the phone. The jackass probably wasn't used to being turned down.

"That's a little presumptuous, don't you think?" Nate asked.

"You're the one calling me so I think I can act however I want." I didn't owe the guy a damn thing.

"Look, I need your professional advice on a matter. This isn't a booty call," Nate said in a humored tone. "Your virtue is safe with me."

I had nothing else better to do on a Saturday night since I went cold turkey from Josh. I made the hour drive with zero expectations in mind, but I wasn't at all surprised when Nate came onto me once I sat down at the bar. He flirted with me like he had the first time and nodded his head toward his office. However, there was a tenseness about him and stress lines around his mouth and eyes that weren't present the first time. I realized right away that he was putting on a show for the club patrons and went along with it, even though the feel of his hand on my back felt all wrong to me.

Nate's demeanor changed the minute we stepped inside his private office. He dropped the suave seducer act and sat down behind his massive desk. Instead of being bent over the desk, as I had been during my last visit, I sat across from him on the other side.

"What's going on?" I asked Nate.

"I think someone wants me dead." Nate gripped the edge of his desk hard enough to turn his knuckles white.

I don't know what I expected to hear from him, but it sure as hell wasn't that. He had my full attention. "What makes you think that, Nate?"

He leaned forward and lowered his voice to almost a whisper and said, "Things have been happening to me that I can't ignore, no matter how much I want to." I found his actions odd at first because we were alone in his private office. Hell, the walls were so thick that I could hardly hear the hard thumping from the club. Then I realized his actions were a sign of fear, not the need for privacy.

"What kind of things, Nate?"

He had released a shaky breath before he began. "I chalked up the first incident to vandalism. I went out to my car to leave one night, and someone had slashed all four tires on my Mercedes. I figured I pissed off a guy when I didn't want to hook up with him for a repeat performance or something."

"And then," I prodded when he went silent for a few moments.

"Then I received an email about a week later, and it basically said I was the scum of the earth and I had to die. The email address was generic, and the reply email I sent was returned with an error message. He's tech savvy, whoever he is." Nate looked away, as if deep in thought.

"Is that all?" It seemed to me like he had more to say, but getting the story from him was like pulling teeth. I had to keep nudging him to tell me what was going on. Hell, he was the one who called me and asked me to meet him, not the other way around.

"I've received a few more emails since the first." Nate paused and swallowed hard before he reached inside his desk and pulled out copies of the emails he received. "This is when I started to get freaked out. I didn't even connect the first two incidents until I received this."

The first email included a picture of Nate checking out the damage to his tires. The email message stated: **I could've killed you then, but what would be the fun in that?**

The second email showed a picture of Nate walking buck-ass naked through his house holding a coffee cup in one hand and his phone up to his ear with the other. There was a second picture of a naked Nate looking out his French door in the direction of the photographer. The email message read: **Such a beautiful cock wasted on a piece of shit excuse for a man. I'm going to cut it off while you're still breathing and shove it in your mouth. I'm going to laugh as you choke to death while deep-throating your own cock.**

"Wow." I slid the emails back across the desk to Nate. "That's some serious shit, Nate."

"That's why I called you. What the fuck do I do?" He ran his hands through his hair, causing the strands to stick up in several different directions. His looks had changed from a confident man to a scared boy.

"You need to call the police here in Cincinnati, Nate. I'm outside your jurisdiction and can't legally help you."

"I know you can't legally help me, but I was hoping to hire you to do it privately. I need to keep this from going public." His dark eyes pleaded for help, but I instinctively knew it would be a mistake to get tangled up with his problems. There was no way to keep that private, even if he did hire a PI to track down the person sending the emails. What then? Was he going to have the guy killed instead of pressing charges against him? A cold chill ran down my spine as I realized there might be truth to my random speculating. "For old times' sake." He had changed his voice to a seductive pitch, but I wasn't biting.

"I'm sorry, Nate, but I honestly can't help you. The CPD can and will, so I strongly recommend you get a report started right away. I'll go with you if you…"

"No!" He spoke loudly and emphatically, leaving no doubt in my mind that he never intended to handle this within the law.

I was not willing to help him skirt the legal process and kill the person threatening him. If he'd spoken his intentions out loud, then I would've been obligated to report the incident to the police myself. All I had to go on was gut instinct and speculation. "Okay," I said throwing up my hands. "I'm not sure what you expected out of me, but I'm about to disappoint you." I pushed my shoulders back, made strong eye contact with him, and carefully enunciated my words so that there would be no confusion about my unwillingness to assist him. "You have no idea who this person is who seems hell bent on seeing you dead. You have no idea about their abilities to carry out their threats. The only course of action you should be considering is calling the police and allowing them to help you. They have a team of tech people who can trace the IP address of where these emails came from. They sent the emails at the same time. Maybe they're using a public computer at one of those cyber cafés, and they have video feed or, if not, the staff might recall the person. Whatever alternative you're considering is probably going to end in a fatality—yours."

Nate pressed his lips firmly together as a stony expression formed on his face. "I guess we're through here."

"I guess we are." I rose to my feet and didn't bother offering him my hand to shake, as I knew he'd reject the offer. He didn't get his way, and his displeasure was plainly etched on his face. "Good luck, Nate." I turned and left his office without a backward glance.

A week later, and the conversation still replayed in my mind. I was wound tighter than a drum and needed a healthy way to get rid of the stress that had my shoulders and neck knotted up. Sally Ann had purchased a gift certificate for a massage for my birthday, but I hadn't planned on using it. I'd only ever had a sensual massage given to me by a lover, so I associated massages as an intimate thing. Plus, the gift certificate was for Curl Up and Dye, and I wasn't sure that I wanted to see Josh so soon after his rejection. It had been a few weeks since then, but I still craved him and his touch. I didn't trust myself not to embarrass us both in his salon if I got close enough to touch him.

I caved in after a few days of popping ibuprofen every six hours to relieve my tension headaches. I called the salon and spoke to Chaz, who got really quiet when he discovered it was me calling. His professionalism kicked in, and he scheduled an evening appointment for me to see their massage therapist, Josi, that same night. I wanted to call and cancel the appointment as soon as I hung up the phone then realized I was acting foolish.

I was bound to run into Josh in our small town; it was a miracle that I hadn't already. I could continue with the way things were and constantly wonder when it would happen, or I could take the situation into my hands—like I did with my frustrated cock each morning—and be mentally prepared to see him. I reasoned that I would be in better control of my hands and mouth if I had the upper hand. That was my story, and I was going to stick with it.

I returned to my desk after I made the call to the salon and found Adrian looking dazed and confused. He was staring at his computer monitor as if he couldn't believe what he was seeing. I felt a tingling sense that Adrian might've found something that broke open Georgia's case, which we needed badly. Nothing had panned out in the weeks after her death, and we desperately needed something to shake loose in our case. I sat down at my desk and waited for him to say something. I didn't have to wait long.

"I can't believe it." He ran his hand over his face and returned his attention to the computer. "The gas station finally sent us the video of the gas pumps for the timeframe on Rocky's receipt." Adrian shook his head in disbelief. "I just can't believe it."

"Is she someone we know?" I assumed his shock had to do with the identity of Rocky's second girlfriend. It still amazed me that the little weasel had a wife and *two* girlfriends. I slid my chair back after Adrian continued to stare at his computer without answering me.

"*Him*," Adrian said about the time I rounded his desk. "We know *him*."

"What?" I leaned over the back of Adrian's chair and stared at the monitor. Adrian rewound the video, and I saw a familiar person pumping gas into Rocky's SUV. "So they went hunting together," I said.

"Keep watching," Adrian replied.

The video played on and Rocky came out of the gas station after a minute or two with his arms laden with snacks and drinks. He walked around to the driver side of the vehicle where the man was pumping gas. Instead of getting in the car as I expected, he walked up to the man and kissed him full on the mouth.

"What?" I stood up straight and watched as Adrian replayed the video after he zoomed in so we could be sure of the other man's identity. "Adrian, isn't that…"

"County Commissioner Jack Wallace," he said before I could.

"Rocky has a wife, girlfriend, *and* a boyfriend?" I asked in awe—but not the good kind.

"It would seem he's just down to a wife and a boyfriend now," Adrian replied. "What we need to find out is how long it's been happening and whether Jack knew about Rocky sleeping with Georgia again. Maybe he was willing to share Rocky with his wife because he's a married man too, but drew the line at sharing him with a girlfriend also."

"I think we need to pay a visit to the county commissioner's office." I walked to my desk and retrieved my jacket. "Let's bring the captain up to speed first."

"Let's do this, partner." Adrian sounded peppier than he had in days unless he was talking about Sally Ann.

I had a strong feeling that we were finally on the right track to solving the case. For me, it had nothing to do with our closing rate and everything to do with getting justice for Georgia Beaumont. Her friends mourned her loss and having the case go unsolved would only stoke the fires of misery. I knew that bringing her killer to justice wouldn't make the pain go away, but it would help to know that he or she didn't still walk among them.

SEVENTEEN

Josh

My body told me Gabe was in my salon before I even saw him or heard his voice. Yes, I was able to hear his voice over the din of hair dryers, music, and gossip. Luckily for me, I was on the very last foil for my client or I might have lost track of the color pattern I'd been working on. I loved doing multi-dimensional colors, but I had to pay close attention so that I didn't fuck it up. The last thing I needed was Detective Distraction waltzing in without an appointment and…

I saw Chaz show him to the sitting area between the salon and massage areas. Gabe happened to look in my direction and our eyes met in my mirror. I narrowed my eyes in speculation and he winked at me. Then my brain chose to function and recall that Sally Ann purchased a gift certificate for Gabe's birthday. That meant he was in my building about to get naked with only a sheet between him and Josi.

Damn that man and all his distracting yumminess!

I turned my focus back to my client because no man was worth fucking up a woman's hair and my reputation. "All right, Mary Beth, you're ready for some time beneath the dryer." I walked her over to a free chair and lowered the dome over her head. "Would you like something to drink or a magazine to look at?"

"Oh, you're such a dear. Could I have the latest HGTV magazine and some sweet tea? Stan and I are planning a kitchen remodel and I'd love to get some ideas while I process."

That meant I had to go into the sitting room where *he* was to get the magazine that Mary Beth wanted. I looked around the salon and hoped that one of the earlier clients had already snatched it up and set it aside, but it just wasn't my day—week, month, or even year. I smiled at Mary Beth who was looking up at me expectantly. "I'll be right back." I turned on her dryer, dug up my courage, and went into the sitting room.

Out of the corner of my eye, I saw Gabe look up from his magazine and lock his focus on me. *Please don't say anything. Please don't say anything.* I willed him not to speak to me so that I could maintain my focus. I began sorting through the magazines on the coffee table in search of the latest HGTV that came in the day before and couldn't find it anywhere, which probably meant...

"Looking for this one?" Gabe wiggled the magazine in front of his chest when I turned my head and looked at him.

"Yes, actually." I was proud of how cool my voice sounded when I spoke because I felt anything but calm on the inside. "My client is getting ready to do a kitchen remodel and would like to look at the magazine."

"What will you give me for it?" The arrogant look on his face and tone of his voice set my teeth to grinding while I dug deep for patience. Too bad I had none for him at that point.

"Not a goddamned thing," I replied vehemently. "I'll just tell Mary Beth that the magazine is gone. She'll think Donna Sumner stole it like she has in the past." I turned and was just about to the doorway of the salon before he caught me. Gabe pressed his body against mine, one arm held me tight against him, and the other held the magazine up in front of me.

"I was only teasing." The heat of his breath tickled my ear, and it was all I could do not to react. "Give this to your client." I took the magazine from his hand then he dropped his arms away from me and stepped back. "Are you going to be around later? I'd like to talk to you."

"We don't have anything to talk about," I replied, hoping he didn't see the small shiver that worked its way down my spine as my body missed his heat.

"Liar." He chuckled as I walked away from him with my spine stiff as a board. The nerve of that asshole.

I retrieved a bottle of sweet tea out of the refrigerator in the small kitchen and then presented the tea and magazine to Mary Beth, who clapped her hands gleefully before she accepted them. I turned my attention to cleaning up my station so that it was pristine and ready for her haircut after her shampoo. I tried my hardest not to think about Gabe being there by focusing on that traitor Chaz. I knew damn well that Gabe wasn't on the schedule that morning when I looked, which meant he called the salon to schedule an appointment earlier in the day and Chaz worked him in without telling me.

I whipped out my phone and sent Chaz a quick text. *I can't believe you didn't tell me that Gabe called and scheduled a massage.*

I looked over and watched as Chaz pulled his phone out of his back pocket. I could feel his humor at my discomfort from across the room.

He smiled the entire time he typed a reply. *Since when have I been required to alert you to a client scheduling an appointment?*

I bit my lip to keep from growling out loud. *Gabe's not a client, jack wagon. He's the enemy, and you should've let me know he was coming into my territory so I could prepare.*

Chaz started laughing in earnest then. *And where's the fun in that?* I was so happy that he was entertained at my expense.

You're fired! I typed and hit send.

Chaz only laughed harder. *Yeah. Yeah. Yeah.* He totally wasn't worried about losing his job.

I slid my phone back in my pocket then grabbed the empty hair dye bowls and headed to the prep room right off the kitchen. I had just walked into the room when I felt, instead of heard, Gabe enter the room behind me. He moved like a ninja for such a big man. Gabe took the bowls from my hand and put them on the counter before he turned and backed me up against the door.

Gabe pressed the length of his body against mine and lowered his mouth to my ear. "How long before your client's dome-looking thing goes off?"

"I'm not doing this with you now or ever, Detective." Too bad he could feel the way my body betrayed me by trembling with want.

"Why so formal after we've been so intimate?" he asked hotly against my ear before he peppered my neck with kisses. "I've had your dick in my mouth so I would think we should be on a first-name basis." He pulled back and looked into my eyes. "In fact, we've been as intimate as two people can be except for having my tongue in your ass." I swear to God that I nearly whimpered. "Is that what it would take for you to go to dinner with me? I've missed you, Josh."

I wanted to believe him, but the memory of his rendezvous with the club owner was still burning in my mind. It gave me the strength I needed to resist him. “You didn’t look very lonely last weekend.”

Gabe straightened to his full height. His furrowed brow formed a deep V over his dark eyes, and he frowned as he looked down at me. “What did you just say?”

“I said that you didn’t…”

“I heard what you said,” Gabe told me.

“Then why’d you ask me to repeat myself, dumb ass?” There was no mistaking the annoyed sarcastic tone of voice I used on him, and I could tell he didn’t like it at all.

“What were you doing at Vibe?” Gabe asked, not even trying to deny he’d been there.

“That’s none of your business,” I said huffily enough to make any soap opera actress happy. “You have some fucking nerve asking what I was doing there when you were hooking up with that sleaze-bag club owner.”

“I wasn’t hooking up with Nate,” Gabe said calmly. “He called me there to get professional advice.”

“Yeah, that’s why you both looked so chummy when he greeted you at the bar.” I narrowed my eyes at him. “Is that how you treat everyone who asks for your opinion on a legal matter?” I had urged myself to calm down because I was giving too much of my feelings away, but I felt like I was on a sinking ship and about to go under at any moment.

“You sure are awfully curious about what I do with other men after you made it clear that you didn’t want anything to do with me.” Gabe placed his hand on the side of my neck so that his thumb rested over my pulse point. “I don’t think you’re as indifferent to me as you’d like to be.”

“You wish,” I said childishly.

“You’re right, I do.” Gabe lowered his mouth to kiss me, but I turned my head away. I would not be his fucking plaything. He grabbed my chin lightly with his hand and turned my head, so I was looking at him again. "I had sex with Nate once, and it was over a year ago. He called me and asked me to talk to him because he's getting death threats through his email."

I gasped in surprise at what Gabe confided in me. "Why would he call you?"

"He's looking to keep things quiet and avoid police involvement," Gabe replied. "I told him he needed to contact the police and that I couldn't help him."

"But why the need for all the touchy feely shit?"

"It was an act so that his patrons wouldn't suspect anything, especially if the person who wanted to kill him was watching." Gabe's eyes were so earnest when he looked into mine. I wanted to believe him, but I didn't know if I could. He must've seen the slight softening I felt because he lowered his head and captured my lips with a kiss. It felt like he poured every emotion he'd felt during the time we spent apart into that kiss; I did the same.

The desire to be one with him, to lie naked beneath him and welcome him into my body got stronger and stronger every time I was near him. Even stronger than the sex was my longing to know more about the man. My hands had been resting on my thighs, but they wanted in on the action. I slipped my hands inside his leather jacket and beneath his sweater to feel the warmth of his taught skin. I slid my hands up between his shoulder blades and raked my nails down his back.

Gabe quickly broke our kiss. "Fuck," he whispered against my lips. "Have dinner with me tonight."

The loud knock on the door I had been leaning against startled me. "Jazz, do you have my client in there with you?" Josi asked loud enough for the entire fucking salon to hear. "I have places to be tonight, so I'm going to need you to turn loose of him so I can work my magic. You'll thank me for it later, sweetie."

Jesus, I would never be able to face the people in my salon again. I stepped away from the door and turned to open it, but Gabe's hand snaked out and grabbed my wrist to stop me. "Gabe, I..."

"Have dinner with me," he repeated. "I told myself I was done with your hot and cold personality. I promised that I'd look for someone who wanted to be with me. But you know what?" I shook my head because I didn't know. "I missed you. I learned that I'd rather be insulted by you than flattered by someone else. Everything inside me screams for me not to give up on you. So, what do you say? Will you have dinner with me?"

"Okay."

I told myself that I only agreed to get him out of my prep room and out of my face, but I wasn't fooling myself. The happy smile that spread across his face made me glad that I accepted. Fuck it! We were just talking dinner.

"What time will you be ready? I can wait around here for you or meet you at the diner." He pushed up against me and lowered his voice. "You better show up if you tell me that you'll meet me at the diner. I'll come looking for you if you don't." The dark promise in his words thrilled me more than they should.

"I'll meet you there at six thirty."

Gabe studied me closely, looking for any hint that I wasn't telling the truth. He must've liked what he saw because he pressed his lips against mine before he let go of my wrist. I stepped aside, and Gabe opened the door.

"You must be Gabe," I heard Josi say.

"Yes, ma'am," I heard him say as they walked away from the door.

I looked at the clock on the wall and saw that I still had at least ten minutes before Mary Beth's hair was processed and ready to wash. I thought I'd hide out in the prep room for the remainder of the time to have a bit of quiet and find my center. My two best friends weren't on the same page as me.

They practically got stuck together in the doorframe as they both tried to walk through the door at the same time. Watching them untangle themselves and fight over who went first was enough to help take my mind off my predicament with Gabe.

"So," Meredith breathlessly said once she freed herself from Chaz. "Did you guys have a quickie in here?"

"Is that hair color in the sink or was Gabe happy to see you?" Chaz nodded toward the sink. One of the bowls from earlier tipped over, and the creamy white hair dye had splattered all over the bottom of the black porcelain sink and did resemble cum.

"I'll never tell," I replied playfully. "Why don't the two of you get back to work and stop harassing me?"

"Fine," Meredith said with an exaggerated eye roll.

"We expect details after the salon closes," Chaz said, retreating from the room backward.

"I can't," I replied. "I'm having dinner with Gabe."

Meredith and Chaz stopped in their tracks and stared at me for a few moments then looked at each other. They wore matching dopey grins on their faces when they focused back on me.

"Upstairs?" Meredith asked.

I shook my head. "Nope."

"At his place?" Chaz asked.

Again, I shook my head. "Negative." I paused for effect to watch them squirm. "I'm meeting him at the diner at six thirty."

There was no immediate reaction from them for several seconds, maybe a full minute, then they looked at each other and let out girlie squeals before they clasped hands and jumped up and down. Their reaction was hilarious, but I wasn't about to let them know it. I nudged—okay, kicked—the door closed in their faces, which only made them laugh and squeal harder.

"What have I done?" I asked out loud once my two friends had moved on.

"Given yourself a fighting chance at happiness," Mere said through the door.

I whipped the door open and found them still standing there.

"I thought you'd gone back to the salon."

"We know, that's why we waited in case you slipped up and mumbled something juicy," Chaz replied.

"There's nothing juicy to confess," I told them. "It's just dinner." The disbelieving looks on their faces would've been comical if panic hadn't started to move in.

"Just breathe, baby," Meredith said, reading me so well.

"It's just dinner," Chaz said, repeating my words.

It's just dinner. It's just dinner. It's just... Dear Lord, what have I done? I prayed that Emma wasn't working in the kitchen that night because news of it would reach my mother before the dinner rolls made it to the table. It was too late to back out, and I surprisingly didn't want to anyway.

EIGHTEEN

Gabe

"You can strip down to your undies or nothing at all," Josi told me. "You'll be covered with a sheet, so you do what makes you feel comfortable. You'll lie down with your face in the hole here," she pointed to the massage table, "and pull the sheet up to your lower back."

"Got it." I gave her a thumbs up.

"I'll just step out for a few minutes," she said before she ducked out of the room.

I removed my clothes, folded them, and laid them on the chair. I didn't have a shy bone in my body, so I didn't hesitate to remove my boxers before I positioned myself on the table and pulled the sheet over my legs and butt.

"Come on in," I said after Josi knocked on the door and asked if I was ready.

I heard Josi sorting through bottles of what I presumed were massage oils then I heard her rubbing slick hands together as she got into position beside the table. I expected it to feel weird having a stranger's hands massage me, but I quickly got past that as soon as she began rubbing my neck.

"Someone has been under a lot of stress," she said softly. "It feels like I'm trying to massage rocks instead of muscles." She dug her thumbs in a particularly troublesome spot, and it felt so good that my eyes rolled up in my head. I made an incoherent noise that made her laugh. "Just close your eyes and relax," she told me. "I'll have you sorted out in no time."

I did as she suggested. I closed my eyes and silently gloated that Josh was finally going to have dinner with me. I meant what I told him too; I would track him down if he stood me up. Josi spread out from my neck to my shoulders, and I felt the tension escape my body with every second of the hour-long massage that Sally Ann gifted me.

Josi worked her way down my spine to just above the sheet and then she moved down to my feet. I'd never had anyone massage my feet before, but knew that I could easily become addicted to it. I was almost sad when she finished my feet and began working my calf muscles with her capable hands. My eyes started to get heavy, and I fought to stay awake.

I must not have been successful at it because the next thing I knew Josh was standing beside me giving me a gentle shake. "I'm starting to get really hungry, sleepy head. Someone promised me dinner."

"Hmm," I said when his hand on my back switched from nudging to massaging. "So good."

"Yeah, Josi has mad skills," Josh said, his voice laced with humor. "I'm going to have to pour you into your car."

"I was talking about you." I was starting to wake fully, and his hands on my bare skin had a completely different effect than what Josi's had. More than just my brain was coming alive. "If you want to eat dinner, then you might want to step back and take your hands with you."

"Are you enjoying my hands on your body, Detective?" Josh dug his hands into my flesh and muscles a little deeper instead of stopping.

I rolled over on my back. "What do you think?" The way my erection tented the white sheet indicated just how much I liked it.

"What do we have here?" Josh slid a hand down my chest and beneath the sheet to fist my cock. "Mmmm, so hard." Josh pulled back the sheet to my knees and stared at my obvious desire for him. "We can't have you walking about in public like this, all cocked and ready to fire. You might scare the good citizens of Blissville."

"What do you suggest?" I asked playfully.

"We need to release the pressure built up inside you, and then you'll be presentable for public." Josh began working my cock with sure strokes while I stared up at him. His face was etched with a serious expression as he focused on giving me pleasure.

After several strokes, he released my dick and reached for the oil that Josi had used on my skin. His eyes took on a wicked gleam as he rubbed the slick oil into his hands. My body tensed with anticipation of having his slick hands back on my cock. Josh fisted my dick with one hand and cupped my balls with the other. I gripped the sides of the table hard as my body jerked with pleasure as he began stroking me again while massaging my balls at the same time.

"Josh… So good."

He laughed in evil delight, causing goose bumps to pebble up all over my skin. I kicked the sheet off my legs and spread them a little to give him better access to my balls. Josh leaned over my body and took advantage of the invitation. I felt his slick finger press against my puckered entrance. He teased me by circling his finger around a few times then pushed lightly against my hole, but didn't penetrate me. I ached to feel the friction of his finger rasping over the sensitive nerve endings. Josh looked at me for permission, and I nodded.

Josh took his time teasing me open while he continued to stroke my dick. My hips reacted to his touch automatically as my body craved more friction on my cock and a deeper penetration in my ass. The devious smile that spread across Josh's face told me he was quite aware of the tormented pleasure he was giving me.

He slid his finger all the way inside me and crooked it up to hit my prostate just right. I drew my knees up and ground my hips down on his fist pressed against my ass. It had been too long since someone touched me so intimately and it drove me insane. I wanted Josh to be naked, so I could see how much he enjoyed pleasing me.

I shifted my hand from the edge of the table and rubbed it over his erection. Josh's moans encouraged me to free his cock, but it wasn't easy to do when he wore such tight jeans. I didn't stop until I had his velvety hardness in my grasp.

"Unh," Josh groaned as I began stroking him at the same pace he worked my cock.

Josh closed his eyes and tilted his head back as pleasure rolled through his body. The only sound in the room were soft moans and the slick sound of his oiled hands working my flesh. I wanted to drop to my knees and take him to the back of my throat, but I was unable to move; a slave to the sensations he gave me, especially when he began working his finger in and out of my ass. It felt so damn good, and I greedily wanted more and more from him until there were no boundaries we didn't cross.

Josh opened his eyes, and I saw so much lust and need in their hazel depths. "I'm going to come."

"Right there with you."

I kept my eyes on him until I saw his body tense and felt the warm splash of his cum on my thigh. I lowered my eyes and watched as he emptied his balls all over my leg and hand. Then I let my body relax and stopped fighting the urge to come. My back arched off the table from the intensity of my orgasm. Josh kept massaging my prostate, causing me to come harder and longer than usual and didn't stop until the last of my seed spilled onto my stomach.

I lay there breathing heavily on the massage table and absorbed the blissful expression on Josh's face. I wanted to hold onto the moment, store it in my memory bank in case he decided to shut me out again. I inherently knew nothing was ever going to be easy with Josh. He was a complex man who held me at arm's length when all I wanted was to hold him in my arms. Something about him made me want to push away every bad memory he had and replace them with happier ones of us.

He could hurt me really bad, in fact, he already had. There was no guarantee that he wouldn't again, and I needed to prepare myself for it, but not that night. Nope, I was getting dinner with him after he blew my mind with a hand job to rival all others. He definitely would've received the gold medal if hand jobs were an Olympic sport.

"Give me a minute to clean up, and we'll go get some dinner." I sat up and swung my legs over the side of the table. I saw Josh stiffen like he was having second thoughts about having dinner with me. My hand snaked out and wrapped around his arm. I tugged him to me until he stood between my legs. "Please."

He thought about it for a while, but this time he kept his eyes locked on mine rather than close them or turn away from me. I saw the apprehension in his eyes and wished that I could say something to ease the doubts he felt. I didn't know who or what caused him to be so gun shy, I only knew I wanted to make it better; if only he would let me.

"Dinner at the diner with you." Josh leaned forward, balancing himself on my thighs. "This doesn't mean that I like you yet or that we're going steady."

"Going steady?" I couldn't help but get a kick out of his old-fashioned phrasing. "And here I hoped to woo you."

Josh rolled his eyes and tried to step back from me, but I gripped his wrists and held him there. I needed a quick taste of him. His eyes watched my mouth as I slowly approached him. His tongue darted out and licked his lips in preparation or excitement. A soft snarl of need had escaped my throat seconds before I captured his lush lips with mine.

Josh didn't bother to fight me either. Instead, he pulled his hands from my grasp, fisted my hair, and became the aggressor in our kiss. He pulled back after our long, passionate exchange and looked into my eyes as he panted against my lips. "You better get cleaned up, or else we won't be leaving here anytime soon." He reached down and tucked his semi-erect penis away then he pulled a towel off the shelf and handed it to me. "You might need two towels." His eyes roamed all over my chest.

I cleaned up and quickly dressed because I hadn't eaten in several hours *and* I was eager to spend time with him. I hoped to get to know him better, perhaps peel off a layer or two as I got closer to the parts of the man he kept hidden. I expected him to drive separately, even though I didn't like it, so I was shocked when he followed me to my Charger. I had clicked the key fob to start the car before we left the warmth of his house. He chuckled when a hard shiver worked its way through my body.

"It's not even that cold yet," Josh said, trailing behind me.

"I'm from Florida," I said by way of explanation.

"Ahhh, then it probably feels like twelve below freezing to you then." He was right, it did.

I unlocked the car as we approached then opened the door for him. Josh stood there staring at me for several seconds before he slid into the car. I got the impression that he wasn't used to kind gestures of any sort when it came to men. I wanted to change that right away.

The diner was busy when we arrived, but not packed. We sat in the car for a few seconds, both of us staring into the big windows of the diner before I turned the engine off. We both knew that what we were about to do was a big deal in the town we lived in. Although they had plenty to talk about lately, Josh and I both knew that we were about to take center stage. We turned and looked at each other, both of us assessing the other.

"I'm going to order the country fried steak dinner," I told him. "It's my favorite thing on the planet."

"Don't tell Emma I said this, but I can make it better than she can."

"Really," I said, turning a little in my seat to face him. "What's it going to take for me to find out?"

"I'll let you know," Josh arrogantly replied as he opened the car door to get out.

His answer surprised me so much that I just sat in the car and watched him for a few moments before I got out to join him at the door to the diner. I opened the door for him once again and received the same surprised look. I was half afraid he would take it the wrong way as if I opened the door for him because I thought him womanly. That was the furthest thing from my mind. My father opened doors for my mom as a sign of respect, not because he thought her weaker than him. I did the same for Josh, and I liked the way I felt when I did it.

I followed Josh into the diner and expected him to lead us to one of the booths in the very back, but he stopped at a table in the middle of the restaurant. He smiled at the confusion he saw in my face. "They're going to be staring at us no matter where we sit. This way they're not all cricking their neck while they gawp at us."

I could feel their eyes on us, and it was unnerving. I eventually ignored it and focused my attention on Josh. "What else do you cook that rivals Emma's food?"

"Everything," he said with a careless shrug. "I love to cook, especially for friends and family."

"Well, hello," a toothy waitress said when she approached our table.

"Hi, Daniella," Josh replied. "Do you ever have any time off? You're here every time I come in lately."

"I've picked up some extra shifts so I can save money to go back to community college for the spring semester," she replied. "So don't be afraid to tip generously for the amazing service you're about to receive."

"Noted," I replied.

"So, will this be one check or two?" she asked.

"One," I replied before Josh even opened his mouth. "It comes to me." I pinned her with a firm look that matched my tone then looked at Josh, who wore a frown. "You can get the check next time."

He dropped his eyes to the menu in front of him, and I was pretty certain he mumbled, "*If* there is a next time."

There would be a next time; I was sure of it.

NINETEEN

Josh

I DIDN'T KNOW WHAT TO MAKE OF GABE AND HIS MANNERS. A PART of me wanted to bristle when he opened my doors because I was more than capable of opening them for myself. I also knew that to him it was a sign of respect, of showing me that I was special to him and that spoke to the part of me that wanted to be loved and cherished. Therefore, I allowed it without fuss. *Pick your battles, Josh.*

"I'll just give you guys a minute to look over the menu. What can I get you to drink?" Daniella asked.

I looked at her like she was nuts because I wanted to drink the same thing I'd ordered there since birth, but then again she had only worked for Emma for a few years, and I had been shaking things up a bit lately. "I think I'll have a Coke," I said, surprising the both of us.

Gabe looked back and forth between Daniella and me, trying to work out why we both seemed surprised by my drink order. It was a nuance of my personality that he'd have to learn for himself. That thought startled me because I realized how much I wanted him to be curious about the inner workings of my personality. To be honest, it scared the shit out of me and made me want to run for the hills. Only Gabe's dark, penetrating gaze kept me in my seat.

"I'll have the same," Gabe told Daniella with a smile. "Do you know what you want to eat?" Gabe asked me once she left to fill our drink order. I swore I heard a snicker coming from one of the tables around us. Apparently, my need for routine and structure was well-known to the entire town.

"Hmmm, I'm not sure." I looked over the menu as if seeing it for the first time. "I think I'll have the Salisbury steak, mashed potatoes, and gravy."

"Really?" Daniella asked when she returned with the drinks. I pinned her with an unhappy look, and she cleared her throat. "Um, I meant to say okay." She pulled the order pad and a pen out of her apron pocket. "Which vegetable would you like to go with that, Josh?"

"Corn."

"Biscuits or rolls?" Daniella asked.

"Rolls."

Daniella turned to Gabe. "And you, sir?"

Gabe kept his eyes on mine the entire time he ordered his dinner. I found it to be quite unnerving, to say the least. I liked being the center of his intense focus when he was fucking me, but not while I was ordering dinner. I wasn't an odd specimen that one needed to study. Yeah, I had quirks, but who the hell didn't?

"I feel like I'm missing something here," he said after a few awkward minutes passed.

"I'm a creature of habit, and lately I've veered off the normal path, and it's creating an uproar," I explained.

"That seems like such a minor thing," Gabe replied. He looked confused as to why people would make a fuss over it.

"Let's put it this way," I said, feeling the need to explain a little more. The guy should know what he was getting into if he… Nope. I stopped myself right there. It was just dinner. "I used to eat the same thing each week and never veered from my routine. I don't like to switch things up."

"Hmmm, interesting." Gabe didn't look too upset about it. "So, what would you normally eat every Monday?"

"Fried chicken dinner."

"Tuesday?"

I narrowed my eyes in irritation. Were we going to go through each day of the week to satisfy his curiosity? "Cheeseburger and chili."

"You never once wanted to eat tuna salad on a Monday night?" Gabe asked.

"Tuna salad is a lunch food, never a dinner food. Dinner food is always hot, regardless of the time of year or temperature outside." He looked at me as if I was a rare species. I wasn't sure how I felt about it. "The only exception to my routine was Sunday."

Gabe put his elbows on the table and lowered his chin into the palms of his hands. "Sunday dinners at your house." He remembered.

"Yes, with my friends since my parents moved to Florida."

"Yeah?" Gabe perked up when he heard the mention of his home state. "Where'd they move to?"

"Boca Raton," I answered. "They sold the house to me and headed for warmer weather so my dad could play golf four times a week, and my mom could knit on her back porch all year long."

"Sounds nice," Gabe said. "Back to Sunday dinners now." He ignored my scowl and kept on talking. "So, I assume that your dinner guests include Meredith and Chaz." I nodded. "Do you ever invite anyone else to Sunday dinner?" I knew he was fishing to see if I ever included guys that I dated in the mix. Ha! Dated? How sad was it that I was twenty-eight years old and on my first real date with a guy? I'd be damned if I told him that because I'd never get his fat head back through the door. The last thing he needed was a swelled ego. I stopped and reminded myself that it was just dinner, not a date. "Sometimes Meredith or Chaz bring a date, but it's usually just the three of us. We don't do so well in the dating department."

"Hmmm, you don't say."

I didn't appreciate Gabe's snark, and I opened my mouth to blast him with enough of my own to peel his skin, but Daniella showed up with our dinners and saved him. "Thank you, Daniella," I said once my plate was in front of me.

"You're welcome, sweetie. Is there anything you fellas need?"

"I'm good," I said and then looked to Gabe. He'd already shoved a forkful of potatoes and gravy in his mouth, so he just shook his head. Damn, he must've fallen on that food like a starving man. At least he didn't pick up his country fried steak with his hands and start eating it. "When was the last time you ate?"

He held up his finger for me to wait a minute. "I think I ate a bag of chips from the vending machine at the station around two this afternoon."

"That's not very healthy." I frowned at the thought of him skipping meals, even though he was a grown-ass man who didn't need me to fuss over him. Why did I even want to fuss over him?

"I don't usually skip meals, but something came up that needed mine and Adrian's immediate attention." Gabe cut a bite of his steak and put it in his mouth. He closed his eyes and moaned like he did during sex.

I noticed a few of the ladies around us sat up and paid closer attention. How could they not? Gabe was gorgeous on every level. I mean, he didn't have a single unattractive feature. "Good?"

"Soooo good." Okay, I'd heard that come from his lips while I was stroking his cock and massaging his prostate. It was bad enough he was making sexy noises in the diner, but then he had to go and add sexy words too.

I leaned forward and lowered my voice so only he could hear me. "You think maybe you could stop working up the female patrons at the diner with your sexy moans and talk."

"Huh?" Gabe looked up at me. I saw the food lust in his eyes and knew he was lost to me for the time being. He was reduced to single grunts, moans, and the most basic language. I had seen the same reaction when we were having sex.

I couldn't help but find the moment both cute and funny. "Never mind. Enjoy your food." I returned to my meal and ignored the secret thrill that worked its way through my body each time I realized that I could reduce him down to his baser needs.

"Do you want dessert?" Gabe took the last piece of his roll and wiped it across his empty plate, looking for the last bit of gravy. "I could use some pie," he said.

I planned to clean my plate as he had, but at a slower pace. "Their banana cream pie is to die for," I told him. "I could go for a piece when I finish my dinner."

"I'll wait." Gabe wiped his mouth one more time and leaned back in his chair. I could feel his eyes on me as I cut my Salisbury steak. I had the feeling that Gabe could be very patient when he decided he wanted something—or someone. "What do you do besides running and yoga to stay so fit. Your abs are tight as hell."

I nearly choked on my food. It wasn't that Gabe asked me in a loud voice, but every nosey ear in the diner had tuned into what we said. Well, if they wanted a fucking show then I'd give them one. "I pole dance." I nearly laughed at the gobsmacked expression on Gabe's face. "It's great for your core muscles."

"Pole dance," Gabe repeated. "Where?" He was trying so hard to look engaged in the conversation when I knew his mind had gone straight to the gutter.

"I have a studio in my attic."

Gabe nearly knocked over his glass of Coke. "Studio?"

"Mmm hmm," I replied nonchalantly. "I took lessons for a while and then decided to turn my attic space into my own studio."

"Are you good at it?" The lust I saw in his eyes nearly made me giddy with pleasure because the thought of my spinning on a pole surpassed his exuberance of the food he just woofed down. Or was he imagining me spinning on his pole?

"Oh yeah," I said confidently. "I've won a few competitions even."

"They have pole dancing competitions?" Gabe looked both shocked and amazed that something like that existed.

"Yep, and they're stiff too."

"Not yet, but it's getting there," Gabe replied.

I had been referring to a tough competition, but I wasn't unaffected by his words. My body responded to the thought of making him hard. My skin suddenly felt too tight to fit my body, and my mouth began to water for something more than the food I had been consuming. I wanted to tell him to order the pie to go, but I cautioned myself to take things slow. There was no doubt in my mind that Gabe would have his fill of me at some point and move on; I had no desire to rush the end.

Daniella arrived just as I finished my last tasty bite of food. "Dessert?"

"Banana cream pie for me," I told her.

"Make that two," Gabe added. "I think I better steer this conversation back to safer topics for public dining," he said once she walked away to get our pie.

"Probably for the best," I agreed. "Did you have a break in Georgia's case today? Was that the emergency that kept you from eating?"

"I wish I could talk about it, but I can't discuss an ongoing case with you," Gabe replied. I could tell by the regret in his eyes that he spoke the truth.

"Fair enough," I replied. I could tell Gabe was relieved that I let it go so easily. Damn, I wasn't difficult to deal with *all* the time. "So, tell me about your family." I thought it was a safe topic. I'd told him a little about my folks, so I thought it fair he did the same.

"My dad is an auto mechanic, and my mother owns a bakery," he replied easily. "They've been married for forty-two years and act as in love now as they always have."

"My parents are like that too," I told him. "I learned to make a lot of noise before I entered a room to give them time to straighten up before I entered. I was happy that they were crazy about each other, but I never wanted to see it for myself." My remark made Gabe laugh and I liked it. "I'm an only child. Do you have any brothers or sisters?"

"No sisters, but I had an older brother." Had, as in past tense. Apparently, it wasn't as safe a topic as I thought.

"I'm sorry, Gabe."

"Thank you," he said softly. I saw the sadness in his eyes and wondered how long ago his brother had died and what happened to him, but I didn't ask my questions. "It was a long time ago. Dylan was a victim of a convenience store robbery gone bad. His case was never solved."

"That's why you became a cop."

"I knew what it felt like to have someone taken away so suddenly and how much it hurts when their killer is never brought to justice. I try so hard to prevent other families from feeling that way." His eyes were locked on a point somewhere over my right shoulder as if lost in thought.

I reached over and placed my hand over his where it rested on the table. I wasn't sure who was more surprised by the gesture—him or me. I simply wanted to give comfort to a man who deserved it, nothing more. I went to pull my hand back once I had his attention, but he snatched my fingers to stop my retreat.

I swallowed down the emotion that had gathered and formed a large lump in my throat. I didn't want to like the things Gabe made me feel, but I did. I didn't want to become dependent on those feelings, but I was worried that I would. I felt panic rising inside me and was about to make a fool of myself when Daniella returned to the table with our pie. I was so happy to see her that I could've jumped up and hugged her.

Gabe reluctantly released my hand, and I could tell by the smile on his face that he sensed just how close I had come to freaking out. "I'm not so scary, you know."

"Said the alligator to the little yappy dog that was standing along the side of the lake before he ate him." I pointed at Gabe with my fork, indicating that he was the alligator in the scenario. Wait! That meant I was the little yappy dog.

"Why'd you have to go and kill the little yappy dog?" He shook his head in disbelief. "Things were going so well until you freaked out because I held your hand."

"I didn't freak out," I replied defensively.

"You started to," Gabe rebutted. "Try not to freak out next time I touch you in public. I promise to keep it clean."

"Next time, huh?"

"Definitely." He laid his fork on his plate and put his full focus on me. "Here's how this will play out. I'm going to walk you to your door and then I'm going to pull you in for the hottest, most incredible kiss you've ever had. It will be so intense that you'll think about it a lot over the next few days. You'll also recall that we had a good time and you're going to want to do it all over again."

"Is that so?" I asked, unable to keep the smile from my face.

He was so damned confident.

"Yeah, it's so."

And it went down exactly as he said, including a kiss hot enough to melt the siding off my house, the daydreaming about the way it made me feel, and the longing to be with him again. *Asshole!*

TWENTY

Gabe

I WAS STILL FLYING HIGH THE NEXT WEEK AFTER MY DINNER DATE with Josh. In my mind, I had a swagger similar to John Travolta in Saturday Night Fever. I wasn't foolish enough to believe it was going to be smooth sailing with Josh. Hell, I hadn't heard a peep from him after I made sure he was safely locked inside his house after our earth-scorching kiss, but it was a start—a fucking good one. He sought me out for sexy time in his salon, for one thing, and he agreed to have dinner with me, for another. Those were both good signs that just maybe we had a fighting chance at… *something.* I really wanted to have something with him. I wasn't willing to risk good fortune up to that point by calling it the "R" word. I just needed to be patient and allow things to happen at their pace and not rush it.

Adrian looked up from his desk and spotted me. He let out a loud whistle then said, "Look at you. You've been strutting your stuff for over a week now. Plus, you sent my wife flowers to thank her for the massage gift certificate she gave you for your birthday. That must've been one hell of a massage to have you looking that happy a week later."

"Good morning, partner." I wasn't about to acknowledge his comments or leering grin.

"It sure looks like it," Adrian replied. "You ready to interview Commissioner Wallace this morning?"

We had gone to his office to talk to him the day we saw the video, but he had taken his family out of town for vacation. I found the timing odd because school wasn't out yet for the Thanksgiving holiday and, according to his secretary, the trip was a spur of the moment decision. It appeared to me that Jack Wallace took his family on a literal guilt trip to Disney World. The longer I cooled my heels, the angrier I became at the situation, but it gave us time to dig a little deeper into Jack Wallace's background.

He had a cousin with an extensive criminal record who looked quite capable of killing a defenseless woman soaking in her bathtub while she read a book. But how did he get in? Did someone make a copy of a key or did he pick the lock? Was it possible we were barking up the wrong tree altogether? Maybe Georgia's death had nothing to do with Rocky or their affair. Someone trashed her house looking for something and didn't bother to take any of her expensive jewelry or high-dollar electronics, which meant they were looking for something very specific. Was it possible that Georgia had information on someone who didn't want it leaked? If so, who had a secret worth killing over?

That brought me back to Jack Wallace. People had killed for a lot less than getting outed to their families. No matter how Jack categorized his sexuality, his affair with Rocky wasn't something he'd want to get out until he was ready—if he ever was ready. I disliked cheaters with a passion, but no matter how angry he made me, I'd never willingly out the man. If we eventually arrested him for any involvement in the crime, there'd be no way of keeping his affair with Rocky quiet.

"I'm ready to solve this case, and I have a strong feeling that Jack Wallace is a piece of the missing puzzle we need to bring Georgia's killer to justice." I was convinced of it. I had that tingling sensation that told me we were on the right path.

"Let's show up at his office and take him by surprise." Adrian rose from his chair and slipped on his jacket.

The short drive to the commissioner's office was quiet. I had expected Adrian to rib me some more, but it was obvious his mind had turned to the case, as had mine. Jack's wide-eyed secretary told us that the county commissioners were all in a meeting and couldn't be disturbed.

"That's not how this works." I pulled back my jacket and showed her the badge I wore clipped on my belt. She knew damn well who I was and her stalling tactics pissed me off. "You either go in there and quietly ask the commissioner to come out and have a private conversation with us, or we go in there ourselves and pull him out. Which do you think he'd prefer?"

Adrian chuckled when the secretary bolted from her chair to get Jack from his meeting. "So, you're the bad cop today?"

I didn't have time to respond before the secretary returned with a thunderous-looking Jack Wallace fast on her heels. "What's the meaning of this?" he demanded hotly.

"Can we talk somewhere private?" Adrian asked him politely.

"Or we can do it right here," I offered, taking my role as bad cop seriously. Wallace didn't need to know I was hesitant to out his cheating ass.

Jack Wallace stood down immediately when he heard the tone of my voice. "Come to my office." He pivoted on his heels, and we followed behind him. "Do I need to have an attorney present?" he asked once he shut the door to his office. He sat behind his desk, but Adrian and I remained standing in front of it in a move to intimidate him.

"Did you do something wrong?" I asked flippantly.

"Having an attorney isn't a sign of guilt, Detective," Wallace sneered at me.

"Of course it's not," Adrian said, using a cajoling tone of voice. "We're not reading your rights, and we're not charging you with a crime, sir. This is simply an interview."

"If it's 'simply an interview' then why the hell didn't you wait until my meeting was over or better yet, schedule a time to meet with me?"

"We get a more honest reaction when we take people by surprise," I told him. "By scheduling an appointment, we give you time to cover all your bases. Oddly, we want the truth and not some sugar-coated version of it or blatant lies."

"You offend me," Wallace said, pointing his finger in my direction.

He offended me too, but I wisely kept my mouth shut. "Let's discuss your trip to Tennessee with the mayor." I wasn't playing around, and he needed to know it.

Wallace turned an ashen color, giving himself away. "I don't know what you're talking about." His denial would have sounded weak and unconvincing to the greenest of rookies.

I placed my hands on his desk and leaned toward him, invading his personal space. "Do not play games with me, Wallace. We have video footage from a gas station showing the two of you together in Knoxville."

"So what. We went on a hunting trip that we didn't want others knowing about." Wallace shrugged. "It's not a big deal."

"If you don't mind me asking," Adrian began, "why did you deny it when Detective Wyatt mentioned it?"

"I do mind, actually," Wallace replied with a sneer. "But I'll tell you anyway. The town thinks that Rocky and I don't get along. In fact, I've run against him for mayor the past few elections. It wouldn't look good to the people who are encouraging me to run again if they knew that Rocky and I were friends."

"Really good friends, I'd say." I laughed derisively at the confused look that crossed Wallace's face. "You don't recall the kiss that you and Rocky shared at the gas pump? Did you not hear me when I said we had video footage of the two of you or did you think I wasn't serious?"

"I-I-I…"

I pinned him with a menacing glare and didn't bother waiting for him to stammer out an excuse. "I can tell you that I'm very serious when it comes to solving homicides."

"H-homicides?" Wallace asked in disbelief. "What… are you implying that *I* killed Georgia Beaumont?"

"Or hired your cousin to do it," I answered.

"You must have some seriously big balls to accuse me of something so heinous." Wallace was either a good actor or innocent, but I wasn't letting up.

"They're pretty damn big," I replied, causing Adrian to snort from beside me. "Look, let's go over some facts. You are having an affair with Rocky Beaumont who, like you, is married and not interested in outing the affair. Rocky was also having an affair with his first wife for the past six months leading up to her death. After Georgia's homicide, someone broke into her house and ransacked the upstairs looking for something but didn't steal any of her expensive jewelry. I find that odd. Do you find it odd, Detective Goode?"

"I find it very odd," he replied. "Here's where we go from hard facts to supposition," Adrian told Wallace. His good cop façade was starting to slip. "It makes me wonder if Georgia had something in her possession that could hurt someone or even multiple people and they wanted to silence her before it got out."

"Rocky was fucking Georgia?" Wallace asked. "After all this time, he went back to her bed?" He sounded angry and disgusted at the thought. "Look," he threw his hands up in the air, "I had nothing to do with Georgia's death. Nothing," he reiterated. "There was no love lost between us, and I was glad when Rocky divorced her, even if it was for Nadine, but that doesn't mean I wanted her dead. She was nothing to Rocky anymore."

"She was *everything* to Rocky," I countered. "He never got over her."

"Lies," Wallace countered.

"Or you're lying to us right now. Suppose Georgia approached you about your affair with Rocky and threatened to go public with it. Perhaps she even said she had evidence to prove it. You have connections to a cousin with a less than savory past—one who's wrapsheet includes arrests for murder. Of course, he's never been convicted because something bad always seems to happen to a witness or they recanted their statements. It seems to me that Andrew Morningside would be the right guy to hire to take care of a nuisance like Georgia."

"I didn't," Wallace denied emphatically. "I wouldn't." He swallowed hard and looked away from me for a few seconds before he returned his eyes to mine. "I was willing to tell my wife about Rocky. I was willing to live openly with him. I told Georgia that when she came to my office and threatened me."

So we were right. "How long did this meeting take place before Georgia died?" Adrian asked.

"A week, maybe two." He shook his head. "A part of me wanted her to out us so we could end all of the lies. Sure, I knew people would be hurt, but I also knew they'd get over it after enough time passed. Georgia was going to do me a favor so I wouldn't have killed her. I haven't talked to Andrew in probably ten years or more."

"Did Rocky feel the same?"

I knew what his answer was by the way his body seemed to deflate right there in his chair. "No," he admitted after a long silence.

"Did Georgia tell you what kind of proof she had of your affair?" I asked.

Wallace raised his head slowly and looked into my eyes. "Rocky and I got careless about a month before she died. My wife and kids went to her folks' house for a long weekend, and he came over. We had always gone out of town for sex, so I was surprised when Rocky called and asked if we could get together. Georgia must've followed him or something. She showed me the photos that she'd taken of us through my bedroom window."

"Does Rocky know about Georgia's visit?" Adrian asked.

Wallace shook his head vigorously. "Not from me. I worried that he'd break off our relationship if he found out. He doesn't know about the photos unless Georgia told him."

"One last question," I said, earning a nod from a defeated Wallace. "Was your trip to Tennessee with him planned or spur of the moment?"

"It was sudden. Rocky said he couldn't take all the stares and whispering after Georgia was killed and needed to get away. My wife thought I went to Columbus to have a weekend with my fraternity brothers. It's something we do several times a year, and sometimes plans are made at the last minute, so I knew she wouldn't question it."

"Thank you for your time," Adrian said, staying with his good cop routine.

"Not like I had a frigging choice," Wallace said under his breath, earning a scowl from me.

Adrian and I showed ourselves out and kept silent until we

got in my car. "He looked and sounded pretty sincere, but I've seen the same from cold, hard killers with no conscience." I looked over at Adrian and said, "Say we give him the benefit of the doubt. He didn't know Rocky was back in Georgia's bed and he was hoping to get outed, which I find hard to believe. Say he didn't hire Andrew to kill Georgia…"

"But there are two other people who might have," Adrian completed as if reading my mind.

"Rocky and Jack's wife, Felicity, would both know about his criminal for a cousin," I added.

"What's the likelihood that Georgia only showed the pictures to Jack and left it at that?" Adrian asked.

"Slim to none." I thought about it for a few seconds and then said, "I think we can rule out Nadine. She wouldn't likely have knowledge about Jack's distant cousin."

"Why do you think Georgia took her affair with Rocky to the grave? Why not rub it in Nadine's face?" Adrian asked. "Especially when Nadine started talking trash to Georgia in the salon."

The mention of the salon brought warm memories of Josh to the forefront of my mind for a few minutes before suspicion wiggled in to ruin it. *Why hadn't I thought about it sooner?* I had already drawn the conclusion that clients got chatty with their stylists, but I didn't truly connect the dots between Georgia and Josh because I was too busy trying to get close to him. *Damn it!*

"I bet Georgia told someone about her affair. It's doubtful she kept it just to herself. She would've told someone she loved and trusted. I think I know just the person."

"Who?" Adrian asked.

"One feisty salon owner," I replied.

"Oh, shit." Adrian was quiet as I drove back to the station. "Why wouldn't he tell you?"

"To protect Georgia's reputation or because I didn't ask." I shook my head in irritation. "Who knows what makes him tick, certainly not me."

"You're not going in there with guns blazing are you?" Adrian asked.

"Verbal ones, maybe," I replied.

"Partner, it sounds like you've already convicted the guy before you've had the chance to talk to him. Don't ruin something good."

I wanted to believe that Josh and I were working toward something good, but how could we if he knew something that big and didn't tell me? Adrian was right though; I was mad at him before I knew the truth. I wanted to drop Adrian off and go to the salon, but I didn't. I knew I wasn't in the right frame of mind to talk to Josh and I was also afraid I was right. If so, where did that leave us?

TWENTY-ONE

Josh

I WOKE UP FEELING GREAT AND TOLD MYSELF THAT IT WAS THE DAY I'd give up being stupid and call Gabe and invite him over. In fact, I gave serious thought to inviting him over to Sunday dinner with Mere and Chaz. That alone was enough to make me pause but even more shocking was how much I missed him in the week that passed since our date.

I missed the sound of his voice, the heat of his body, the taste of his mouth, and especially the look in his eyes that said I was special to him. I was half convinced that I saw things that weren't there because I wanted it to be true. Then I'd recall the way his eyes would gleam when he smiled over something that I said, whether I intended to be funny or not. Yes, it was time to be brave and see where things would lead with Gabe.

Bright sunlight streamed in through the windows of the salon when I went downstairs, but I wasn't fooled into believing the outdoor temperature was anything other than freezing. I could see the ice clinging to the bare tree branches and grass. I couldn't help but hear Gabe's grumbling in my head about the frigid weather. I decided I would show him all the benefits of cold weather, namely cuddling together under a blanket—preferably naked with his dick in my ass.

Someone cleared their throat behind me, and I turned to find Meredith watching me with a huge smile on her face. "Deep in thought over your guy, I see."

"He's not my..."

"Shut up, Jazz." She rolled her eyes and went to her station that was directly across from mine to get ready for her day. "Lady Chatterbox is first up this morning," Meredith told me.

I was grateful for the change of subject because I didn't know how to talk about Gabe and the way he made me feel. That was a first for us; I'd always been able to talk to Mere about anything and everything. I worried that her feelings were hurt, but the smile she sent me through the reflection in the mirror told me that things between us were good.

"Why are the chattiest ones morning people?" I asked her. "We're all going to need an extra dose of caffeine to handle her."

"You know it," Meredith replied.

I added an extra scoop and a half of ground coffee beans for a stronger brew when I made our pot of coffee. We drank our heavenly nectar from the gods and embraced the calm silence before our day began. Chaz was next to arrive, and he went straight to the coffee pot with a wave of his hand as his only greeting. He looked exhausted as if he hadn't slept in a week. Something was going on with him, but I couldn't figure it out. I respected his privacy and hoped that he'd come to Meredith or me if he needed us.

I looked over at Meredith to find her watching him closely. "He'll let us know if he needs us," I told her.

"I hope you're right," she replied.

"When aren't I?"

She placed her finger over her lips, tilted her head to the side, and pretended to think about it for a few seconds. "You want to go there?" she asked.

"Not really," I replied honestly, earning a delighted laugh from her.

Too soon we gave up our quiet and embraced the day when our first clients showed up. My mood stayed high through the morning into early afternoon but took a dive when the dark clouds moved in and eclipsed the sun. It felt like a premonition of something bad to come, but I couldn't figure out what it could be until I saw Gabe enter the salon right before we closed for the day. The expression on his face was every bit as dark and threatening as the snow storm we were sure to get that evening.

Meredith and Chaz shot me inquisitive looks but didn't comment. I also saw Meredith hesitate to leave me alone with Gabe, but I nodded to let her know that I would be okay. The last thing I worried about was Gabe hurting me physically; I wished I could be as certain about him not breaking my heart. The tight clench of his jaw warned me that doom and heartache lurched around the corner.

"Why do you look so angry with me?" I asked, breaking the ice. No sense in beating around the bush.

"Did you know that Georgia was having an affair with Rocky?" he asked.

"What?" I was surprised that his thunderous countenance was work-related and that it was aimed at me.

"Did Georgia Beaumont tell you she was sleeping with Rocky?" He enunciated each word as if I would have a hard time understanding him.

I felt my spine stiffen at the same time I got hot all over. The implication that I knew something that could help Gabe with his case and deliberately kept it to myself pissed me off. I knew that I hadn't let him get to know me very well, but his question felt like a low blow to me. "Why would I keep something like that from you?"

"You didn't answer my question." Gabe paced a few steps then stopped and faced me once again. "Did you know?"

"I knew…"

"Fucking figures." Gabe threw his hand in the air and then turned away from me. His posture was stiff and foreboding.

I was so shocked by his behavior that it took me a few long seconds to respond to his rudeness. "You didn't let me finish before you judged and executed me, asshole." I held my chin high and glared at him when he turned back to face me. "I knew—or suspected, really—that she was seeing *someone*, but I didn't know who."

"How did you know or suspect she was seeing someone? Did she tell you anything at all?" Gabe asked, his voice a little less hostile and accusatory.

"It wasn't what she said but how she acted that made me think she was finally moving on from Rocky. Well, that's what I thought at the time. I didn't say anything to you because I didn't have any facts to share." The sting of his suspicion hadn't lessened inside me, so I didn't bother to modulate my tone. "You never answered *my* question."

"I just figured you were either protecting her confidence, being stubborn, or high drama." I got madder and madder with every stupid word that left his mouth. How was it that I ever fantasized about his lips on my body?

"Stubborn or high drama?" I asked, advancing on him. Maybe later I'd get a chuckle over the contrite expression on his face or the way he backed up as if *I* was a physical threat to *him*. "That's what you think about me, Gabe? I'm just a big motherfucking drama queen?"

"Drama king," he replied in a pathetic attempt at humor as if that made it better.

"I. Am. Not. High. Drama." People assumed that about me because I was a tad flamboyant and I styled hair. I did more than style hair; I was a motherfucking business owner who probably pulled in the highest salary in my town. I refused to be talked down to by anyone, especially the man I ignorantly gave my body to. "Get out, Gabe."

"What?" His mouth dropped open, and he blinked rapidly in confusion. "You're throwing me out?" he asked in disbelief.

"I'm pretty sure I was clear." My body began to shake with rage and hurt. I fucking knew I couldn't trust him. Regardless of what he had said on prior occasions, the truth came out. He thought I was a girlie guy who was prone to drama. He also believed I was dishonest. To him, I was the Dishonest Drama Diva. "I want you to leave." I could feel tears burning the back of my eyes, and I'd be damned before I let him see just how badly his words had hurt me.

"Come on, Josh. Don't be this way." His pleas were falling on deaf ears. "What did I say or do that warrants you kicking me out? You're the one who kept crucial information from me when I interviewed you *twice* after Georgia's death. I should be the one throwing a hissy fit." His face paled when he heard the sharp intake of air I pulled into my lungs. "Okay, that was wrong of me to say. I didn't mean that or my comments earlier about…"

"Get. Out. Now." If he wanted to see a hissy fit, then I would gladly show him one.

"Josh, please…" Gabe took a few steps toward me but stopped when I shook my head no.

I'd cave if he touched me. I'd listen to his apology and accept his claim that emasculating me wasn't his intention because that was what I wanted to believe. I didn't realize just how much I wanted to believe in him—us—until any hope we had exploded into so many pieces that they couldn't be put back together again.

"This isn't over," Gabe said firmly. He could believe what he wanted. I followed him to the door so that I could lock up after him. Gabe turned and reached for me, but I evaded his hands.

"Goodbye." I kept my eyes locked on his so he could see how sure I was.

He said nothing else before he turned to leave. I refused to watch him walk away from me because I knew it was the last time. I flipped the lock and stumbled my way upstairs and into the shower before I lost it.

It had always been the place I felt safe enough to cry. It had started in high school when I released the heartache through a torrent of tears after getting bullied at school for being gay. It continued to be my safe harbor with every crushing blow to my heart from failed attempts at relationships with guys who only wanted me for sex.

I stood under the hot spray of water until the last tear fell from my eyes and then I got out and dried off. I decided it would be the last time that I let Gabe Wyatt hurt me. And while I wasn't convinced I'd die alone, I was sure that Gabe wasn't the one I would share my life with.

Thanksgiving was around the corner, and I knew I had two choices. I could stay home and be lonely, even though I'd join Meredith or Chaz's family for dinner, or I could fly down and see my folks. The salon was closed that week, and I thought that several days under a warm sun could do a world of good for me. I retrieved my laptop from my bedroom and ordered a roundtrip ticket before I could talk myself out of it.

I decided to call my mom the next day because I wasn't in the mood for the probing questions she would ask me. I made a mental note to visit home more often so she wouldn't be so damn suspicious when I did. As much as she drove me crazy, I loved her and missed her very much.

I spent the rest of the night losing myself in television shows to put Gabe out of my mind. I resolved to forget him anytime his image crept past the bitch-slapping reality show marathon I watched. He wasn't for me; I had known it before just as I knew it then. Too bad I hadn't listened to myself the first time because I would've avoided the false hope and heartache.

"Live and learn," I said out loud.

I began dreaming of Gabe and what could've been that night and the several nights that followed. Thoughts of him haunted me during my time in Florida and overshadowed what could've been a lovely trip. My dreams were so realistic, more so than the ones I had about the guy who tried to kill me in my bedroom. I heard his voice, saw his face, and felt his touch so vibrantly that I would wake up and expect to find him beside me. In many ways, shattered dreams of hope were far worse than scary dreams.

I knew my mother sensed I was going through something, but she surprisingly didn't pester me until I came clean. Maybe she realized that this heartache was so much stronger than any I'd felt before and I needed more time. Whatever her reason, I was grateful for the reprieve.

I was thrilled to see how happy and active my folks were in their retirement community. It seemed like they had plans every single night with their friends and I didn't want my unplanned visit to ruin them. The downside was that I had a lot of time on my hands to think. I replayed and relived every single second of my argument with Gabe until I thought I would lose my mind.

Yes, he said hurtful things to me, but I knew in my heart that he was not a cruel person. After enough time had passed, my wounded heart allowed me to acknowledge the regret I had seen in his eyes when he realized how deep his words cut me. I began to think that maybe I overreacted and should've given him the opportunity to apologize instead of throwing him out.

I wanted to call him or text him, but the fear that I had pushed him too far paralyzed me. How much forgiveness could one guy have? I was afraid to find out so I thought it would be best for me to leave things alone and move forward without him. That was easy to do when I was over a thousand miles away from him. I knew I would struggle with moving on from him a lot more when I returned home.

I just kept praying to whoever was listening to help me avoid running into him until I felt stronger in my conviction that we were better apart than together. It seemed like they were honoring my request until I dropped by The Brew to get a peppermint flavored hot chocolate the Sunday after I returned home from Florida. I had placed my drink order and even added a few sugar cookies that were decorated to look like snowmen when I felt his presence. I fucking hated that he still had that effect on me, even though I gave my heart and body strict instructions to ignore him.

Don't look. Don't look. Of course, I looked and hated myself for it afterward. Gabe was sitting at a table drinking coffee and eating pastries with Kyle. He looked so cozy and happy to be with him that I honestly felt ill. It reminded me that I was probably nothing more than a distraction for him while he and Kyle worked through their problems. It looked like they were once again a happy couple from the way they sat smiling at one another.

The barista called my name to give me my order just then, and Gabe looked away from Kyle in search of me. I turned my head before his eyes could connect with mine because I couldn't face him yet. It was too soon; I was too raw. I ended up leaving the shop without my hot chocolate and cookies, but I didn't care. I needed to get as far away from him as fast as I could.

I would've run home if it didn't look so cowardly. I settled for a brisk power walk and was proud of the distance I had made when I heard Gabe call my name. *Don't stop. Don't stop.* Of course, I stopped and turned to look at him. His long legs ate up the distance between us, and he stood in front of me in a blink of an eye.

"You forgot your hot chocolate and cookies." I looked away from his dark, mesmerizing eyes and saw that he held my hot chocolate in one hand and bag of cookies in the other. "Um, you also forgot your car." He tipped his head backward and sure enough, there was my Mini where I had parked her. In my haste to get away from him, I had forgotten that I'd driven to The Brew instead of walked.

"Fuck!" My humiliation had hit an all new low.

"Josh, can we please talk?" Gabe asked. Damn those puppy dog eyes of his.

"Gabe, I don't think we have much to talk about," I told him, trying so hard to hold on to my anger and disappointment that he had turned out just the way I thought he would. I was a fool to think that he missed me like I did him and was glad I hadn't embarrassed myself by reaching out to him while I was away.

"Okay, how about I talk, and you listen," he suggested. "I'll try hard not to insult you with every word that comes out of my mouth."

"Every other word," I said, giving him a little bit of slack. I took my hot chocolate and bag of goodies from him and walked to my car. I opened the passenger door and put my drink in the holder and laid the cookies on the seat before I shut the door and turned back to face him.

I expected Gabe to say something, but instead, he cupped his hands around the back of my neck and pulled me to him for a kiss. I wanted to be disgusted by the taste of him on my tongue, but I wasn't. I should've pushed him away, but instead, I melted against him. My brain screamed *danger*, but my heart was so happy that we were in his arms again. Damn, I had missed his mouth. Gabe pulled back after too short of a kiss. "I've really missed you, Josh. I'm sorry for the hurtful things I said to you. I truly am."

"You didn't look like it," I said, trying to grasp onto any reason to not let him back in my life. His words, his kiss, and the heat from his body were making me weak. "You looked kind of cozy with Doctor Dimples." Gabe's lips quirked up into a crooked smile over Kyle's nickname.

"We just showed up this morning at the same time, both of us commiserating over the fact that the guys we want don't want us in return." He grabbed hold of the thin beard covering my chin and tugged. "I think listening to his woes was the first time I smiled since you threw me out of your salon. He's an even bigger idiot than I am."

"I think I should be the judge of that," I replied. A wild thought occurred to me, and I tried to stomp it down, but instead, I heard myself ask, "What are you doing for dinner tonight?"

"Are you inviting me to Sunday dinner?" He looked so hopeful that I couldn't resist him.

"I guess I am." I also knew that I'd be fixing country fried steak and all the fixings instead of the pork roast I originally planned.

"What time and what can I bring?"

"Six o'clock and just bring yourself." His smile nearly blinded me, and I hated to say anything that would cause it to dim, but I had to make it very clear how I felt. "Gabe, I've worked very hard to get where I am in life now. I seldom let people close enough to hurt me, but I made an exception for you. I don't ever give second chances, so please don't make me regret this."

"I won't." He looked very confident.

"Don't be late for dinner," I warned him.

"I won't."

I raised up and kissed his lips softly, surprising the hell out of both of us. I didn't know what it was about him that made me want to throw caution out the window. It didn't work out so well the first time, and I had no guarantee it would work better a second time. I just knew I'd regret it for the rest of my life if I didn't at least try.

TWENTY-TWO

Gabe

I HAD ALL AFTERNOON TO GET WORKED UP OVER HAVING SUNDAY dinner at Josh's house with his friends, who were more like family to him. I knew it was a big fucking deal to get the invite and I didn't want to do anything to blow it. He was giving me another chance, and that was an even bigger fucking deal. I was terrified of screwing it up. No one had ever made me as nervous as Josh Roman—not even dangerous felons. I didn't even know what that meant, but I knew I had to find out. I was a moth to his bright, burning flame.

Buddy's head was cocked to the side as he studied me from his end of the couch. He must've sensed my inner turmoil because he lay down and placed his head on my thigh to give me comfort. I dropped my hand to scratch his ears and felt calm descend over my frazzled nerves. It was easy to see why they brought pets into hospitals to visit with patients.

I watched football with Buddy for most of the afternoon and then I took a long hot shower to ease any remaining nerves I had left. I knew I couldn't go to his house acting like a damn fool. Josh told me I didn't have to bring anything, but my mom taught me it was bad manners to show up empty handed. Even if my mom didn't contribute with food, she'd bring the host flowers or wine. Would Josh think I was insulting him if I brought flowers?

There were no wine sales on Sunday in Ohio, but I had a bottle of Prosecco that I'd received as a birthday gift. I was mostly a beer guy, so I was saving the Prosecco for a special occasion. I honestly couldn't think of anything more special than being invited to Josh's house for Sunday dinner. My mom had always put sliced strawberries in the bottom of the champagne flutes to make it look extra special.

I made a quick stop at the store to grab some strawberries, and a Christmassy floral bouquet snagged my attention. The arrangement had white roses and red carnations, with glittery gold-painted pine cones mixed in with the greens. I picked it up after hesitating for a minute. In a way, this felt like a test for both of us. I needed to be able to act on my impulses and instincts without constantly worrying that I was going to piss him off. He needed to accept my offerings for what they were—a gift for someone who was special to me.

I arrived at his house the same time as Meredith. She grinned like the Cheshire Cat when she saw what I brought with me. "He invited you to dinner?" she asked.

"Yep." My nerves about being there also extended to spending time with his friends. I wanted them to approve of me, but I knew I hadn't given them much to like up to that point.

To my surprise, Meredith clapped gleefully, bouncing up and down. "It's about damn time you morons start figuring things out. I'm so tired of him moping about."

"He's been moping?" It was nice to know that I wasn't the only one. I felt hope bloom in my chest.

My question was met with an exaggerated eye roll. "I can't even begin to describe it. Hell, he ran off to Florida for Thanksgiving to lick his wounds and I hoped he'd be better when he got back, but he wasn't."

So that was where he went. I had stopped by a few times to apologize in person for being an ass; for overreacting to the situation with Georgia and saying stupid things out of frustration. "He wasn't the only one," I assured Meredith.

"Even better," she said, earning a confused look from me. "If you were both miserable then it means the attraction isn't one-sided." She stopped me just before she opened the back door to Josh's house. "There will be no place on this planet that you can hide from me if you hurt him. Your badge won't save you either. Understand?"

"Yes, ma'am." Everyone needed a friend like Meredith in their corner.

The sound of soft music playing eased my nerves a bit, and the mouth-watering smells coming from his kitchen made my stomach growl, reminding me that I hadn't had anything to eat since the pastry from The Brew. Josh was in the kitchen with his back to us when we went upstairs.

"Hey, handsome," Meredith called out.

Josh spun around with a huge smile on his face until he saw me standing there beside Meredith. His smile faltered and my heart fell to my knees. His gaze shifted away from my eyes to what I held in my hands. "You didn't have to bring anything," Josh said when his eyes met mine again. I was happy to see his smile return, even happier that it was a more intimate smile, if not as grand as the one he bestowed upon Meredith.

"My mom always said it was bad manners not to bring something for your host," I told him.

The three of us stood there awkwardly until Meredith said, "I'm going to set the table like I always do. You can oversee the drinks since you brought us booze, Gabe."

"Okay," I said, following her into the kitchen. "I'm going to need some champagne flutes and a knife."

Meredith pulled down what she needed and what I had requested before she left me alone with Josh in the kitchen. "These are for you." I held out the flowers to him.

Josh took them from me and dropped his nose to smell the roses. "They're very beautiful," he said, looking back into my eyes. "Thank you." Then he surprised me by wrapping his free hand around my neck and pulling me down for a soft kiss like he'd given me outside The Brew that morning. The delighted squeal that Meredith let out reminded me that we weren't alone. If I were lucky, Josh would let me stick around for a little bit after his friends left. I owed him a sincere, heartfelt apology.

"Whoa," said a surprised Chaz when he arrived. "I don't believe what I'm seeing."

"Hi, Chaz."

"Hi." He smiled like a goon as he looked between Josh and me. "You've never invited a guy to Sunday dinner," Chaz told Josh. I was sure that Josh didn't appreciate his friend broadcasting that little tidbit, but I sure as hell did.

"You," Josh said, pointing to Chaz, "enough with the oversharing. You," he said turning to me, "wipe that smirk off your face and pour us some drinks."

I didn't wipe the smirk off my face, but I settled in at the counter next to Josh who returned to the stove to check on the potatoes. I washed the berries then focused on cutting them and not my finger, I wasn't a clumsy person in general, but Josh always had me so tied up in knots that I never knew what to expect out of myself. I placed the berries in the bottom of four flutes and then poured Prosecco in each one.

I leaned toward Josh and whispered, "Thank you for inviting me to dinner." I gave him a quick peck at his temple then carried the drinks to the dining area. I saw the arrangement I gave Josh sitting in a place of honor in the center of the table and was glad that I'd listened to my instincts.

I sat in the living room area and chatted about mundane things like adjusting to Ohio winters after living in Florida all my life with Chaz and Meredith while Josh mashed potatoes. I mentioned helping Josh, but Meredith's arm snaked out and grabbed me before I could get up to go back into the kitchen.

"He doesn't like sharing his kitchen space, and he has this down to a fine art. We're better off to let the master do what he does best and not get in the way," she told me. Her expression held a sincere warning, and I heeded it well. She and Chaz knew the man best, and I trusted their guidance.

"Don't try to fix something that isn't broken," Chaz advised sagely.

"Time to eat," Josh called out.

I followed behind Meredith and Chaz, unsure of where I should sit at the table. Josh set the platters and bowls of delicious looking food on the table while Meredith and Chaz took a seat on either side of the oval dining room table. Josh gestured for me to have a seat at the foot of the table opposite of him. I thought it was charming when Meredith said grace over the food once we had all settled in our chairs.

Chaz reached for the platter with the country fried steaks on them and served himself one before he passed the platter to me. I forked a piece of heaven and put it on my plate then passed the platter to Meredith, who served herself before handing the platter to Josh. To my way of thinking, Josh should have served himself first since he did all the work, but I knew from experience that it didn't work like that. The same pattern continued with the mashed potatoes, gravy, lima beans, and dinner rolls. There wasn't an inch of the plate showing by the time the food had been passed around.

"Dig in," Josh said.

He didn't have to tell me twice. I chose to take my time and savor the meal rather than hoover it down like I wanted to. "This *is* better than Emma's," I said after my first bite of perfectly breaded fried steak. The sweet smile Josh gave me had my heart speeding up; I found myself wanting to put that smile on his face more often.

"Tell me about yourself, Gabe?" Chaz asked me in between bites. I felt like I was interviewing for a job.

"What would you like to know?" I asked.

"Let's start with your hobbies," Chaz said after thinking about it for a few seconds.

"I play softball on the police department's team in the spring and summer, I lift weights a lot, and I'm trying to teach my dog some new tricks."

"What position do you play?" Meredith asked.

"I'm pretty versatile," I told Meredith, whose brief smile told me her mind had headed straight to the gutter. "I mostly pitch though."

Chaz snorted and muttered, "I bet." Josh smacked him upside the back of the head, which caused him to laugh hard. Meredith gave in to the urge to laugh too.

"You two fools sound like cackling hyenas. Gabe was talking about his softball team so get your minds out of the gutter," Josh said firmly, but his twitching lips told me that he wanted to laugh along with them.

"Oh, you were asking about *softball* positions?" I asked Meredith. "I play center field." My response only made Chaz and Meredith laugh harder. Josh narrowed his eyes in mock irritation at me while I just kept eating. It truly was the best country fried steak I'd ever had.

"I almost squirted Prosecco out my nose," Meredith said once she stopped giggling. "Oh, that was some funny shit."

"I'm almost afraid to ask anything else," Chaz said to Meredith. "He might tell us whether he's cut, uncut, or his number of inches right here at the dinner table."

"Cut and more than you could handle, dumbass," Josh told Chaz. "Shut up and eat your food."

I nearly choked on the bite of lima beans I had just scooped into my mouth. A person shouldn't gasp while trying to swallow food at the same time. It had a disastrous effect. My eyes watered and tears ran down my face as I tried to right myself.

Josh went to the kitchen and returned with a glass of water. "Here drink this." The cold water soothed my irritated throat. "I'm sorry I made you choke," he said, stroking the back of my head. "We have terribly inappropriate conversations during dinner, and you're probably not used to it. I should've warned you instead of branding you by fire."

"It's worse than a locker room," I told him. My voice sounded raspy, so I drank some more water until there was nothing left.

"Do you want another glass?" Josh asked me. I saw worry in his eyes, and I smiled to assure him that I was fine.

"I'm good." I turned my attention back to the other people at the table. "What he said," I replied in response to Chaz's remark about my dick. Meredith bit her lip to keep from laughing, and Chaz didn't even bother trying to hold back.

Josh nudged my shoulder with his elbow and said, "Don't encourage them," before he returned to his chair.

"What made you want to be a cop?" Meredith asked.

Josh's eyes nearly bugged out of his head with worry that the question would upset me. "It's okay," I told him before I turned to Meredith. "My older brother was killed during a convenience store robbery when he was seventeen, and I was fifteen. His killer was never arrested, and it was a horrible feeling. I never wanted another family to feel that way, so I became a cop."

"I am so sorry," Meredith said, covering her heart with her hand.

"That's rough," Chaz said somberly.

"It was rough and to be honest that kind of hurt never goes away, but you learn to handle it better after time. Holidays and birthdays are the absolute hardest, but Dylan would kick my ass if I didn't try to make the best of every moment. I was so lucky to have him as a big brother for fifteen years, so I try to focus on that more than his loss."

Josh looked at me with wet eyes and a soft smile. "He'd be proud of you." His words meant more to me than I could say. Dylan was so much more to me than a brother; he was my champion and hero. I hoped I had the opportunity to tell Josh all about him someday.

We ate the rest of our meal in silence, and I worried that my response about my brother ruined dinner. Meredith pushed back from the table and made a big production of stretching and yawning. She gave me a warm smile then placed her hand on Josh's.

"Dinner was scrumptious, Jazz. Thank you so much." She stretched and yawned again before she said, "I'm worn out though so I'm going to head on home." She looked pointedly at Chaz across the table. "You're tired too and need to go home to rest."

"But we haven't had dessert yet."

"Get it to go," Meredith said in a no-nonsense voice.

Chaz looked at Josh and then me in confusion, and then I saw realization dawn on his face. "You know what," he said, rising from his chair, "I'm stuffed. I couldn't eat another bite."

"You guys don't have to rush off," Josh said.

"I'm very tired," Meredith said, slipping on her coat. "I hope I can stay awake long enough to get home." The twinkle in her eyes contradicted her statement.

"So stuffed," Chaz said, rubbing his stomach. "I need to get home and put on some sweats to give my gut some room before I explode."

"See you Tuesday." Meredith dropped a kiss on Josh's cheek.

"Tuesday," Chaz repeated and kissed Josh's other cheek.

I blinked, and the duo was downstairs and out the back door. "Let me help you clean this mess up and then I'd like to talk."

"Talk?" Josh asked.

"Yes, talk," I replied. "I have some groveling and apologizing to do. You won't want to miss it."

Josh removed his cloth napkin from his lap and tossed it on the table. "In that case, cleanup can wait."

TWENTY-THREE

Josh

I SCOOTED BACK MY CHAIR AND ROSE TO MY FEET. "WHY DON'T WE go into the living room so we can be more comfortable when you beg and grovel."

Gabe smirked as he stood up. "I didn't say anything about begging," he replied. "I believe I said apologize and grovel."

"Same difference." I waved it off dismissingly. "Would you like to have dessert first? I baked banana pudding with meringue on top." I remembered the way his eyes glazed over the first time I mentioned making the pudding when at the pet store.

Gabe's eyes widened with food lust that almost rivaled the look he gave me when I got naked for him. "Let me get the apologizing over with first."

"Don't forget the groveling," I reminded him. "It's my favorite part." I led us into the living room and sat on my sofa. Gabe sat beside me, and I morphed my expression into one of vast confusion. "Oh, you're not doing this from your knees?" I released a playful sigh.

"Apologizing and groveling will not be the activity I do from my knees." Gabe chuckled, which meant he could tell by the expression on my face where my mind had immediately gone. I was about ready to forget the apologizing and groveling portions of the evening for more satisfying parts. "Seriously," he said, steering me back to the present. "I can't believe I'm about to say this, but I think we need to talk out what happened between us. That's what mature adults do, right?"

"I think so," I replied. "Not sure who the hell you're calling an adult though." I attempted humor to relieve the tension building up inside me. Truthfully, I'd never had a mature relationship, so I had no clue what it entailed, but I suspected that Gabe was right and we both needed to talk about what happened the night we argued in my salon. Gabe's throaty laugh at my response sent thrills throughout my body and threatened to derail his good intentions. I told myself to calm the fuck down because there would be time for sexy stuff afterward.

"I make no excuses for the stupid things I said or the references to being high drama," Gabe began. "I do not ever think of you as feminine nor do I think you're a queen of any sort. I want that to be very clear between us." He reached over and clasped my hands in his much bigger ones. "I need to think about what I say before I speak because it's obviously a sore button with you. I also need you to stop punishing me for someone else's mistakes. I know that people have hurt you in the past, but I'm not them." His words surprised me, and I sat up straighter. "I messed up that first night we met months ago. I've apologized for it. I've told you that I don't think that way about you. I need for you to believe it though, it's the only way we're going to have a chance at... *something*."

I knew that he was right about me lumping him in with the others and he had a valid point about me punishing him for past hurts. I nodded my head in agreement while my brain tried to form the words I wanted to say. "Some hurts run bone deep, and they can skew the way you see, hear, and interpret things. I will try harder not to jump all over everything you say and twist them into something you didn't mean. I also need you to trust me, Gabe. Trust that if I knew something that would help you solve a case, especially one involving my friend, I would tell you. Trust is very important if we're going to have a chance at... *something*." He smiled when I used his same phrasing. "I'm not always an easy person to get along with, but I hope you think I'm worth the hassle because I... like you."

"You are worth it, Josh." Gabe tugged my hands until I was almost on his lap. "I... like you too." The deep timbre of his voice made me want to rub against him like a kitten. When he pressed his lips to mine, I melted against him and kissed him with every ounce of longing I had while we were separated.

For the first time since I'd met him, I wasn't in a rush to get naked beneath him. I was willing to savor every second that we had. I didn't try to rustle up resentment to push him away; I held him close. I didn't warp my mind with all the things that could go wrong; I focused on everything that was right.

Gabe pulled back from our kiss and smiled down at me. "You know what we need to do now don't you?"

My hard cock knew exactly what we needed to do next. I rose to my feet and held out my hand to him. I started to head to my bedroom, but Gabe tugged me back. I turned and looked at him in confusion. He pointed to the mess on the dining room table that was waiting. I cocked a brow at him. "You'd choose to clean the dishes over getting naked with me? I think it's been way too long since you've been inside me, but if you'd rather scrape pans…"

Gabe yanked me into his arms and kissed me savagely to show me exactly what he'd prefer to be doing right then. "I'd choose to get you naked over breathing." He began walking me backward to my room. "I'll help you with the dishes after I show you just how much I *like* you."

It was amazing to me how much things improved after we exchanged a few sentences. It wasn't like Gabe, and I sat on my couch and divulged every feeling we'd ever had. We told each other exactly how we felt about the argument we had and talked about how we could avoid it in the future. I felt like there was solid ground beneath our feet for the first time.

The confidence I felt spilled over into the bedroom. I felt bolder as I undressed Gabe and touched his body. I wanted to take the time to learn all the nuances of him and what drove him wild. I needed to hear him moan my name and dig his fingers into my skin because he couldn't get enough of me. Gabe seemed willing and patient enough to let me have my way.

I pushed on his broad chest until he lay flat on his back in the center of my bed. I placed my lips just beneath his jaw on his neck and began my journey of exploration. I loved the way his muscles jerked beneath his skin when I reached an exceptionally sensitive spot, like his ribs beneath his armpits or the crease between his thigh and pelvis. I adored how his nipples pebbled beneath my tongue and the way his cock flexed when I licked a path from root to tip.

The sexy way he growled when I sucked his cock to the back of my throat had me leaking. Gabe white-knuckled my comforter as he fought hard not to fuck my mouth. I loved the dominant side of him that liked to take control and fuck me hard, but I also liked that he was willing to temper that to give me what I needed.

When I felt he'd had enough torture, I slowly released his cock from my mouth and reached for the condoms and lubricant. Gabe sat up and grabbed me before I had a chance to do anything else. He pulled me until I straddled him with my knees on either side of his face. Seemingly out of patience, Gabe lifted his head and swirled his tongue around the tip of my cock before he sucked it into his mouth. His big hands grabbed my ass cheeks and urged me to fuck his mouth.

Once I found my rhythm, he released my ass, and I missed the feel of his hands on my body. They weren't gone long before they returned slicked with lube. I'm not sure what incoherent ramblings left my mouth when his finger first slipped inside my tight entrance to tease my prostate as he blew me.

"Jesus, Gabe," were the only two words I recognized. Then he breached my hole with two fingers, and it felt so damn good I nearly forgot how to breathe. "Gabe," I said pleadingly.

Gabe slid his fingers from my ass, and I could hear him ripping the condom wrapper open before he rolled it on his cock. Once he was ready, he pulled his mouth off my dick and scooted me down until I hovered above his erection. He slid a hand between my legs and held his cock steady while I lowered myself down on him.

I loved the slight bite and burn as my ass stretched to accept his penetration. Gabe's lashes lowered over irises so dark with need that they appeared black. His brilliant eyes opened once more when I began to move, and he watched every roll of my hips as I rode his cock. Then I moved my hands behind me to rest on his strong thighs and parted my knees wide so he could watch his cock disappearing inside of me.

"So hot." He shifted his eyes back up to my face as he reached down and fisted my dick. "Eyes on me," he said when mine started to close.

I felt my resolve to take things slower fade as my orgasm built inside me. Gabe grabbed my hips and rolled me to my back. He slipped his arms beneath my legs and placed them up over his shoulders before he held my ass in a death grip.

"It's been too long since I've had you, Josh. I can't do slow right now." He almost sounded apologetic, and I might've laughed if I wasn't feeling just as desperate.

"Fuck!" I shouted as he started to pound in and out of me. "Gabe." I gripped his biceps and held on for dear life as he fucked me hard enough to slam the headboard against the wall, repeatedly. The way he tagged my prostate felt so good, I could've cried.

"Stroke your cock," he demanded, which told me he was close and didn't want to come before me.

I felt his eyes on my hand as I worked my dick up and down. It didn't take long before an orgasm exploded inside of me so strong that every molecule of my being was affected. Gabe released my legs and collapsed on top of me once the last drop of cum fell from my cock. He gathered me close and captured my mouth in a fierce kiss as he rode my ass hard. When he came, I held him tight against me, capturing his gasps and groans in my mouth.

I felt alive for the first time since he walked out of my salon. I wasn't foolish enough to think it was the last argument we would have, but I felt we would be smarter when it happened again. I didn't want to think about future fights or anything else besides holding onto the happiness I felt at being pinned to the bed by a guy who probably weighed close to a hundred pounds more than me.

"Am I squishing you?" Gabe asked.

"Huh-uh," I replied.

Gabe lifted and braced his weight on his forearms. He looked at me skeptically through eyes that showed how content he felt. He lifted a hand and brushed my hair off my forehead tenderly.

"Come back down here," I said tugging on his arms.

"How about we take a shower to get cleaned up and then I'll help you clean the kitchen before I go home." I didn't like the sound of him going home, but I understood it. As much as I wanted him to stay, I also needed time to absorb the new changes in my life.

"Sounds perfect."

I lingered in the shower a lot longer with Gabe than I would've if I had been alone. I had a lot of fun touching his soapy, wet body and he seemed to enjoy doing the same to me. The only thing wetter and hotter than the temperature of the water were the kisses we shared. It didn't take long for our bodies to recover from our recent orgasms and our erections looked like dueling swords not long after we slipped beneath the spray.

Gabe coated his hand with shower gel then fisted our cocks together and began stroking them. Gasps for air and moans of pleasure echoed throughout the enclosed shower as he jerked us to orgasm again. I collapsed against the cold tiled wall when he finished, certain that my legs had turned into jelly.

"You ruined me," I told him.

"For other men? I sure hope so," he said arrogantly.

"I was thinking about the run I had planned in the morning, but you might also be right."

Gabe tugged me into his arms then slapped my ass playfully. "I adore that mouth of yours. So full of sass."

It was a good thing he liked it because that part of me was never going away. There were several things I knew I could work on to make things go smoother between us, but I refused to alter my personality, just as I wouldn't ask that of him.

True to his word, Gabe helped me carry the dishes from the table to the kitchen with the intent to help me clean up the dinner mess. His cell phone rang in his pocket midway through the cleanup. He looked at the caller ID and said, "It's Adrian." He grinned as he tapped the button to answer the phone. "Hey, partner. What's up?" The smile slid off Gabe's face. "I'm sorry, man. I was in the shower. What's wrong?" Gabe listened intently to whatever Adrian said. "Did he make it?" He heard my sharp intake of breath and reached out a hand to calm me. "I'll be there in ten minutes or less, Adrian."

"What happened?" I asked as soon as he ended the call.

"Rocky Beaumont was involved in a serious car accident just outside of town," Gabe told me. I couldn't tell by his facial expression or his tone if Rocky survived. "It doesn't look good," he said somberly. "Let me help you finish…"

"No," I said, cutting him off. "You go do what you need to, and I'll finish the cleanup." I pulled him down for a quick kiss. "Will Buddy be okay tonight? Do you need me to do something for him?" Gabe's eyes had been all business seconds before but softened with my gesture.

"He has plenty of food, water, and the full run of the house, so he'll be okay while I'm gone." He lowered his forehead to mine. "Thank you for understanding and for offering to look after Buddy. I am sorry to run out on you."

"It's fine. Just be careful, okay?" I breathed him in one last time and stepped away so that I wouldn't hold him up any longer. "I do like you after all."

"I really like you too."

I wasn't sure how long I stood in that same spot after Gabe kissed me soundly before he left. Diva winding herself through my legs finally pulled me back down to earth. "You want to help me clean the kitchen, Diva?" She walked away from me with her tail swishing from side to side. "I take that as a big no. Do you have some big cat emergency you need to attend to also? Hmmm?" She didn't dignify my question with a response, although she probably wished she could flip me her middle claw.

After I had cleaned the kitchen, I got ready for bed. I said a silent prayer that Gabe and the other officers stayed safe on the blustery night. I replayed the way Gabe told me that he really liked me and remembering the timbre of his voice made my toes curl. I couldn't fall asleep no matter how many times I told myself that Gabe was a seasoned veteran and knew his job well. I tossed and turned for what seemed like half the night until I heard my phone vibrate on my nightstand with an incoming text message.

Just got home. Wanted you to know I was okay. Gabe hadn't promised to text when he got home nor did I ask, but I appreciated his thoughtfulness.

I'm glad you're home safe. Thank you for telling me.

I put my phone down and nestled back down under the covers. I felt my eyelids getting heavy as sleepiness crept in. I thought it was amazing how one simple text could have such an impact on me. Then I realized that nothing about my *something* with Gabe was simple, but I honestly wouldn't have it any other way.

TWENTY-FOUR

Gabe

I MIGHT'VE BEEN BLURRY-EYED FROM A SHORT NIGHT OF SLEEP when I returned to the station the following morning, but I was the happiest I'd been in a very long time. It seemed like Josh and I was finally on the same page, and things were moving forward—where life was taking us, I didn't know. We finally admitted that we liked each other and that there was *something* between us. Texting him to let him know I got home safe just felt like the right thing to do. Receiving his immediate response, as if he had been waiting to hear from me, warmed me and made it possible to get a few hours of much-needed sleep.

The only dark scourge in my life was Georgia Beaumont's unsolved homicide and the attempt on her ex-husband. The tow truck operator discovered that Rocky's brake lines were cut when he pulled the wrecked car from where it slid off the road and wrapped around a tree at the bottom of a steep hill. Rocky was still clinging to life when I showed up back at the station, but it wasn't looking good for him.

I would've loved to pin both things on Jack Wallace, but we could find no hard evidence tying him to either crime. He voluntarily allowed us to look at his phone records instead of making us get a court order. He seemed sincere when he said he didn't care if his relationship with Rocky was outed. The question was, did Jack feel the same way once he discovered that Rocky had been sleeping with Georgia?

Adrian and I hadn't ruled out the use of a burner phone when Wallace's records didn't turn up anything suspicious. We had spent days going through the call logs hoping to find a call or text to Andrew Morningside, but we found nothing.

"The only people who might want Rocky dead and have known ties to a dangerous felon are the Wallaces." Adrian handed me a cup of coffee, which I accepted gratefully. "I'd bet your next paycheck that one of them hired the hit on Georgia and then Rocky."

"My next paycheck?" I asked.

"I have a baby coming, partner. I can't afford to bet my paycheck. Sally Ann has huge plans for a nursery, and I'll be damned if I let her down." Adrian propped up his feet on the desk. "We haven't interviewed the wife. I think it's time we did that."

"I have to wonder if Jack Wallace was Georgia's first attempt at blackmail or if she had practice." There had been absolutely nothing in the contents of her safe deposit box that her lawyer turned over to indicate that Georgia had been up to no good. Her entire estate was to be sold with the proceeds going to various charities for children. There seemed to be no one else who might want to hurt Georgia outside of Rocky, Nadine, and the Wallaces. *Unless*, Georgia had been trying to blackmail someone else. "Georgia had to have a cache of evidence somewhere in that house. Either the vandal found it, or it's still there."

"There are probably only a few living people who might know the secret hiding spots in that old house." Adrian rubbed his chin while he thought it over. "Mrs. Honeycutt is definitely one of them, but she certainly would've told us something if she knew it."

"Not if she was trying to protect Georgia's reputation," I replied to Adrian. "We might have to get a little tougher with Mrs. Honeycutt." I knew I'd have to be the one to do it. "The other person would be Nadine, who was Georgia's personal assistant for a few years, but she's got her hands full right now."

"Still, she should want to help find the person responsible for nearly killing her husband," Adrian replied. "But let's start with Mrs. Honeycutt." He cocked his head to the side and asked, "Did you bring your bad cop with you today?"

"Always."

Adrian called Mrs. Honeycutt and asked her to meet us back at the house. The only other person who had a key was Georgia's attorney, but he wasn't quick to do anything. As predicted, Mrs. Honeycutt readily agreed to assist us.

Once inside the house, I turned to face her. "Mrs. Honeycutt, you've been very helpful to us so far, but I can't help but feel you're holding something back." Mrs. Honeycutt began clutching her pearls nervously, so I pressed on, but not as hard as I went on Jack Wallace. I didn't believe she would require that level of intensity, to tell the truth. "Now, it's come to our attention that Georgia might've had possession of some documents that were damaging to certain people's reputations and they could be the reason for her death."

Mrs. Honeycutt shook her head hard enough to loosen her

bun. “No. Rocky killed her. I just know it.” She wanted it to be so, but that didn’t mean it was. “That’s probably why he wrecked his car while driving drunk.” There had been no alcohol in his system so either she was speculating, or that was the early morning gossip. We weren’t sharing with anyone that Rocky’s accident wasn’t really an accident at all.

“We’ve been told that some of the documents that Georgia had incriminated Rocky in illegal activity,” Adrian said, lying through his pretty white teeth. “They might be the motive that he had to have her killed.” Lying to an elderly lady wasn’t fun, but it was necessary to get to the truth. “Please help us, Mrs. Honeycutt.”

She closed her eyes for several long seconds as she pondered what to do. I could see the confliction in her eyes when she reopened them. “I think I know where they might be.” We followed her to the library where she moved a few books on a shelf to reveal a button hidden in the panel of the bookcase. “This house was part of the Underground Railroad and was used as a haven for slaves as they made their journey north.” Mrs. Honeycutt pushed the button, and the entire bookcase swung outward to reveal a staircase down to what appeared to be a cellar.

“I hate dark, dank places,” Adrian said.

I didn’t like them either, but I knew we were on to something. I didn’t find a light switch, but I wasn’t surprised because the house was built before electricity was invented. It had been renovated many times since then, but the room remained a secret because it wasn’t included in the renovations. “We’re going to need flashlights,” I told Adrian.

“I’ll get them,” he replied.

Mrs. Honeycutt wrung her hands nervously. “I’ve never been down there before, but Georgia was very familiar with the room. This would’ve been the place she used to hide things she didn’t want discovered.”

“You did the right thing by telling us,” I told Mrs. Honeycutt, although I wished she'd done it sooner.

Adrian returned a few minutes later. "Here you go, partner."

I took the flashlight he offered and tested it to make sure it worked before I led the way down the ancient steps that creaked and moaned with every step we took. "We'll go back up one at a time," I told him, concerned our combined weight might cause the staircase to collapse.

"Fine, I'll go first," Adrian said without hesitation. "Good thing Mrs. Honeycutt stayed upstairs. She can call for help if this fucker gives way," he added after the stairs began to tremble after a particularly loud groan.

After careful maneuvering, we made it safely down to the cellar. I shined my flashlight around the large, cavernous concrete room. I could easily imagine men, women, and children hiding down here feeling both fear that they would get caught and exhilaration at the prospect of becoming free. If those walls could've talked, they would've had a lot to say. I wished they could help reveal where in the hell Georgia might've hidden the evidence of her blackmail scheme. There were several shelves that looked to hold canned goods and storage trunks placed throughout the room. Unfortunately, there was no X that marked the spot.

"Let's split up," Adrian said. "I'll go right, you go left, and we'll meet back in the middle."

"Sounds good to me." I began looking through trunk after trunk but found nothing but clothes from previous decades or even centuries. I heard a thud and what sounded like Adrian groaning. "You okay, partner?" Adrian didn't respond, and I worried that he'd done something to hurt himself. "Adrian?" I called out once more and then rose to my feet from where I'd been kneeling over a trunk.

A cold chill worked its way through my body that had nothing to do with the damp coldness of the cellar as I made my way to where I had last seen Adrian. The beam of my flashlight landed on Adrian lying prone on the floor. I rushed to his side and knelt beside him. There was a bloody gash on his forehead, and a large goose egg was starting to form. I pressed my fingers against his pulse point and found that he was still alive, just unconscious. I looked around for the source of his injury but found nothing.

I suddenly had a sense that Adrian and I weren't alone in the cellar. I circumvented my training to make sure the space was clear of threat in my rush to help Adrian. I switched my flashlight to my left hand and reached for my gun with my right as I rose to my feet. I heard a noise behind me and spun around with my gun out in front of me.

I walked toward the noise with my gun and flashlight sweeping from left to right as I went. I had just rounded a corner of shelves set up in the middle of the room when something hit me hard in the back of the head. I dropped my gun and flashlight as I fell to the concrete below. The last thing I saw in the beam of my flashlight before I lost consciousness were small feet encased in black leather flats.

Next thing I knew, I heard Adrian's voice calling my name as he felt around my head and neck for injuries. I slowly opened my eyes, but the room was as dark as when I'd had my eyes closed. "She must've taken our flashlights," I told Adrian.

"Thank fuck you're alive," my partner said in relief. "She took our fucking guns and phones too. I can't believe a seventy-year-old woman outsmarted me."

"She moved like a ninja," I told Adrian. "How the hell didn't we hear her walk down those rickety-ass steps?"

"There must be another entrance to this room," he replied. "We'll never find it in the dark though. Our only way out is to take those fucking steps."

I tried to get up, but a wave of dizziness and nausea hit me hard. "I need a minute," I told Adrian. "I can't see it, but I know the room is spinning. I'll be ready…"

"You're not going anywhere," Adrian said, cutting me off. "You must've really pissed her off because she did a number on your head." Adrian patted me gently on the shoulder before he stood up. "I'll feel my way up the staircase to the door. There has to be a way to release the door from the inside."

I wanted to argue with him that I was fine to make the trip upstairs, but I knew he was right after another failed attempt to sit up. "Be careful," I told Adrian. "Sally Ann needs you returning home in one piece."

"At this moment, I wish she hadn't talked me into giving up cigarettes because I'd at least have a lighter on hand." Adrian began the slow journey around the obstacles to find the staircase. "I have a general idea of where it is," he told me.

"Keep talking to me so that I know you're okay," I called out to him.

"Will do."

I couldn't say for sure how long we'd been down there because I didn't know how long we had been knocked unconscious. It seemed like it took days of Adrian shuffling around the room and slowly walking up the creaking steps before he reached the top. He found the door release relatively fast once he reached the door. Of course, I kept fading in and out the entire time so it could've taken him twenty minutes or twenty days.

"Hang in there, Gabe," I heard him call from the top of the steps. "I'm going to use the landline to call for help."

"Okay, partner," I said, my words slurring.

The last thing I had remembered before my world went dark again was Adrian hollering down the steps, "The cavalry is on the way."

TWENTY-FIVE

Josh

I WOKE UP FEELING AT PEACE WITH MY LIFE EVEN THOUGH I ONLY had a few hours of sleep. The world seemed like a brighter, better place. I realized that I was well and truly on my way to falling in l-l-like with him. Okay, it was stronger than like, but I was nowhere near ready to admit that to myself.

I lingered a little longer over my coffee than I normally would have, therefore it was closer to mid-morning before I got in the shower. I paid special attention when I styled my hair and trimmed my beard because I was almost certain I'd be seeing Gabe again after he was through working for the day. I fed my pets and headed down to the salon around noon to work on inventory and review the schedule for the upcoming week.

I cranked up the music louder than I would if I had clients inside and got to work. I finished up the inventory and schedule quickly and decided to restock the stations. My mind was on Gabe the entire time and more than once I caught myself grinning like a fool in the mirror's reflection. "Take it easy, kid," I told my reflection. "Rome wasn't built in a day and neither will your faith in... *somethings*."

The phone rang several times while I worked, but I let it go to voicemail since the salon was closed. Chaz would return the calls and schedule appointments when he came to work on Tuesday morning. I noticed that the phone was busier than usual, but didn't give it much thought. I wished that I had when I heard loud knocking on the front door of the salon. I turned around and saw a frazzled looking Adrian standing on my porch. Our eyes met, and he waved his hand urgently for me to come to the door.

I knew whatever he had to say wasn't good news, but that didn't stop me from going to him. "What's wrong?" I asked Adrian. He was wearing a large bandage on his forehead and didn't look so good, but he was at my salon, and Gabe wasn't. I tried so hard not to panic, but it wasn't working and was evident in my voice when I asked, "Where's Gabe?"

"He's at County General," Adrian replied. "Our cell phones were taken, so I didn't have your personal number, only the salon. I drove over here to get you when you didn't answer the phone. Grab your coat, and I'll take you to him."

I quickly grabbed my coat and followed him to his car that he'd left running out front. "What happened, Adrian?" I asked once we were on the road. My heart was up in my throat by that time.

"We were following a lead and let our guard down when we

shouldn't have." He removed one hand from the steering wheel and pointed to his bandaged head. "Stupid. Stupid. Stupid."

"I'm freaking out here, Adrian. What kind of condition is he in?" Against my better judgment, I had let my guard down to have a chance with Gabe. I was terrified of losing him.

"I'm sorry, kid. I didn't mean to scare you half to death." Adrian took his hand off the wheel again, but that time it was to ruffle my hair. I saw that I'd have to set down some rules with Adrian about calling me a kid and touching my hair, but it could wait until after I was sure that Gabe was okay. "Gabe's in stable condition, but he has one hell of a concussion. He'll probably be staying at Casa de County General for a few days."

"He's going to be okay though, right?" I was relieved to hear that he hadn't been shot or stabbed, but head wounds could be tricky.

"He's tough, and you'll be the incentive he needs to get better." Adrian glanced briefly in my direction and offered me an assuring smile. I hoped he was right about all of it. I assumed Gabe was plenty tough enough, but I wanted to be his incentive to heal.

We were given his room number right away when we arrived at the hospital. My heart pounded in my chest, and the sound of my blood rushing through my veins roared in my ears. I became light-headed and dizzy outside his room and realized I'd been holding my breath.

"I need a minute," I told Adrian. "I don't want him to see me like this." He was the one injured for fuck's sake. I needed to get my shit together and be strong. I got my breathing under control and said, "I'm ready." I forced a smile on my face when Adrian opened the door, but it quickly fell when I saw Gabe lying in bed, his head wrapped in white gauze. "Gabe!" I rushed to his bed and reached for his hand.

Gabe's eyelashes fluttered then his eyes opened slowly. He had blinked several times before he was able to focus on me. "Hurts." His slurred word broke my heart, but the way he reached for me with his hand pieced it back together again. "Come here." He seemed uncoordinated as he tugged me down for a sweet kiss. "Better now." He dropped back to sleep, and I just stood there staring down at him.

I finally looked over at Adrian. "Is there anyone we should call for him. His parents?"

Adrian shook his head. "I'd say yes if he were gravely injured. I think it's best to let him call his folks when he's feeling better." He reached into his pocket and pulled out a set of keys. "These are Gabe's," he said, "I'm going to get Buddy and take him home with me while Gabe is here. Do you want me to come get you later tonight?"

"I'm not leaving," I told Adrian. "I'll call my friends if I need anything from home."

Adrian nodded in approval. "He'll be just fine," he told me. "I'm going to head back to the station so I can help with the search for the person who did this to us." I wanted to ask who it was, but I knew he couldn't answer me.

"Take care of yourself, Adrian."

"I'll be back later to check in on you both." He offered me a quick wave before he took off, eager to find the person responsible for putting Gabe in the hospital.

Once I was alone with Gabe, I looked down at his serene face as he slept. "What am I going to do with you, Gabe?" I released his hand long enough to pull a chair beside his bed. "Look, I think we need to come to an understanding," I said seriously as if he was listening to me. "I probably more than like you, but I'm not ready to tell you that yet. I want the chance to tell you someday, so can you stop getting hurt?" Of course, he said nothing. "I'll take your silence as agreement."

A nurse came in around an hour later and woke Gabe up to ask him a series of questions. I was happy to learn that he knew the year, his birthdate, and who the president was. He looked happy to see that I was still there. "Hi, beautiful." He chuckled and then moaned in pain after I looked around to see who he was addressing. "You, Josh."

"Those must be some serious drugs," I told the nurse as she replaced the IV bags.

She laughed quietly and said, "They're pretty good but not as good as he'd like after being knocked in the head as hard as he was. He can have some more potent stuff a little later." She looked at me and smiled when she finished. "Do you want me to have a cot brought in so you can stay with your boyfriend."

"That would be great." I didn't know if Gabe considered us boyfriends, but it didn't matter. I was staying.

"I'm glad you're here," Gabe said when we were alone again. He cleared his throat like it was really dry.

"Let me get you something to drink." I poured a cup of ice water from the pitcher beside his bed and held the straw up to his mouth so he could sip it. "Slowly," I told him when he wanted to gulp it. "Little sips until we see if your stomach will keep it down."

"I'm sorry if you were scared." Gabe reached a shaky hand up toward my face, and I met him halfway to help him conserve energy. I was hoping he'd be able to stay awake for longer periods of time.

"I was at first, but Adrian assured me that you were okay."

"Where is Adrian?" Gabe asked

"He went back to the station to help with the search." I brushed my hand along the side of his face. "I'm sorry that you're in pain."

"I can't believe a seventy-year-old woman got the drop on us," Gabe said. I must've misunderstood him, or his head injury was worse than I thought. "Wanda Honeycutt should win an academy award for best actress in a homicide investigation."

"Wanda Honeycutt?" I asked. "Seriously?"

"Spawn of Satan," Gabe replied. "If she didn't kill Georgia then she sure as hell knows who did."

"I can't believe it," I said, recalling the sweet lady who taught bible school to me as a child.

"Believe it, babe." Gabe squinted his eyes while he concentrated, and I realized he wasn't aware of what he had called me.

My heart realized it though and thumped a little harder and faster at the cheesy endearment. I never considered myself a guy who wanted to be called "babe." I always thought I'd want to be called something more exotic and less commonplace until the word rolled off Gabe's tongue.

"What?" Gabe asked. I looked at him in confusion because I hadn't said anything. "You have a strange look on your face. Did I say something stupid because I'm going to blame it on the concussion, the drugs, or something else."

"No, Gabe. What you said was right, not wrong."

That look of intense concentration crossed his face again. He could've been struggling to remember what he'd just said or straining to fart; it was a tossup. "I called you 'babe.' You're not freaking out," he told me.

"Nope."

"It's because you *like* me." His eyes were starting to get heavy again as sleep beckoned him.

"I sure do." My words earned a sweet smile.

"I *like* you a lot," he replied. "I can't wait to get out of here so I can show you." He let out a growl that was about intimidating as a kitten's meow.

I bit my lip to keep from laughing. "Okay, tiger, but how about you get some rest first."

"Mmkay."

Once he had drifted back to sleep, I pulled my phone out and dialed Meredith. Of course, the story had already started to circulate throughout the town, and she'd called me twelve times since I had arrived at the hospital. I had my phone on silent and didn't realize I missed her calls. I felt terrible for causing her distress, which I told her as soon as she answered the phone.

"You're not forgiven," she said huffily.

"Can I please ask a favor? I need a few things from home…"

"Already have them," she said from behind me as she entered the hospital room. I spun around and saw that Chaz had come with her.

"I'm so happy to see you," I said in relief.

"Jazz, I'm right here. You don't have to talk to me through the phone." She disconnected the call and slipped the phone into her pocket.

"Oh," I said, feeling like a complete idiot. I put my phone back in the pocket of my jeans.

"We brought you some clothes, a warm blanket, and a pillow," Chaz said. "Are you okay?"

"I am now that I've seen him with my own eyes," I answered.

"Is he going to be okay?" Mere asked. "Hell, I'd heard about twelve renditions of the story—from him only needing stitches to him needing an undertaker."

"Don't say that." I clutched my stomach.

"We'll hang out with you for a bit to keep you company," Chaz said.

"Thank you," I told them. If my friends stayed and kept me occupied, then maybe I wouldn't fixate on how close I could've come to losing Gabe.

Adrian and Sally Ann showed up a little while later and brought some dinner. The nurse hadn't been back in to wake Gabe yet, and he was sleeping soundly, with only a few occasional moans. Each time he made a noise, I reached for him, and he would calm down like my presence comforted him.

A different nurse came in not long after we'd eaten and she performed the same tasks as the first nurse I met. She was just as friendly, took the time to introduce herself to all of us, and asked if there was anything she could bring Gabe. "Some broth maybe?" she asked him.

"That would be nice," he replied. Once the nurse left to get him broth, he looked at Adrian with a fierce expression. "Please tell me that you've found her."

"Fucking-A," he replied, "but she's not talking."

"Yet," Gabe replied. "I won't be in this hospital bed forever." The fierce determination in his voice had me wiggling in my chair. I knew damned well he wasn't going to rough up Wanda Honeycutt, but I believed in his ability to get her to confess. "Are they searching her house for evidence of the crimes? I reckon she could've stabbed Georgia easily enough if she snuck up on her. It would explain why there were no strange prints and no forced entry. I somehow don't see her climbing beneath Rocky's car and cutting the brake lines though."

"I'm with you, partner. We've been operating on the notion that the two events are related, but what if they're not? It sounds like the pair had their share of people who might want to harm them. We'll dig deep and won't leave any stone unturned," Adrian said. "Right now, you need to worry about getting better."

"I'll be back on the job in no time," he said confidently, but the way he started to wilt said otherwise. He didn't stay awake long enough to sip the broth the nurse brought in for him.

Everyone left me alone with Gabe with promises to be back the next day. I was grateful for the quiet so I could just sit and watch him sleep. I eventually lay on my cot beside him, content to hear his soft snores while he rested peacefully.

TWENTY-SIX

Gabe

My return to active duty wasn't as fast as I had boasted about in my hospital room. The captain forced me to take an additional week off after I was released from the hospital, so I missed out on the Wanda Honeycutt investigation, but Adrian kept me apprised every step of the way.

When the police department searched her house, they found the evidence that Georgia used in her attempt to blackmail Jack Wallace. That alone wasn't sufficient evidence to tie her to the homicide because she could've easily said she was holding it for Georgia. But when coupled with the pair of shoes they found in her garage that had minuscule drops of blood on them; things started to look up.

That wasn't the only thing interesting they found in Wanda's garage. They found a pair of snips that had brake fluid on them. After some digging, we discovered that Wanda's grandfather, and then later her father, owned an auto repair shop many years prior. In fact, it was so long ago that only the oldest citizens remembered it. Adrian's grandfather had told him about it, so the search team knew to look for any tool sharp enough to cut brake lines.

"I still can't believe she crawled beneath his car in the winter and cut the lines," I had said to Adrian when he stopped over after they concluded the search.

"That's how much she hated him." Adrian shook his head.

Adrian, the best partner on the planet, snuck me into the station so I could watch the interrogation through a monitor in the equipment room. Captain Reardon was too busy playing the role of bad cop to know that I was in the station. When faced with the evidence against her, Wanda Honeycutt confessed to everything but the vandalism. She was adamant that she didn't do it and we couldn't prove differently, so unfortunately, that part of the case was still open.

"Georgia was going to replace me," she said tearfully. "I didn't have a choice. No one could take care of her like I did." Her voice and expression switched rapidly from sad to angry. "That was the thanks she was going to give me after everything I did for her after that bastard broke her heart. She was going to take him back and start a new life that didn't include me. She thought I was too old to do my job." By that time, Wanda's eyes were protruding from her sockets and veins were popped out on her forehead. "They both got what they deserved." Spittle flew from her mouth, and she pounded the table angrily with her small, balled-up fists.

"I don't think she's sane," I told Adrian once we left the station. "I don't see her doing hard time. Do you?"

"Probably not, partner."

"Thank you for today, Adrian." I reached over and held up my fist for a bump. "It means a lot to me."

"Anytime."

I got out and entered through the back of the salon and found Josh waiting for me upstairs with his hands on his hips. I wisely kept my mouth shut, but he honestly looked like a pissed off diva—not unlike the reality housewife shows he seemed to be addicted to watching.

"Where have you been?"

"Um..."

"Was that Adrian I saw bringing you home? Were you at the police station after they put you on leave for a week?"

"I..."

"Gabe, what am I going to do with you?" Josh asked.

The best thing to come out of my injury and downtime at work was getting to spend it with Josh, who insisted I come home with him for a few days so he could look after me once I was released from County General. I wanted to bristle and say that I didn't need babying, but I saw something in his eyes that cautioned me to keep silent and accept his offer. It wasn't the warning look I received when I returned from sneaking off to the police station with Adrian. No, that look was softer and affectionate. What kind of dumbass resisted Josh's hard-to-obtain affections?

Josh packed a bag for me, grabbed Buddy's dishes and toys, and moved us into his house. I worried that Buddy and Diva wouldn't get along. I had visions of Buddy chasing her through the house and making her miserable, but he completely ignored her. True to her name, Diva wanted no part of being ignored. She would puff up on the back of the couch in hopes of getting his attention, but Buddy continued to ignore her in favor of playing with Jazzy the ferret.

Diva would even jump in front of him and hiss in hopes of getting his attention, but he continued to play hard to get until she gave up. Only then did he press his nose to hers to introduce himself.

I thought my dog might be onto something with his tactics and took mental notes for the next time Josh baited me into an argument. I think he wanted to push me to see if I'd run off or stick around. I had no intention of running from him, and it was past time Josh realized it.

I spent those days at Josh's house soaking up his affections and resting. Adrian and Sally Ann frequently visited, as did Josh's salon employees, who I learned he loved and treated like family. When Josh was busy downstairs, I entertained myself with television, movies, or coloring in the adult coloring book full of swear words that Sally Ann gave me. Hell, even I learned new words that I didn't know and did my damnedest to teach them to Savage.

Josh wasn't impressed when he came home the second day of my stay and Savage squawked out, "Fucknugget," as loud as he could. I tried to shrug like I didn't know where he'd heard it, but it wasn't very convincing when I was doubled over in a fit of laughter.

"Oh, it hurts," I said, in between peals of laughter.

"It's going to hurt really bad if you keep it up," Josh said, trying for fierce, but miserably failing as he fought back laughter.

"Fucknugget!" Savage squawked again.

"That's enough out of you, Savage," Josh said firmly before turning on me. "I can't have him talking like that when he's down in my salon."

"Really, Josh? I seem to recall the ladies hysterically laughing when Savage confessed that he liked big cocks and couldn't lie." I looked at him pointedly, but he ignored me and turned his ire back to the bird.

"Bad bird," Josh said to Savage.

"Up yours," was Savage's reply. Damn, I loved that dirty bird.

My favorite part was the nights, of course. Josh curled into me, and I had never slept better in my life, except the first night when he was instructed to wake me every two hours. He didn't exactly follow the script when he asked questions like, "Who's your daddy?" or "How many cocks do you see?" as he pulled down his brightly colored bikini briefs to flash me.

Josh seemed to enjoy sleeping next to me just as much, except the night when he woke us both from thrashing around in the bed. I recognized that he was having a terrible nightmare and carefully woke him up. His eyes had been wide with fright before he closed them in relief that it had only been a bad dream.

"Do you have these often?" I asked him while holding his shaking body close.

"I don't have them as frequently as I did after it happened." He looked up at me and clarified what he was talking about because my mind was spinning all kinds of terrible things that could've happened to him. "I was dreaming about Bianca's killer and the night he tried to kill me too."

"It's completely normal to have nightmares after a traumatic event like that," I told Josh. I rubbed my cheek against the top of his head and breathed him in and tried not to think about how close I had come to losing him that night. "Have you talked to someone about them?"

"No," he said softly. "They are getting better though. I'm not sure what triggered it, maybe it was the thriller we watched tonight or maybe I can't get closure until I know all the facts that led to him killing Bianca. Hell, I refused to learn his name thinking that I could shut out what he did to me by not giving it any attention."

"It didn't work like you'd hoped, huh?"

"No." Josh got quiet, and I thought he'd drifted back to sleep, but then he said, "Tell me about him."

"Are you sure?" I asked. I didn't want to do anything to make things worse for him. I knew that everyone processed and healed from trauma differently.

"I am." He sounded certain, and I had to trust that he knew what was best for him.

"His name was Oscar Davidson." I ran my hand up and down Josh's back and let my fingers bounce along the bones of his spine to soothe him. "According to his wife, he confessed to her that he'd purchased a love potion from Bianca that was supposed to make her fall in love with him again. She said they'd drifted apart the last few years of their marriage and it was his attempt to put things back together again." I dropped a kiss on Josh's head while hoping that we never drifted apart. I'd been down that road before, and it was a helpless feeling. "He apparently slipped the potion in her drink, and instead of falling all over him, she confessed to being in love with his friend. That's when he lost his shit and told her about the love potion."

"Ouch," Josh said. "Do you believe in that love potion stuff?"

"I'm not sure I believe it, but Oscar was convinced," I replied. "His wife said that he came back and raged at Bianca for selling him the wrong kind of potion. That was when he practically ran you over on the sidewalk." I pulled him tighter to me. "She knew he was upset, but she had no idea he was planning to kill Bianca."

"Then he saw the media release that contained his police sketch and description of his car and knew it had been me who reported him." He turned his face up to mine and asked, "How did he know where I lived?"

"He remembered you from the incident and probably came to town looking for you. As small as this town is, it probably was easy for him to do. He probably staked out Bianca's house and saw you running then followed to see where you lived." A hard tremor shook Josh's body. "He's dead now and can't hurt you. I'll do my best to make sure no one ever hurts you again."

After several seconds of silence, Josh said sleepily, "You have the power to hurt me more than anyone." It was a heartfelt confession that his feelings for me ran deeper than *like* and it warmed my heart.

"That's not going to happen," I told Josh confidently. "I'm going to fuck up, and you're going to set me straight. We're going to figure this out because the alternative is unacceptable to me."

"To me too," Josh confessed, his voice fading as he was on the verge of falling back to sleep.

Sleep didn't come to me as quickly. I held Josh tight and continued to run my hand up and down his back, but it was more for my peace of mind at that point. I thought about the words we exchanged and realized just how much I meant what I said. Josh was quickly coming to mean so much to me in a frighteningly short amount of time. I expected to be alarmed by the swift changes in my life, but instead, I embraced them wholeheartedly.

As I lay there, another pressing thought occurred to me. Christmas was around the corner, and I had no idea what the hell to get Josh. I wanted his gift to be poignant and meaningful on our first Christmas together, not something frivolous. I smiled in the darkness of Josh's bedroom when the idea of his perfect gift came to me. It was going to be a Christmas he'd never forget.

TWENTY-SEVEN

Josh

JUST LIKE THE SONG SAID, IT WAS THE MOST WONDERFUL TIME OF the year. It was Christmas Eve, and I was surrounded by people that I loved, great food, and a festive feel in the air. I sat quietly sipping a glass of wine and watched Gabe interact with Meredith and Chaz, who honestly adored that man. It was almost gross how they hero-worshipped him. Okay, so the man saved my life and probably my heart, but I thought it was best to keep him grounded rather than inflate his ego too much.

Gabe and Buddy had moved back to his house, and I missed them more than I was ready to acknowledge. I still saw them nearly every day, and we slept over at one another's homes a few nights a week. I missed them when they weren't with me, but I knew it was important to do things right and not rush into a situation that neither one of us were ready for yet.

I learned new, adorable things about him every day, such as his love for all things Christmas. I thought I was Christmas crazy, but Gabe took the cake and ate the whole damn thing without sharing. He sang along with the music, made a list of the shows he wanted to watch then searched to see when they were airing, and woofed down cookies faster than I baked them. He even bought us matching Henley pajama shirts and flannel bottoms with snowmen on them. Then there was the date to Cincinnati to ice skate, which was the sweetest thing since he hated being cold. I kept him as warm as I could with hot chocolate, and later, my body when we returned home.

As was our tradition, Meredith and Chaz came over for dinner and a gift exchange on Christmas Eve. I loved every minute of having them there, but I was ready for them to go home so I could be alone with Gabe. I had already decided that we would exchange our gifts that night rather than wait for Christmas morning. I knew I would be too excited to sleep. Still, I didn't rudely push my friends out the door after we ate. I cherished every second we had together; near-death experiences made a person appreciate things more. Even so, I got a little anxious as the clock ticked closer and closer to midnight.

Gabe decided that Chaz and Meredith had too much to drink to drive, so he drove them home while I tidied up things. He was back before I finished and immediately jumped in to help me. After we had finished, Gabe tugged me close and cupped my face in his hands.

"I thought they'd never leave," he confessed. "You know how

much I adore them, but I've been dying to do this." He started to lower his head for a kiss that I knew would put the jolly in "Holly Jolly Christmas," so I stopped him. "What?" he asked in confusion.

"I want you to open your gifts first," I told him. "If you kiss me now then we won't get to them for hours."

"It's not Christmas yet," he said.

I pointed to the digital clock on the microwave that read 12:01. "It is now."

I could tell that Gabe was trying to play off that he wasn't excited to exchange gifts, but I knew better. He hurried to the tree and began pulling out wrapped gifts and sorting them into two piles, one for him and one for me. "Let's do this," he said.

I walked to the tree at a more leisurely pace, even though I felt like a five-year-old again on the inside. Gabe reached for my hand and tugged me down to sit beside him. "You open your gifts first," I told him.

"No way." Gabe shook his head. "We take turns."

I handed him one of his gifts, and he handed me one of mine. We argued about who went first and then we ripped into them at the same time. I pulled out a dress shirt like the one he destroyed the day of Georgia's funeral. He opened a box set of the *Lethal Weapon* movies he adored. Next, I opened a stuffed, purple hippopotamus because I loved to sing that song as loud as I could just to irritate him.

"There," he said triumphantly, "you received a hippo for Christmas so you can stop singing about it." That didn't stop me from humming the melody of the song for a few seconds.

Gabe's funny gift from me was a coffee cup with a giant rooster on it that said: **I got a big cock!** I thought it went well with his collection and his laughter told me he agreed. "I'm going to use this one at work," he proclaimed, causing me to groan.

Gabe looked nervous when he handed me my final gift, which made me feel a little better because I felt the same about the one last gift he had yet to unwrap. "I hope you like it," he said.

"I'm sure I will." I unwrapped the gift and sat staring at it for a second. He gave me the movie *Meet the Parents.* It was a great movie, but I didn't understand why he was nervous. Unless… I looked up at him and found him grinning at me.

"Open it."

I gasped when I saw that two airline tickets to Miami were inside. "Chaz has always wanted to go to Miami," I said, using humor to cover the overwhelming joy I felt in my heart. Gabe was taking me home to meet his parents, and by doing so, he showed me how much I meant to him.

"Ha ha," Gabe replied. "I figured February would be enough notice to plan time away."

"It's perfect." Then I thanked him with a kiss. "I'm worried my gift is a letdown after yours."

"Not a chance." Gabe ripped the paper off excitedly before opening the small box. He slipped his hand beneath the medallion hanging from a leather cord so that it sat in his palm. "Saint Michael, the patron saint of police officers." He looked up, and his eyes were soft with affection when they locked on mine.

"For the next time you piss off a seventy-year-old woman." Again with the humor.

"I love this, Josh." He accepted my smartass remarks for what they were and moved on. "It's beautiful, and I'll wear it every day." He gave me a crooked grin. "I never know when those seventy-year-old women will strike." It was his turn to show me with lips and tongue how much he liked my gift.

Our presents were soon forgotten, just as I knew they would be, and our clothes went flying. I had never once in my life thought about making love next to a Christmas tree, but it was beyond romantic. So much so, that I didn't realize I had thought about our sexy time as making love until I was lying beside him as he slept in my bed. I started to panic at first, but then I pushed it aside. The guys who had hurt me in the past and made me feel unworthy of love were not Gabe. How we met no longer mattered to me, only our future did.

I wanted to think that our future, as the Christmas season, looked merry and bright.

EPILOGUE

Gabe

One month later...

My phone ringing brought me out of a deep sleep. I had to untangle myself from Josh to roll over and pick it up from the night table. I squinted sleepily at the display, which said it was an unknown caller.

"Detective Wyatt," I said into the phone.

"Sorry to wake you, Detective," said a voice I vaguely

recognized. "This is Sheriff Arless Tucker with the Carter County police department."

I sat up straight, going on high alert. I knew that the sheriff of our county wasn't calling me in the middle of the night for good reasons. "What can I do for you, Sheriff?"

"I'm at the scene of what appears to be a homicide on highway twenty-two, and I was hoping to get your assistance," Sheriff Tucker said.

I was confused about why he'd be calling me because our jurisdiction didn't extend out to the county highways. "Sure, Sheriff Tucker, but can I ask why you're calling me?"

"The victim has been run off the road and then shot in the head." Again, I wasn't sure where I came into play in any of it. "There was no ID on the victim, but we did find your business card in his wallet. Can you come down and ID the body?"

"Yes, sir. I'll be there in fifteen minutes." A sick feeling came over me as I realized who the victim most likely was.

To be continued…

ACKNOWLEDGMENTS

First, I need to thank my husband and children for their constant support and encouragement. It's not easy living with a writer who often disappears into a fictional world for long periods of time. They do so many things to help me out so that I can realize my dream. I love you guys more than words can ever express.

Many thanks go out to my three best friends, Anne, Deena, and Kerry. They've stood by me, cheered me on, picked me up, and held my hand through some really rough patches this year. I love you girls so very much. I wish everyone had friends like you because the world would be a much kinder place.

To my creative dream team, thanks seems hardly enough for all that you do. Pam Ebeler of Undivided Editing thank you for your tireless work, feedback, and many laughs while editing. Jay Aheer of Simply Defined art is just an incredible artist and I love how she brings my words to life. Stacey Blake of Champagne Formats is also an amazing artist who does incredible interior formatting and designing for e-books and paperbacks. New to my team is Judy Zweifel of Judys' Proofreading. She does an amazing job of finding the tiniest details that make a book shine.

I would like to thank my beta readers for all the honest feedback they give me on my storyline. I appreciate you guys so much. Aimee's ARC angels are Anne, Kerry, Jason, Jodie, Kim, and Laurel. Thank you for all that you do!

ABOUT THE AUTHOR

I am a wife and mother to three kids, three dogs, and a cat. When I'm not dreaming up stories, I like to lose myself in a good book, cook or bake. I'm a girly tomboy who paints her fingernails while watching sports and yelling at the referees. I will always choose the book over the movie. I believe in happily-ever-after. Love inspires everything that I do. Music keeps me sane.

I'd love to hear from you.
You can reach me at:

Twitter - www.twitter.com/AimeeNWalker
Facebook – www.facebook.com/aimeenicole.walker
Blog – AimeeNicoleWalker.blogspot.com

Made in the USA
Middletown, DE
13 April 2018